THE FLU HEALING 2

A PERMUTED PRESS book

ISBN (trade paperback): 978-1-61868-1-607
ISBN (eBook): 978-1-61868-1-614

Cover art by Travis Franklin

This book is a work of fiction. People, places, events, and situations are the product of the author's imagination. Any resemblance to actual persons, living or dead, or historical events, is purely coincidental.

PERMUTED
PRESS

JOURNAL ENTRY

<u>October 14th</u>

My name is Christian Hughes, but everyone calls me Chris. I'm thirteen. This is my first entry. I don't know how much I'll write or for how long.

My pap said I should write in a journal. He said it would help me get my feelings out. Don't need to write in it every day, just when I feel like I have something on my mind. I asked him if he ever had one, he said he didn't but saw no reason why I shouldn't. I'm the talker.

I don't know what I'm gonna write. Maybe tomorrow I will. Kind of explain what all happened and why I am writing.

In the morning we leave. Not for long and not far away.

I don't even know what's outside my town. Heck, I was rarely outside of my town before this all happened.

My stepfather is taking me and my little brother away. Just a trip. Just us three.

He said so we can find ourselves.

I hope he's right. I hope I find myself. Because right now, I am so lost.

1. THE FIRST STEP

October 15th

Two hours into the journey, Mick Owens pulled over. There was a rest area just before the end of the Ohio turnpike and it was a perfect place to stop.

Their drive had been an easy one, not that two hours in a car was all that long. It was peaceful driving. They spotted one car on the road and they were headed in the opposite direction. One car in two hours. It was only highway driving and what was ahead scared him.

Civilization. Or what was left of it.

The boys didn't say much. Mick didn't expect them to. It was part of the reason he was taking the boys away for a spell. Perhaps the further away from home, from the hurt, the more they would be themselves, if that was ever possible again.

They had lost. Mick and the boys had lost. Their mother, their grandmother, brother … it was too much to handle.

Mick not only saw those around him succumb to the flu and lose their lives, he had watched the spark of life leave Chris and Tigger.

Then again, it had only been a week. Time would heal. For that Mick prayed.

There wasn't a soul at the rest area; it was eerily deserted and Mick put the SUV in park. Fall had set in and the leaves covered the parking lot like a layer of snow. Untouched, because no cars had passed through them.

He looked in the rearview mirror to six year old Tigger who due to a medical condition, was no bigger than a three year old. Tigger wiggled.

"You have to take a leak, Tig?" Mick asked.

"No." He shook his head. "I'm just dancing."

"I'm sure." Mick opened his door. "Chris, take your brother while I top off the gas."

"Sure." Chris started to open his door but stopped. He looked through the windshield at the silent rest area building. "You ain't wanting me to take him in there, are you?"

"No, I—"

"Cause it's not like I'm scared or anything, just ... it's ..."

"Chris," Mick said softly, "just take him a few feet from the truck. Not too far. I don't want you boys far from me at all."

Again, Chris started to open the door. "Why you topping off the gas, Mick? We running low already?"

"No," Mick answered, shifting his eyes to the rearview mirror and to Tigger who wiggled more intensely. "I'd rather not stop when we are near Pittsburgh."

"Cause that seems kind of fast, doesn't it?"

"What's seems kind of fast?"

"That we're running low on gas."

"We aren't running low on gas, I just wanna top off."

"What if we run out?"

"Chris ..."

"I mean, with no electricity, how we gonna get gas?"

"I brought plenty."

"How do you know?" Chris asked.

"I know. We're not going all that far. Now take your brother to pee."

From the backseat, Tigger said quietly, "Too late."

Mick grumbled with a slight exhale and stepped out of the SUV. "I'll get you fresh pants."

"I'll help ya, Tig, get you all dry," Chris said. "Shame Mick made you pee your pants like that." He too slid out, looked at Mick, and gave a smile. Not wide, but a smile that indicated he was kidding him.

A moment of breathlessness hit Mick and he was glad to see it. Chris hadn't smiled in a week. Not that there was any reason to, but even when his father died long before the flu, Chris found a reason to smile.

Not this time, though. Mick hoped that somehow he'd put some 'at ease' on the thirteen year old boy's face, in fact, he hoped that outcome for them all.

* * *

It had been weeks since Tom Roberts had opened his video store. He closed it for a spell when the government ordered all unnecessary businesses shut their doors. Then Mick shut the proverbial doors to Lodi, Ohio and Tom opened his store again. But not for long. A month or so, and then Lodi suffered the same fate as the rest of the world.

It faced the flu.

Tom was one of the first to get it. Lodi was ready, under the watchful eye of Lars Rayburn and the CDC, prepped with an experimental treatment.

The treatment worked on Tom. It worked on a lot of people, but it failed on so many. Tom didn't just suffer from the after effects of the flu, he suffered from a broken heart he was certain would never mend.

His wife Marian … gone.

His daughter Dylan … gone.

And his grandson Dustin … gone.

Three times, three ways, Tom was crushed. The love of his life, the one he gave life, and his grandson.

Losing Marian was tough; he loved her and always would. Tom was certain, even if there were plenty of people left in the world, he'd never find another Marian.

Dylan was his flesh and blood and only child. It wasn't right that he had to stay on this earth while watching his child leave. No parent should watch their child die.

If Tom could have changed places with any of them, he would have.

A pain shot through his heart when he thought of Dustin. How incredibly special Dustin was. Tom recalled when Dustin was born. How a spark of life like he had never before felt ignited within his being at the first moment he laid eyes on the baby boy.

It was an indescribable love that only a grandparent could feel. As if God Himself had reached into Tom's heart and lit it aflame with an emotion he never realized he had.

From that moment on Tom was hooked on Dustin as if the child were an addictive drug. He loved his other grandchildren just the same, but Dustin ... was his boy, the son he never had. He loved the fishing trips Dylan thought were too boring. Dustin did it all.

How Tom loved to torment the teenager when he waited on a new release at the video store. Tom would tell him he rented it out. Dustin would pout, whine and then switch up and say, "That's okay. I'll wait. It'll be worth it. Thanks, Pap."

Pap.

The bright young man, who so diligently watched for signs of the flu, was on target. He made it to treatment with minimal symptoms and was a prime candidate for success.

It didn't work on him. It ravaged him in a way that was inhumane.

Nothing ... *nothing* Dustin did in his young life warranted the suffering he experienced and nothing Dylan ever did warranted her having to witness it.

Perhaps that was why Dylan opted out.

When she knew she was going to die, she asked to die, before the horrendous end. And for that, Tom was grateful. Though he didn't want to see Dylan go, he didn't want to see her suffer. Somewhere inside he found a tiny bit of comfort knowing that his wife, daughter and grandson were together.

How long had he stood at the door to the video store? Key in hand, movies from the house tucked under his arm. He stood there for a while. Not in contemplation of opening the store, but in thought. He actually did think about closing the store forever. After all, there wouldn't be any new releases, not for a long time. No one had money, so there was no economical reason. But Dustin loved the store and a return to some sort of normalcy was in order, even if it began with a simple video store.

He looked down to his keys, his vision blurred. Tom was tired, he hadn't slept much. He hoped that was the reason for his eyes blurring, because if he needed new glasses he was in trouble. There wasn't an ophthalmologist in Lodi.

Something so simple as a pair of glasses, Tom thought, *will be something difficult to get.*

"Oh my God." The male voice was tired, raspy, but familiar. He chanted out the words in shock. "Oh my God."

Tom turned around. Ross Jenkins owned the local funeral home. He wasn't an older man, just middle aged, and his face was worn and drawn, much like everyone else's. He stopped about four feet from the store steps.

"Hey there, Ross."

"Tom? Tell me you're opening the store. You'd be the first you know, to reopen."

"Yeah, think I will," Tom said. "Maybe I'll start a chain reaction. Who knows? I know it's early and all—"

"No," Ross interrupted. "Timing is perfect. People need to see that life goes on." He sighed. "Even if it starts with a video store."

"I appreciate it. And if you aren't so busy, maybe you'd like to come in and help me get this place back in order? I'm sure it's dusty."

"I'd like that," Ross said, moving toward the steps.

After a pause, Tom stuck in the keys and unlocked the door. A smell of dust and 'stale' pelted him. He held the door open for Ross. "Come on in. I'll hit the switch in the back. At least the power's on, even if it's on roll outs."

Ross stepped to the door. "It's good to see you, Tom."

Tom nodded.

"I'm sorry for your loss with Marian, Dylan and Dustin."

Tom nodded again with a closed mouth. "And I'm sorry too, for Jill, Ben, Gary, Steve, and Lizzy."

"Thank you."

For simplicity, Tom could have just said he was sorry for the loss of Ross' family. But he didn't, he couldn't. Doing so would lump them all together and somehow Tom felt as if that slighted them. He supposed the 'sorry for your loss' comments would be regular things in Lodi for a long time. And the list of names would be long and recited.

That was life in Lodi. No one was just a statistic or resident. They were people with names and families. Everyone in Lodi knew everyone, that was what made it so hard.

At some point though, even early, a sign that life has to keep moving on, had to be delivered.

One step at a time.

Tom walked into his store.

2. AN OUNCE OF HEALING

The small fire crackled and Mick poked it with a stick. He had cooked some canned ham and beans for him and the boys. Tigger was out like a light, fast asleep on the ground, curled up on a sleeping bag that twisted around his body.

Chris sat on a mini seat, elbows on knees, staring at the fire.

Mick glanced across to him many times.

They had never reached their destination of West Virginia. They got as far as the interchange where I-79 split and met with 1-279 just 12 miles before Pittsburgh and a roadblock kept them from going any further.

It appeared as if an exodus out of the city had taken place. Vehicles had used both lanes on all roads to leave, but had been halted by a military blockade. A traffic jam so bad, no one could even turn around. Mick hadn't even heard of any military blockades. Then again, Mick had focused only on Lodi.

He didn't stop to see if there were people or bodies in the cars. The boys didn't need to see that. There was no way to go around it, so Mick, not wanting to waste the gas, headed north.

He located a campsite just outside of Erie. The switch up

would save them gas, Mick told Chris.

It wasn't what Mick expected.

People had flocked to the campsite. It seemed this particular one tried to do what Lodi had done - seal off the site. The two trucks that served as guard were empty, and were only blocking the entrance. Mick was able to move one and pass around. The winding road into the campsite was deceiving, giving the illusion of desolation. The road was covered with leaves, like at the rest stop, and had no tracks. Mick was certain no one would be there, until they passed the gate.

Upon entering, Mick could see a ton of RV's parked, and tents set up. That was in the distance. Up close, in a section near the fence, were mounds. Rows and rows of fresh dirt mounds.

Graves.

People had fled there and people had died there.

Someone had to be there, or at least was at one time, because someone had buried those who passed. There was at least one survivor, Mick figured.

No sooner did they pull into the site when a man waved for them to stop. Mick slowed down and the man, in his thirties, stepped to the window.

"Hey, there," he said to Mick. "Passing through or staying?"

"Um, a little of both," Mick replied. "Was wanting to get my boys away from home for a while, you know. Couldn't get by Pittsburgh to get to West Virginia. Not on our gas rations."

"I hear you." He extended his hand into the window. "I'm Ethan."

"Mick Owens," Mick said, introducing himself.

"Where you guys from?"

"Ohio. Lodi, Ohio."

"No, shit? Your town fared pretty well, I hear."

Mick gave him a sad look. "Better than some, but we got

hit. We …" Mick paused and looked at Chris. "We got hit."

"I see. Well, you are more than welcome to stay. You can pitch a tent, or the Charles' camper is empty. They left for the city when they got sick. Just parked it and took their truck." He pointed. "It's right over there."

"We appreciate it. Thank you."

"We'll be seeing you," Ethan said.

Mick nodded conveying another 'thank you' and pulled in the direction of the camper.

"We ain't staying in there, are we, Mick?" Chris asked. "People got sick and died in there."

"They didn't die in there, you heard the man. They moved on. We can stay in the truck, but I didn't bring a tent," Mick replied. "Why I don't check it out before we make the call. Okay?"

"I suppose that'll work."

Mick reached over and squeezed Chris' leg, and pulled in front of the camper. It was a nice sized one and newer.

Mick checked it out, then Chris. Tigger didn't really mind one way or another. Chris gave his seal of approval and Mick was glad. He wanted to stop for a little bit.

They were out of Lodi, away from familiar surroundings. Around people they didn't know. And there were 'people' there; one person was more than Mick had expected to see outside of Lodi.

Just after they parked, and pulled some things out of the SUV, a woman named Madge came over.

To Mick, she looked injured. Not physically, but emotionally like everyone else. Chris and Tigger were outside when Mick stepped from the camper.

"I saw the truck," she said. "I was hoping the boy wasn't driving it." She smiled. "My name is Madge; you met my son Ethan when you pulled in. Here …" She handed him a plate. "It's a casserole. You and the boys eat. Have some lunch. You must be hungry."

"Thank you, ma'am," Mick said. "That is very kind of

you. We'll enjoy it."

She produced a sad smile. "It's good ... good to see children with a grownup. Are they your children? Or did you find them?"

"They're my sons."

She pursed her lips as if she held back tears. "That's wonderful and finally nice to see. I'll let you get settled. If you need anything, just ask anyone here. We're all pretty tight."

"I will, thank you."

She cleared her throat, ran her hand over Tigger's head, folded her arms tight to her body and walked off.

Chris nudged into Mick and peeked at the plate. "What did she make?"

"Doesn't matter," Mick told him. "We're eating it. Gonna be polite."

"Don't you think that was an odd thing to ask?" Chris questioned. "You know, about us being yours?"

Mick tilted his head. "I guess it is."

"Man, you have to wonder how many kids there are without parents for her to greet us like that." After a sigh, Chris took the plate. "Come on, Tig, let's eat before Mick eats this all. You know how big his stomach is."

Mick didn't say anything. In fact, the plate slipped from his hand without him noticing. He heard what Chris said and then he saw a child, then another. Four or five sat across the campsite; another small group was on the playground area.

Where were all the adults? Mick spotted maybe two more. They had to be inside.

No sooner did Mick have that thought when he had another: *Oh my God, the children.*

He had never thought beyond the walls of Lodi. It never crossed his mind that there would be countless children left without parents, not just parents who lost a child.

A 'snap' of the fire snapped Mick from his thoughts.

However, the thoughts of children alone stayed with him through the course of the day and as he watched his own son, Chris, looking so lost.

"You okay?" Mick asked.

"Yeah," Chris said. "Just thinking."

Mick reached into his shirt pocket and pulled out his phone that he had charged in the truck and he powered it up. He wasn't a making a phone call. Cell phones had gone down. He was using it for a fix. A Dylan and Dustin fix.

There were 875 pictures on his phone and close to a hundred videos. Mick was grateful for each and every one. But he guessed one day, that number would be small. Because to make up for a lifetime lost, 1000 images just would never be enough.

"What are you doing?" Chris asked as he sat down next to him.

"I need to see your mom and brother," Mick said softly.

Chris' breath shivered loudly. "Me, too. Can I …can look with you?"

"Without a doubt."

Chris moved closer, right next to him. Mick brought his arm around the boy, bringing him close and huddling in to share the phone.

Chris rested his head against Mick. "Mick, you think we'll ever feel normal again?"

"I think that's a pretty tough question to answer. I think that time will ease some of the pain. It'll never be like it used to be. But I think we'll get used to feeling a hint of pain and then that will become the new normal."

After a pause, Chris said, "That wasn't very helpful."

"It's the best I can do."

"I'll take it."

Mick gently kissed the top of Chris' head and together, slowly, they looked through the pictures.

* * *

Arcata, California

Before Lexi Martin was educated at the University of Pittsburgh School of Medicine, she was educated on the streets of Detroit, Michigan. That alone, she believed, would be the schooling she needed for what was ahead. More so than any other education she had received.

Her father lost his job at the plant, her mother worked as a waitress and sales clerk, and Lexi dropped out of high school at fifteen to work under the table for the Lees at their dry cleaning business. Eventually she got her GED, went to community college, then a local university, scoring highest in her class before getting accepted into Pitt.

That was quite an accomplishment.

While most med students were about the age of 27 when they did their internships, Lexi was already well into her thirties.

She scored high and did remarkably well. She had all intentions of returning to Detroit, working at a clinic, and giving back to her community. But on a whim, she applied at the Centers for Disease Control, and was surprised when she got the position of field doctor.

Even five years at the CDC didn't prepare her for the field of death she faced when the flu brought an end to life as she knew it. She was sent to Anchorage, Alaska, and Anchorage was the first major city in the United States to die out.

Watching what this particular strain of the flu did make Lexi grateful she'd never taken the time to have children.

She prayed and hoped that elsewhere it wouldn't be so bad. The flu started in Alaska. An accident at a lab facility embedded deep in the wilderness would have — should have — been contained, but a local Eskimo barter carried not only the good but also the germ to a neighboring village.

It had spread through the villages, and continued to

spread throughout the population because of two men. One of them beat the flu; the other, Lexi heard he had died.

One man, Bill Daniels, lost his fiancé and had no other family. When the flu was all said and done in Anchorage, Bill had left with Lexi, being a helping hand in any way he could. News had reached them that the flu was now a worldwide pandemic, and the CDC moved Lexi to California. For one month, she and Bill moved to three different small towns. The last of which, Arcata, held on tight until the first week of October, then most of them died.

The former population of 18,000 was now maybe … population 1,500. Maybe.

Most of the people of Arcata were struggling with how they could survive. They were in a good position for fishing, but were still reeling from their losses and not thinking properly.

Taking in their final California sunset, Lexi shared a package of peanut butter crackers with Bill as they sat on the beach. It was probably the last fresh pack for a very long time.

"Last radio contact," Lexi said, "the last two remaining CDC men were heading to Lodi."

"You think they did?" Bill asked.

"If Kurt said they did, they did." Lexi smiled. "He was a good man to work for at the CDC."

Bill reached for the bottle of whiskey they had dug into the sand. "When was it we last heard that broadcast?"

"Six days ago." Lexi nodded at Bill's silent offer to refresh her glass. "I can only assume that the president is still trying. And I think that town he mentioned is Lodi."

Bill downed a quick drink and poured another. "We could stay here."

"I know," Lexi said. "And I know the people here may be sad to see us go. But we've been ready to go for two weeks. Packed, planned and ready." She sipped her drink. "More than heading to Lodi, I think I need to see what's left of this country."

Bill choked out a laugh.

"What?" she questioned.

"A little post-apocalypse sightseeing?"

"Well when you put it like that ..." Lexi shook her head. "Yeah, I guess. Aren't you curious?"

"I'm very curious. Could be dangerous."

"I know. But I feel safe with our plan. I feel safe with you." She stared at him.

"I appreciate that." Bill lifted his glass to hers. "Then we go. We'll leave tomorrow, first thing."

Lexi clicked her glass to his, took a drink, then she sank into thoughts of the journey ahead, while watching the rest of the sunset with Bill.

JOURNAL ENTRY

October 16th

I really don't know what to write. I'm not feeling any better. We had tuna casserole yesterday; I think that's what it was. It was good. Mick didn't really give us a choice, we had to eat it. A lady brought it by.

Tigger and Mick are still sleeping. I fell asleep for a little bit, but I had another nightmare. I don't tell anyone, not even Mick, about my nightmares. Maybe because I'm thinking he's got his own to deal with.

I dreamt of my brother. I always dream of my brother. Not Tigger, but Dustin. Tigger is young. I don't think he knows yet what happened. He asks all the time about Mom and Dustin. He nods when we tell him they ain't coming back, but I don't think he understands.

I'm glad about that. The less he knows, the less he will hurt.

Last night me and Mick looked at pictures of my mom and Dustin and our old life.

I kept thinking how it was Monday.

Monday was me and Dustin's night. We watched wrestling every Monday. He was my best friend in the whole world. We had big plans and now they're gone. What am I gonna do? How am I gonna even wanna grow up and do things without my brother?

It hurts to even think about him. It hurts to think about my mom. She was my hero. I wish I would have told her that.

I'm scared, cause I know they're gone and I'm afraid I'll forget what they look like or sound like. I'm so glad Mick has that phone.

It's worth more than all the food and water in the world. I just hope that phone never breaks, never stops working, because in that phone is all I have left of them.

I know it sounds stupid, but that's how I feel.

I just miss them so much. It's wrong, it's so wrong what happened.

We all take it one day at a time. Right now, I just hate the days because I don't have my brother and mom anymore.

Just sucks.

3. SPACE BETWEEN

The knock on the camper door surprised Mick. He was cleaning up after breakfast, the boys were working on a puzzle. He wanted them to go out, mingle with the other kids, but neither of them showed any interest.

Ethan stood in the doorway when Mick opened it. "Sorry, to bother you," he said.

"No. No bother. Did you want to come in?"

Ethan lifted his hand waving it back and forth. "There are two reasons, I came by. One … later this afternoon, I wanna gather up some of the kids and take them fishing. We try to hit the lake every couple days. Catching is good. Wanted to invite you and your boys."

"We'll be happy to join you."

"Great. A-and the o-other thing is …" Ethan stammered some, almost nervous about approaching Mick, "I don't have many men in this camp. I realize you aren't staying, but Liam's back is bothering him and I was wondering if I can pull you away to help me check out Rosemont."

"I'm sorry, Rosemont?"

"Small town about twenty miles west of here. They finished their flu less than a week ago. Heard it was a long, dragged out thing there. Thought they beat it, didn't, it came back sort of thing."

Mick twitched his head. "I'm confused."

"Small towns got hit last, you know."

"I'm well aware," Mick said.

"I been hitting them. Can't get into the cities, which saddens me."

"Ethan, I understand that. Are you going to the town for supplies?"

"No … for kids. A lot of kids are left alone. We been bringing them here until we can figure out what to do with them."

Mick heard a shuffle behind him and looked back; Chris had stood up. Obviously it caught the young boy's attention.

Ethan continued. "I suppose in while it will be futile, but I wanna try. At least I can say I tried. I'd go alone, but I just want back up in case there is trouble. Haven't seen trouble in a while, thank God."

Mick lowered his head. "I … I can't leave my boys, I'm sorry."

"Mick," Chris exclaimed, "you have to go. I'll watch Tigger. I'm grown enough."

"And my mom is right nearby," Ethan said. "I know you don't have reason to trust us, but it's safe here. I promise. We won't be gone more than two hours."

Mick opened his mouth to talk and Chris interrupted. "And you don't have reason not to trust him either, Mick."

Open mouthed, Mick turned to him. "I can't leave you boys and I don't want to take you."

"I said I can watch Tigger," Chris huffed. "You have to, Mick."

"Why are you so insistent about this, Chris?"

"Because, what if there are kids in this Rose town? Which, by the way, has the same name as your mom. It's a sign, Mick. And wouldn't you want someone to come get me and Tig, if we were all alone in this world?"

Ethan pointed. "That's a bright, caring kid there."

"Yeah, yeah, he is." Mick nodded. "I'll grab my coat, be right with you."

"Thank you. I'll let my mother know to keep an ear out."

Mick shut the door. "You put me on the spot," he told Chris.

"Yeah, well, I can't believe you don't want to go."

"It's not that I don't want to go …."

"You're afraid, huh?" Chris asked. "It's okay to be afraid."

Mick closed his eyes. "It's not that."

"Then what is it?"

"Nothing. It was me not wanting to leave you, but that's settled. Let me find my jacket and gun." Mick slipped by Chris. But he wasn't honest, he *was* afraid. Not of anything bad or possible trouble, but more so of what he'd find. It had been a while since the flu. If a child survived the flu, what were the chances that they survived … life? Mick wasn't quite sure he could take seeing anymore bad.

* * *

Tom watched the third truck pull down the main street of Lodi. He'd been going since sunrise, making plans for survival runs, getting food and supplies, then determining a distribution center. Lodi had acquired a few more residents in the last couple days. Tom worried. He didn't want to take on any leadership position, but with Mick gone and not really stepping up to the organization plate, Tom figured someone had to so it. The two guys from the CDC were more concerned about the national level.

Tom worried about Lodi. That was it. What happened outside of it, well, that wasn't his concern.

He made a notation on his clipboard and turned around, surprised to see Lars Rayburn standing there.

"You're up early," Tom said. "Aren't you the noon riser?"

"I used to be before this ordeal," Lars said. "But this morning, I went out with Will and guess what?"

"I'm game, what?"

"Looks pretty steady on the power and landlines. Nothing giving way."

"Now, if we can just get word out to others on how to get things up and running," Tom said. "Maybe we should think about sending Will and someone else out there to help."

"That's possible. But is it safe?" Lars asked. "Have we heard anything?"

Tom shook his head. "When all this started going down, there was some trouble. Since then, haven't heard much. Wish there was a way to get in touch with Mick. Hopefully he'll bring back some insight. But to be honest, Lars, my concern isn't going out for food now. There's plenty out there, lying around. But for how long? There were no crops this year, everyone got sick. It's time to start planning long term," Tom said. "And to be honest, I'm not knowing where to begin."

* * *

The town of Rosemont wasn't all that different from Lodi. It was set off a highway, nestled back off the back roads. There wasn't a town square, just businesses.

"How do you propose finding these kids?" Mick asked Ethan.

"Like I do in every town. First I ask, then I drive the residential streets. Looking for signs. The flu hit in the summer, so I look for bikes, toys, swing sets, stuff like that. Then I listen. You get real quiet and you listen. With no sounds of life, it's easy to hear a crying kid."

"How many have you found?"

Ethan exhaled. "Nineteen so far. We placed almost half of them."

"Placed?"

"Yeah, folks that pass through like you. Lost their own kids, they take a liking and take on an orphan. Me and my mother use good judgment. Don't think we're just sending them out to bad people."

"No, no, I wasn't thinking that." Mick indicated with his head then pointed. "There's a man up there."

The man on the street was packing his car. He looked over at the truck as Ethan slowed down.

Ethan wound down his window. "Morning, sir."

"We don't have anything. The town is wiped out," the man said. "If that's what you're looking for."

Ethan shook his head. "No. I've been hitting a lot of small towns. Looking for kids that may be left alone after their parents died."

"Noble cause," the man replied. "Why?"

"Ever since two were left orphaned at our camp," Ethan said, "I wondered how many others were out there."

"Well …" the man shrugged, "most of this town died from the flu. We thought, you know, we had it beat. We had a small outbreak and then about ten days ago, it just wiped us out. Returned with a vengeance. We lost our last person about four days ago."

Mick understood that, and his head lowered.

"I think I'm the last of the people here. Maybe the Morgans, but I'm not sure. They're over on Carson Street, four blocks down and to your left. They may know more, but I'm really not sure about any kids. I'm alone."

Mick leaned forward. "Sir, I'm from a town called Lodi. Lodi, Ohio."

"Lodi," he said airily. "I heard about that town on the news. It was flu free."

"Not entirely," Mick said. "We suffered a lot of deaths. But the town is still functioning. Maybe you should head there."

"Maybe I will. Good luck with your search."

Ethan nodded a thank you and drove on looking for Carson Street. The population sign read 1600, so they knew the town wasn't all that big, but it was definitely deserted.

The businesses hadn't been boarded up, yet the doors were open.

Out in front of the small volunteer fire station a tent was erected. Possibly a help station at one time. But that man by the truck was the only person they saw.

Carson Street proved futile, as there was no one there. It was barren and Mick and Ethan even called out. They'd walk, call out, listen and walk.

From the map, Mick saw there were about six patches of residential areas. He understood Ethan's plight and reasoning, but didn't see how he was going to find anyone in a town such as Rosemont. Really, it was a small town. Would there be children left alone?

The third patch of residential homes was a small mobile home area set just down a small hill from a day care center. They pulled the truck down and began their search.

Mick remained cool, calm, and indifferent until he saw the doll on the street. Just lying there, its legs broken, probably from being run over. It was dirty, the hair frizzy, and Mick bent down to lift it.

Was the child who loved that doll still alive? He imagined in his mind the family leaving to get help and the doll dropped. So much screamed at Mick about all that happened to the world, all that was lost, when he saw that doll. Just as his fingers gripped it, he heard it.

So did Ethan, because he turned his head to Mick. "You hear that?"

It was high pitched sound, achy, and almost catlike.

"Animal?" Mick asked.

Ethan shook his head and called, "Hello!"

Again, the noise came to them, faint but close.

Mick spun to the tan mobile home. "There."

"You sure?"

"I think."

A few more steps and another cry out, and Mick was certain he and Ethan were entering the right home. The second they stepped into the mobile home, the familiar smell of death pelted Mick. It was raw, overpowering and the trailer was warm, which seemed to breed the odor. It didn't take long, only a few steps, to find not only the source of the smell, but the cause of the noise.

The body of a woman lay on the sofa. She was covered in a blanket, her eyes wide open, face grey. In the center of the living room was a portable playpen. Inside, surrounded by empty bottles was a child. It was apparent by the amount of bottles the mother had done all that she could. That perhaps as she lay dying she prayed that someone would find her child before it was too late.

The boy was no older than two, and was lying on his side. His skin was dry, cracked and pale. His tiny mouth was open and his eyes sunken in. He blinked once, as if trying to focus on Mick, then whimpered out a labored, faint cry.

"Oh my God." Mick rushed to the playpen. He knew the second he placed his hands on the child, that it wasn't the flu. The toddler was starving and severely dehydrated. "Oh my God," he said again as he lifted the child.

His heart broke. The child was listless, only able to squeal, and it was apparent that the simple noise took everything from him. He locked eyes with Mick and Mick just wanted to cry. Just crumble and cry.

"We gotta get fluids into that child," Ethan said, rushing to the playpen and lifting a bottle. He raced to the kitchen and looked. "Nothing here."

Mick just stared at the child, the slowly brought him to his chest. His little hands tried so hard to grab on to Mick, but he didn't have the energy.

"I got water in the truck," Ethan said, rushing from the kitchen to the door. "Let's go."

Mick just stood there.

"Mick, come on. We got to help this child."

After only a nod, Mick, cradling the toddler, quickly

followed Ethan.

Help the child? Mick thought, *Was that even possible?*

JOURNAL ENTRY

I thought I'd write a little while me and Tig were just hanging back in the camper. We're waiting on Mick, he won't be long. Tig keeps looking out the window. We can hear kids out there playing.

They're laughing. I don't understand that. How can they laugh? A part of me feels as if I am not allowed to laugh. That if I smile, it would be wrong.

Not that I want to smile. I don't have it in me and I don't think anything, right now, can make me smile. Not a real one or big.

I had the weirdest thought. I wonder if my dad was psychic. Maybe he knew deep inside that something was gonna happen, something big and sad, and that was why he took his own life.

I didn't understand it when he did it. I mean, why? But now, I'm a little jealous. Why?

Because he didn't have to see it happen.

He didn't have to watch Dustin die. What my brother went through was bad. Really bad. He was so sick and he did not deserve to feel that much pain.

Yet, he wasn't scared. How can you know you're gonna die and not be scared? I am proud of my big brother. I wonder if my dad was there waiting on Dustin, saying, "Come on, guy, we have to greet a lot of people.' I wonder if they were sad or happy when my mom got there.

Like I said, a part of me is jealous. I know that sounds stupid. But my dad gets to be with Dustin, my gram, my mom. I get Mick and Tig. Don't get me wrong, I love Mick and Tigger. I just wish our family wasn't broken up.

I'd give anything to have it be normal.

I'd give anything to have my mom and brother back.

What's gonna happen now to this world? I'm pretty sure I'll never go to school again. Never have my friends. Probably never go to college. What about the dreams that I had, that my brother had?

They're just gone.

I'm smart enough to know that water isn't always good enough to drink when you find it, and the cans of food on the shelf at the store ain't gonna last forever.

Maybe it's something I should leave for the grownups to worry about. But something tells me I'm gonna have to be a grown up long before I'm ready.

It ain't fair that this happened.

But what can you do?

4. LIFE

"I seen this before but not this bad," Ethan told Mick as they placed the baby on a dampened cloth. Internally, that wet towel would do nothing, but Baby Boy Doe was like prune. Literally like a prune.

Putting liquids in his bottle were futile, as Doe wouldn't drink or swallow; he could barely react at all.

"Come on, little man," Mick pleaded. "You got to drink, something, please drink something."

"He needs more than water. Maybe they got some of the electrolyte stuff in town in one of the stores. It won't hurt to look."

Mick was at a loss. As an officer of the law he had some knowledge of emergency medicine, but it was basic. First aid, CPR, stuff like that.

Baby Boy Doe was naked, his legs barely squirmed, and Mick held him as they got in the truck.

"Ethan, you said you seen this before?"

Ethan soaked a paper towel with water. "About a week ago when we found Billy, yes. He's six, like your boy. He was dehydrated to the point he couldn't swallow. He was able to have some reaction. Most of the young ones are starving, thirsty." He handed the wet towel to Mick. "Put this in his mouth. Maybe he'll suck on it and get just enough into his system so that he'll take a bottle."

Ethan shut the door and walked to his side of the truck.

The water from the towel rolled down Mick's hand and he brought it to the boy's mouth. He opened his mouth some and placed the cloth inside. The baby barely reacted.

"Massage his throat," Ethan instructed. "Help him to swallow, keep him up, you don't want him to choke."

"So you have done this before?"

"Yeah, but he wasn't this bad. No one was. I don't know." Ethan started the truck. "I saw that little gas station up there, maybe they have something."

Mick kept constant eye contact with the baby. He didn't know why the child pulled at his heart so. He kept encouraging the baby to take the cloth, swallow, anything.

Baby Boy Doe's breathing was rapid, and his protruding stomach snapped back and forth with each breath.

"What did you do before this world went to shit?" Mick asked.

"I was school teacher."

It made immediate sense to Mick, why Ethan thought of children first, how he cared so much about those left behind. He could see Patrick doing the same had he survived the flu.

"Mick, you seem like a level headed guy," Ethan said. "But right now, you're frazzled. Relax, trust me he can sense it."

"How did this happen, Ethan?" Mick asked with such heartbreak. "How?"

"What do you mean?"

"I mean, apparently his mom tried, you know? But he was forgotten. He was just forgotten. How?"

"Mick, think about it. I don't mean to dredge up anything, but when you were suffering your loss, when you and your family were going through the hell of the flu, did you stop to think? Did you at all, stop and wonder, let's say, about the Smiths down the street, how they had two boys and what would become of them? Did you wonder at all about the kids?"

"I did. Yes, I ran my town," Mick said. "And our whole town became like a family when the flu hit. We went door to door."

Ethan exhaled. "That was Lodi. It isn't the way it was. Unfortunately, unlike Lodi, no one really cared what happened outside their own home. You folks were just different."

Ethan's words hit hard to Mick and rang a painful reality. Yes, the people of Lodi cared for each other, came together and rallied to each other's aid. But in essence, Mick did the same as everyone else in the country. He didn't care about what was happening outside his house. Only difference was, All of Lodi was his house.

After thinking about it, Mick simply said. "No, no we weren't. We were the same, Ethan, just on a different scale."

Mick held the baby with the cloth to his mouth. How ironic that such a small, helpless child could bring such a big revelation. Mick had only focused on what happened to his home, his family, and for the first time, the hard reality of what had happened to the world pummeled him.

* * *

Rose Owens was still angry with her son. It wasn't like when he was a teenager and didn't check in. Mick was a grown man. In fact, he was the Chief of Police in the small town of Lodi, Ohio. But he had left.

He stated he had good reasons, but to Rose there wasn't any good reason to up and leave the town that you had led through such a horrendous ordeal.

She credited her son and a couple of others with saving the lives of half the population of Lodi. Half. While the loss seemed great when spoken, it paled in comparison to the rest of the world.

Rose thought about the rest of the world; she was certain her son did not.

To him, Mick had lost his world - the love of his life and the boy who was no less than a son to him. He didn't care hide nor hair about anything except what he lost and what he still had remaining.

Tigger and Chris.

Rose was sure she didn't play into the 'still had' factor, or else he wouldn't have left. She understood his reasoning, but she didn't like it. There were too many painful memories in Lodi and Mick wanted to take the boys away. She wasn't sure where, though. Tom's family cabin in West Virginia? Would they even get that far? Rose doubted it.

Mick made decisions his entire life based on the passion in his gut and not the knowledge in his head and that worried Rose. The boys had just lost their mother, brother and grandmother. As much as a testosterone filled getaway seemed like the thing to do, Rose wondered if Mick had a clue what was outside the town limits.

Rose had returned to Lodi at the height of the flu epidemic. She watched people panic, rush to the streets, to the hospitals, break into stores. She saw the confusion and chaos. And it wasn't long before that Lodi put up an iron wall to keep people out. A wall many tried to break through.

Mick was there to hold it; he was the one who kept law and order. And now there was only one deputy remaining, one law enforcement agent. Mick was gone.

Did he suddenly think with the end of the flu, so came the end of any threat? Rose thought it unfair of him and selfish. Yes, he was hurt. But so were the boys. And so was everyone else in Lodi.

Being hurt and emotional left one vulnerable. What kind of world remained out there where he was taking the boys? Nothing was hunky dory anymore - she knew that. Rose's gut wrenched with worry for her son and grandsons. Mick was a big man, but was he big and strong enough to keep those boys safe?

Mick and those boys were all she had left in the world.

And while she prayed for their safety, she grew angrier by the hour. They had been gone a little over a day and it was a day too long.

She stayed in her home, declining dinner with Tom and Lars, who supported Mick's decision. Of course they would. They weren't out in the world like she was. Tom checked off a clipboard, sending out trucks for supplies and opened a video store.

Rose couldn't sit idly by, pretending that all was fine while watching a movie she picked up at Tom's. If things were going bad during the flu, the bad didn't die off.

The bad may have paused, but for how long? Her instincts told her something was awry. Tom told her she was crazy.

Her son stood well over six foot five, and Rose pushed six foot with her boots on. She had a thick, tough body that didn't waver in strength even though she was sixty-two.

Nor did her attitude. She was tough as nails, and barely flinched, even in the worst stages of the flu.

In the morning, after Tom sent out the trucks, Rose got on her motorcycle and decided to do what no one had in a week. She went out to check the perimeter of the town.

The 'iron wall' of strength that Mick had erected to protect the main entrances to Lodi was gone. The trucks were moved, and the motorcycle brigade gone. Most of the bikers had packed up and left after they helped bury bodies. They went out to find their families. The few remaining soldiers had left as well.

Then, so did Mick.

Rose didn't see anything, of course; it was flat. But it was when she was visiting the new cemetery outside of Lodi, that she smelled it.

Smoke.

Something about it made her hair stand on edge. She focused her view to the trees in the distance and couldn't see anything. It could have been someone starting a fireplace.

After all, the air did have a chill. Maybe she was being neurotic and looking for something, and maybe it was coming from within Lodi. She just thought it was odd that she had to go outside of her community to grab the scent.

From the cemetery she couldn't tell, couldn't get a good direction or lock on it. There was only one way to find out, so Rose hopped back on her bike, and headed back into town.

* * *

Doe's lips moved, and they closed some against the cloth. Mick smiled in relief. "He's responding."

"Finally," Ethan stated. "Let's see if he'll take the bottle yet."

Mick removed the soaking cloth and tried enticing the toddler with the bottle. He didn't seem ready to take it. "Not yet. But he looks better, doesn't he?"

Ethan tilted his head. "A little, not much. We're getting there."

They had driven back into town. The man who was packing was long gone. The gas station didn't have the electrolyte drink and they used up more time looking for it. Finally they located a child's version of it and were getting some results.

It helped Doe but it wasn't what he really needed. At the fire station and EMT garage there were no IVs, and nothing else that would help.

Ethan scratched his head. "This little one has to be seen by a medical professional. Unfortunately, I haven't a clue where we'd find one."

"I actually do," Mick said. "Lodi. Lars Rayburn is there."

"Lodi isn't that far, a couple hours' drive. This child, if you keep trying to hydrate him, could survive that and stand a fighting chance."

"I know. I guess, I'll have to cut the trip with the boys

short. I'm certain they'll understand."

"You carry that cell phone. Does it work? Maybe you can call that doctor."

Mick shook his head. "Cell phones went down a few days ago. Actually, one of the last calls received by Lodi was from the president."

"Of?"

"The United States."

"Wow, I thought he was dead. What did he want?"

"Since two of his government guys were in Lodi, he was letting them know he was trying to … restructure … or whatever."

"That's good to hear," Ethan said. "Will it work?"

"Can't think about that right now," Mick said. "Let's get this baby some help."

Ethan gave a nod, handed the rest of the infant electrolyte water to Mick and both men got in the truck.

Mick continued to try; intently focusing on the baby, and suddenly, saving the child was most important to him in the world.

* * *

"What are you writing?" Tigger asked, peering over Chris' shoulder.

Chris repositioned himself at the tiny kitchen table in the camper. "Stuff."

"A story?"

"No. Well, sort of." Chris shrugged. "Just stuff that happened, my thoughts."

"Can you read them to me?"

"I can tell them to you."

"Yeah, but I miss stories. No one reads me stories anymore."

Chris closed the cover to the notebook. "I'll read you a story tonight before bed, okay?"

Tigger nodded then climbed up to sit across from Chris. It was a task for him, being so small. He exhaled, a breath too big to come from him, as he perched his chin against the palms of his hands and peered with a sideways glance out the window.

"What's up little man? You bored? Wanna play a game?"

"Would you be mad if I said I wanted to play with the kids?"

"Now why would I be mad about that?" Chris asked. "You're a kid, of course, you wanna play. Can you wait for Mick to get back?"

"I guess. But what if they stop playing by then? They look like they're having fun."

Chris peered out the window. 'Yeah they do."

"Don't you wanna go play? You're still a kid, too."

Chris stared at his little brother. He reached across the table and rubbed his hand over Tigger's wiry hair. "Yeah, I am, dude. Grab your coat and hat. Let's go out."

Tigger grinned, widely. He jumped from the table and raced for his things.

Chris swept up the notebook, deciding he'd take it with him in case he got bored. He doubted it though. Maybe what he needed was to get out and be a kid again.

* * *

Lodi, Ohio

Tom had barely returned to the store when Henry Davis popped in. Director of the CDC, Henry had run most of the country when the president went into lockdown. He kept statistics along with Dr. Kurt Wilson of the World Health Organization. The two men, stuck in a room, lone survivors, were some of the few who hadn't fled their post, the two man epicenter that ran America. Henry and Kurt had instituted the Lars Rayburn Therapy against the flu. It was a long shot, but one that had to take. Henry was the one responsible for the organization of the plan. He had sent supplies to Lodi to help the residents fight off the flu, to help it be the one town that successfully safeguarded itself. And then Henry, and Kurt, with nowhere else to go, no family, had come to Lodi as well.

They arrived right when the town, who all believed had escaped the devastation of the flu, was hit.

"Renting a movie?" Tom asked.

"No, no," Henry said. "Need you to call an immediate meeting of that council you put together."

"Mick ain't here," Tom said. "He's a big part of that."

"Well, this will have to go forward without Mick," Henry told him. "I heard from the president again. I was finally able to make radio contact."

Tom whistled. "Been over a week. Didn't think we'd hear anything from the outside after the cell phones went down."

"Fortunately," Henry said, "it looks like they may be able to connect again. They're hoping in a few days the phones will work."

"Hot dog, that's a good thing. Mick has that cell phone for pictures. Won't he be surprised when I call him?" Tom said. "Is that what the meeting's about?"

"No." Henry shook his head. "At last contact they were thinking about making Lodi a central station since we held on to civilization the most. But the president said they're gonna try to establish from where they are. At least until they can pull more reserve troops in. They locked in contact with some. Apparently, it's not safe out there. When they sent out scouts, they were ambushed."

"By whom?" Tom asked with shock. "Who the hell wants to ambush anyone? Is there even anyone left?"

"Tom, you aren't that naive."

Tom gave a half shrug. "I guess after nothing happened, after the flu finished, I kind of gave props to humanity in good faith."

"We all did. But that's not the case," Henry said. "People are trying to reestablish their own lives now. They are emerging. Survivors. People are hungry, they're desperate."

"You been talking to Rose?" Tom asked. "'Cause she says the same thing."

"Haven't spoken to her. But, if you could get everyone together, that would be a good thing. Meet tonight?"

Tom nodded. "Josh Hayward is part of the council, I sent him out for a run. I'll tell him when he gets back." Tom glanced down at his watch and stared.

"What's wrong?"

Tom shook his head. "Nothing. They're just late. Probably fine."

"I'm sure they are."

"Tom, come to Diggins Drug store. Now!"

Rose had called for him. Not by a phone or radio; she had actually called. She shouted loudly, at the top of her lungs, like a mother calling her kids in for supper.

"Tom Roberts! Come to Diggins now!"

Tom slammed his hand to the counter. "Now what in the world is up with that woman? I swear she lost her mind with the flu."

"She doesn't sound like she's in trouble."

"No, she does not." Tom cringed at the call again. "Will you excuse me?"

Henry swiped his hand over his mouth to hide his smirk. "Of course."

Tom walked around the counter and outside. Rose continued to call steadily. Diggins was only a block down the street and her voice grew louder the closer he drew to the store.

"I hear ya!" Tom shouted. "Stop calling my name for crying out loud." Tom stopped before the store, and looked left and right. "Where are you?"

"Up here." Rose waved from the rooftop.

"What in the hell woman? Are you stuck up there?"

"Tom Roberts, you think I'd be stuck up and here and scream for *you* to help me?"

Tom was about to respond, but felt a tap on his shoulder and turned to find Lars standing there. "Where'd you come from?"

Lars pointed to the store. "I was in there finishing off the shelves for inventory. Why is she on the roof screaming your name?"

"I don't know. If you were in there, why didn't you see what she wanted?"

"Would you?"

"Good point." Tom aimed his voice upwards. "What do you need, Rose?"

"Come up here, please. Thank you."

After an exhale, Tom looked to Lars. "Join me?"

"Why not?"

* * *

Diggins was the tallest building in Lodi. Apartments perched above the drugstore, and the only way to the roof was to walk the four flights of stairs. When Tom and Lars reached the top, Rose was looking out, facing the town.

Tom took a second to catch his breath. "Okay, Rose, this better be good."

"Oh my God," Lars whispered.

Tom turned to him. "Oh my God … what?" He saw that Lars was staring outward. Before he could see what it was that caught Lars' attention, Rose stepped to him.

"That's what I called you for," she said. "When I was out at the cemetery, I smelled the smoke but couldn't see it. I figured it may be a fireplace or something, then I came up here. At first, I still couldn't see it, and then it started. And in the few minutes it took for you guys to get here, it went from a wisp to *that*." She pointed. "Fuck me, right?"

Tom was about to question the need for her use of

obscenities, even though swearing was a natural part of Rose's vocabulary, but he wanted to sputter the same exact words when she sidestepped and he saw.

In the distance, thick black smoke billowed into the sky. So much that it started to create its own cloud formation.

Rose handed Lars the binoculars. "Like I said, a few minutes ago, it was a thin trickle. Now look at it."

Binoculars in hand, Lars moved closer to the roof's edge. "How the hell can something be on fire?"

"Whatever it is, it's big. Big enough for us to see." Tom reached for the binoculars. "Looks like it's burning near Wadsworth."

"No, Tom," Rose said solemnly. "That fire is *Wadsworth* burning."

JOURNAL ENTRY

On my thirteenth birthday, my brother Dustin gave me a copy of The Best of WrestleMania. *Not that I didn't have it. I did. But one night when we were playing around, we broke it. My mom said she wouldn't get me another. Man.*

But my brother did and we watched that for three days straight. We always vowed we'd be a wrestling duo, the ultimate tag team.

That ain't happening now. I doubt wrestling would even come back. Even though I think it's important.

I remember, right after the flu started. Things were still semi normal in the world, the news wasn't on all the time. But I knew that it was pretty bad when they cancelled Monday night wrestling. They never cancel wrestling. But they did and it never came back.

I wonder if any of the wrestlers got sick. They probably did.

Me and Dustin talked about that. I guess it was a pretty shallow thing to talk about when the world was dying. I guess this whole entry is pretty shallow.

But I wanted to talk about wrestling. I miss it. I miss my whole old life.

5. DESPERATE

When Jonah Briggs was eight years old, he positioned himself on the limb of a tree and deliberately jumped onto the back of the neighborhood bully to stop him from beating up another child. From that moment on, Briggs knew he wanted to be a hero.

A big and brawny guy, quiet most of the time, he joined the United States Army before he even graduated high school. He spent the summer before his senior year in basic training. But that was what he wanted.

There was never a doubt in his mind. He served his country well and with everything he had. Unfortunately, after seventeen years of service, he was dishonorably discharged for inhumane interrogations of prisoners of war.

Briggs felt he was a pawn, had been set up; after all, he was only doing what he was told to do.

But he found other means of protecting his country. Without missing a beat he was hired by a private security company and worked a lot of overseas security details. Within three years of being part of that security company, Briggs acquired Commanding Officer status of Defend USA, a nonprofit, private militia and survival group, the largest in the state of New York.

Briggs joined the company early, when it was still in its infancy. Once he was in the private security sector he recruited a lot of his fellow workers. All of which, at one time, had served their country in an official capacity.

Defend USA grew rapidly. Its motto of defending America from any and all threats, whether manmade or natural, and standing with her to rebuild and protect against invasion or civil unrest, was relentlessly repeated when the flu began.

In fact, Briggs sent out emails to its members and families stating that he had a friend in the government that told him the flu would and could be man's extinction level event. Briggs knew of the Alaska outbreak before anyone else and he knew when it crossed the border of being contained. He encouraged Defend USA members and their families to stockpile, to prepare.

When the western states began shutting down, he encouraged them to isolate themselves and move to defend America's grounds. He sent invites to come to the New York Base. While there was only sufficient housing for a thousand, there was enough acreage to accommodate everyone. People came, and then as time moved on, people flocked there.

Briggs worked with a neighboring community and the mayor there. He also set up communications with other militia units and a post-pandemic plan, should power be extinguished.

It had been 30 days since the height of the flu, and the population of Briggs camp of members and refugees, along with the small town, capped 18,000 people. When the flu wiped through them, only thirty percent survived.

They vowed to rebuild. To restore law and order, to maintain survival, a means of power had to be established. Someone had to be in charge of the resources – of the food, the power, the water, and to protect the land against foreign invaders. Someone had to make sure everyone had enough.

If someone didn't step up to the plate, chaos would ensue. Briggs stepped up to the plate.

Through post-flu networking he knew of many surviving

small towns, but that wasn't where he'd start. To build up his forces, he'd start small - the lone survivors, the starving camps. He'd build a security force.

It was his agenda to recruit everyone. For order to be restored, for civilization to work again, everyone had to participate. Every man, woman, child, small town or little group. No one would be excluded from the rebuilding.

Like before the pandemic, people would pay their taxes, only their taxes would be paid in goods, services, and so forth. It was the only way.

The United States would not survive if it were divided and Briggs was going to do everything and anything he could to ensure that would not be the case. Anything.

At the last census on October 11th, Briggs had 4,000 people. He kept a skeleton crew at camp to work on organizing stock and incoming supplies, the rest he divided into groups and sent them out. Their mission was simple: organize the towns, secure their involvement, recruit members, deal with criminals, and seize property and supplies by order of the new government. They were to "deal with" insurgents and those who resisted. Above all, should force be necessary, at any cost, they were to protect themselves from harm.

The problem was, Briggs wasn't specific enough and left it up to the judgment of the leader of each individual search team. That was his first mistake.

* * *

Her name didn't matter, mainly because she wouldn't be alive long enough to tell it to anyone. But what she went through *did* matter.

She had survived the flu. She didn't even get it, but her husband did, and so did her mother and three young children. They all died. She watched them all die and she, too, wanted to die.

Her parents divorced when she was teenager, but she never lost contact with her father. When she'd last spoken to him, he hadn't gotten sick. She tried several times to kill herself, but never was able to finish the job. Finally, after virtually trying to starve herself, she left her Virginia home to trek north to find her father. She didn't think too much about running out of gasoline, until she did and couldn't refuel her car because the pumps were empty. After two days of walking, she met up with a kind man, who said that he too was heading north. He had supplies and so did she.

Safety in numbers.

He was about the same age, and like her, wasn't a survival savvy person, but they got along. The trip was taking longer than expected. Many of the roads were closed off or blocked and they had to take back routes. They pulled over for the night, with high hopes of reaching their destination the next day. They set up camp not far from the road, maybe twenty feet back.

Just after breakfast, while he was kicking dirt on the fire to extinguish it, laughter and then a deep cough caught their attention. After having survived the flu, she was certain that coughing would always and forever give her shivers.

To their shock, there were four men and they picked through the truck, taking what they wanted. Her travel companion hollered for them to stop, even showed anger, raging at the men bravely. One shot to the head and he fell; she screamed and took off running. A part of her hoped all they wanted was the supplies, but two of them pursued her. She wasn't fast enough.

One of the men backhanded her, causing her to spin and fall to the ground. She scurried back, staring up at the intimidating man.

"Please, please," she begged. Her insides trembled. "Don't hurt me. Just take what you want. Please! Just take what you want and leave."

He did. Before she knew it, he had flipped her over,

ripped down her pants and raped her. She had neither time to react, nor the emotional or physical strength to stop him. She went numb.

Grasping her hair, the man took her body with relentless, brutal thrusts. Her hands dug into the dirt for support, and her neck was arched so far back, she couldn't scream.

He finished and dropped her face first into the ground, her fingers clutching the dirt. While she lay there crying, the other man rolled her over.

Almost angrily, he pulled her pants the rest of the way from her body and tossed them to the side. She tried to slide back, to move away, but he grabbed her leg and dropped to his knees. Just as he was about to mount her, a bellowing voice blasted. "Enough! What the fuck? This isn't why we're here. Let's go assholes."

He released her and stood. Her assailants replied something to the man who had charged at them but she couldn't make out what it was. She was hyperventilating.

Thinking, *thank God,* she rolled over, sobbing uncontrollably into the ground. Lifting her eyes, she spotted her pants and she raised herself to her knees to crawl in an attempt to retrieve them. She had moved no more than a foot when her hair was grabbed once more, her head tilted back, and she felt a painful, burning tear against her throat, just before she was dropped again to the ground. A few seconds later, she heard them leave. At least she thought she did.

Weakly, she brought herself to a kneel and put her hands to her neck. She felt the wound and the warm sensation of blood as it poured over her fingertips. She reached her pants, sliding them to her and placed them hard to her throat to try to stop the bleeding.

It took everything she had to stand and she stumbled as she did.

Her body teetered back and forth. Everything swirled around her. She heard the sound of a vehicle. The loss of blood caused confusion; she didn't know if it was them returning or someone else coming, but she knew the road wasn't that far.

Holding her pants to her wound, she staggered to get to the road.

* * *

"Ethan, watch out!" Mick yelled when he saw the person stumble onto the road.

Ethan had been engrossed in conversation with Mick, but caught the warning and slammed on the brakes.

Mick clutched tightly to Baby Doe as the truck swerved, back end out, until it came to an abrupt, screeching halt.

Mick braced the dashboard to stop both him and the child from flinging forward.

"Holy shit." Ethan put the truck in park. "I didn't hit them, did I?"

"No."

Ethan jumped from the truck first, and Mick was barely out when he heard Ethan moan, "Oh my God."

It wasn't what Mick expected to see. The woman, half naked, lay on the road in front of the truck. Her legs were muddy and bloody, and she clutched tightly to a pair of pants.

Mick handed Ethan the baby, and crouched down.

"Is she dead?" Ethan asked.

Mick reached for her neck, for a pulse. The woman blinked. "No," he replied, then saw the pants, saturated with blood. Her fingers were rigid around the fabric.

Her lips parted and she gasped, "Help … me."

Mick didn't get a chance to do anything. The woman's head tilted, her eyes transfixed, and she went still.

After closing his eyes briefly, Mick pulled the pants away from her neck. "Her neck's been sliced." He slowly stood. "Ethan, get the baby back in the truck."

"What about her?"

"I'll handle this." Mick lifted the woman's body and carried her to the side of the road. As he laid her down, he saw the single blanket lying near the still smoldering fire.

He was about to grab that blanket and cover the woman when he saw the body of the man. He had been shot in the head.

There were no other supplies except for that blanket. A dead man and a half naked woman with her throat slit; Mick didn't need to be a master detective to know it was an ambush.

He drew his revolver and looked around. Whoever had done it was gone, but it had been recent. The bodies were still warm. He took a moment to move the woman and man next to each other and he covered them both before returning to the truck.

"What the hell happened?" Ethan asked.

"Best I can figure, those two were camping and they were ambushed."

"For what? She was naked, Mick, you don't think …"

"More than likely, yes."

"Christ. That's wrong. It's sick. Didn't we have enough death in this world?" He handed over Baby Doe to Mick. "And it's scary, too. So close to camp."

Mick's head sprang up as he took hold of the baby. "Oh God."

"What?" Ethan asked.

"It is close. Too close. We need to get moving. Now."

Ethan didn't hesitate; he slammed his foot to the gas and sped away.

* * *

Tigger looked happy as he ran about. At least Chris thought he did. Madge told the kids that she was getting lunch and if no one wasted anything, they'd get to go fishing.

"There's a lake, you know," Jake, a boy of twelve, told Chris. He introduced himself at least three times. He seemed nice enough, but nervous. He was a skinny African American boy, with huge hazel eyes. He kept lifting and adjusting his baseball cap, probably to cover his hair that needed a cut.

He took a liking to Chris, maybe because they were near the same age. There were seven kids not including Chris and Tigger. Two were about the same age as Tigger. One was smaller, a little girl, who was maybe three. And aside from Jake, the other two were older.

But all of them played. Right in that spot near the edge of camp.

"It's a nice lake," Jake said. "We been there. Ethan said before the flu, fishing was tough there. Now there's lots. Used to be some old guy that lived in the cabin that took care of the lake but he died. Good thing the flu didn't kill the fish."

"Good thing," Chris echoed.

"That your brother?" Jake asked.

"Yep, he is."

"Real brother or after-flu brother?"

Chris snickered. "He's my real brother."

"You're lucky, my family died in the flu."

"All of them?"

"Yep. We came up here hoping to stay clear of getting sick. But it didn't work."

"I'm sorry," Chris said honestly. "That's horrible. I know how you feel. We came here to get away 'cause we lost our mom and brother."

"You took a vacation?"

"My stepfather's idea," Chris said.

"Your stepfather? You're lucky you still have family." Jake sighed. "Some people came, you know, and took some kids with them. I guess 'cause their own died, but they left the older ones. That was before Emmie. Someone surely would have taken her." He pointed to the little girl. "She got here just before you. Ethan found her on the road. She was just walking by herself."

"Wow, that's terrible." Chris shook his head. "Well, you know, you are welcome to come with us when we leave and go back home."

"Really?"

"Oh, sure, unless you wanna stay here. But we have a nice town, too."

"We should bring Emmie ..." Suddenly, Jake laughed. "Look at her chasing your brother. She must like him 'cause they're same age."

"He's just small. Born with a condition that don't allow him to grow." Chris stood when he saw Tigger diligently trying to avoid the little girl who clung to him. He called to his brother. "Tig!"

"She won't stop kissing me, Chris," Tigger said. "I tried to tell her I'm not looking for a relationship, but she can't talk."

Chris smiled. "Be nice." Just as Chris reached down to Tigger's arm, the heard a loud bang.

"What was that?" Tigger asked.

"I don't know." Chris shook his head.

Two more bangs caused Chris to not only jolt, but he grabbed on to Tigger for dear life and headed for the mobile home.

* * *

Tom didn't stop. With determined steps, he strode directly to his store, went in the back and grabbed his shotgun.

A short distance radio was all he had to work with as a fast, effective means to get hold of those he had deemed able bodied enough to be the 'watchdogs' of Lodi.

Reality hit Tom when he arrived at his truck to find Rose waiting to go and about three other men.

He turned to Lars. "Is this it?"

"I can go," Lars said. "I don't have a problem."

"No, I need you here in case something goes wrong," Tom told him. "Where are our young fit men?"

"You sent four of them out on the trucks," Lars replied. "We can't spare Buzz, he's all we have around here as trained law. And Tom, most of our young and fit died in the flu. The majority of our surviving adult male population is over forty."

Tom closed his eyes. "Well, I said I needed four men. Glad I have these guys." He waved out his hand. "Load in." It was then he saw Rose getting ready to jump in the truck. "Rose, what in tarnation are you doing?"

"Going."

"I wanted men to go."

"Yeah, well, tough," Rose said. "I'm a better shot."

"Still, Rose, you're a woman."

"You gotta problem with women?"

Tom stammered for an answer.

"You tell me if you don't think I'm tougher than most of the fucking men in Lodi. You tell me that, I'll stay back."

Tom stared and then growled. "I can't. You got me beat, that's for sure. Get in."

Rose did and then Tom opened his driver's door and got into the truck.

Lars walked around and closed it. "Be careful, Tom. I hope everything is okay."

"Well …" Tom twitched his head and spoke calmly. "My trucks are two hours late and our closest town is aflame. I'd say chances are it's not." He nodded to Lars, started his truck and took off.

* * *

Las Vegas, NV

One of Lexi's biggest fears was that she and Bill would run out of gas or the car would break down in the desert.

They had a plan for gas on the journey. A small generator would help to pump gas from the storage wells at abandoned stations. Unfortunately, a long stretch of road through the California desert didn't reveal a gas station and they traveled on a wing and a prayer that they wouldn't break down or run out.

They used their last five gallon container to make it the rest of the way. They sputtered the final distance into Sin City, pulling over at a station just before town.

Vegas looked orange. A dusty hue covered the city and the sun reflected off the buildings causing the illusion of fire. Dirt and sand covered the gas station lot and they almost had to dig their way to the reserve well.

The highway wasn't much different. It looked like a sandstorm had moved in, but Bill told her, no movement on the road, no clearing of the dirt and sand. With the steady, warm air, sand just rolled in.

"I always wanted to see Vegas," Lexi told Bill.

"Then we might as well stop for the night."

Not that it was anywhere near nightfall, but they had a country to cross. At least that was the plan.

It was scary though, what would Vegas hold? Would anyone be there? Maybe on the outskirts, but on the strip?

"I was here once," Bill said. "Isabella and I came here to get married."

"I didn't know you were married."

"We chickened out."

Lexi laughed with a toss of her head and then she saw what looked like a light. Actually, the hotel name seemed to be illuminated.

"Do they have power there?" she asked.

"Has to be an optical illusion," Bill suggested. "It has to

be. Or a mirage?"

"Ha, ha, ha, the irony," Lexi said as they pulled slowly down the strip. "Wait, " she instructed.

Bill did. "What's up?"

"Pull over."

He turned the wheel, pulling the car under the protective covering of the hotel's 'drop off' area. "What's going on?"

"I saw something." Lexi opened the car door and gasped as the heat once again pelted her. She waved her hand and focused, then crossed the street. "There. Look." She pointed.

Footprints danced about the sand. It looked like more than one person; in fact, there were several sets.

"You gotta be kidding me," Bill said. "Vegas is still running."

"They have to be fresh or they wouldn't still be here, not with the way the sand is blowing. They lead that way."

Her indication was once again to the hotel in the distance that appeared to have power. They followed the footprints to the huge casino. They knew right away, the establishment did indeed have power.

The opening of the doors brought the cool, crisp, welcoming wave of air conditioning.

There wasn't a soul about, yet there were numerous electronic machines beeping and music was playing. That and another sound … coughing.

Bill looked left to right, and walked by the rows of brightly lit video slot machines. He motioned his head toward the source of the sound.

Beeping, music, coughing.

"Hello?" Lexi called.

No reply.

"Over there," Bill whispered, placing a guiding hand on Lexi's arm.

A few more steps and a turn of the bend brought them to the source. A man in his fifties, sat before the video slot machine. He sipped from a bottle of whiskey as he tapped the slot machine buttons.

The machine went wild with noise. He coughed uncontrollably.

"Hello?" Lexi tried again.

"I thought I heard someone," he said, not turning from the slot machine. "Welcome to Vegas."

"Are you the only one here?" Bill asked.

He shook his head. "Nah, there's others. They're around. We got the power back on. Machines work. Bar's open."

Lexi looked at Bill then to the man. "Are you alright?"

"Yep." He slammed his hand on the machine and coughed. "Damn it, all these years I come here. Now that it doesn't matter … how about this …" He looked at Lexi and Bill. "I got the progressive jackpot."

Lexi finally got a look at his face. She saw the gray pallor, dark circles under his eyes, cracked and bleeding lips, and mucus dripping down his chin. He returned to his game. Lexi lifted her eyes to Bill. "The progressive …" she whispered. "That's not all he's got."

6. GONE

The second they turned on to the roadway leading to the camp, Mick knew. His gut screamed to him that they were too late, that something had happened within the camp.

The two trucks that had served as a blockade were moved completely off the road and as they approached the fence, they saw that not only was it down, but small fires sent warning smoke signals in the air.

"No!" Ethan cried. He sped up, drove quickly through the gate and stopped suddenly in the middle of the camp. He flung open the truck door and raced out.

Mick didn't hesitate either, but he was hindered by the baby in his arms.

Ethan's hands went to his head in disbelief and he spun in circles. Three of the campers were burned, two of the wheels on Mick's SUV had been removed, and his camper door was wide open.

There was a silence to the camp. No sounds at all. And no children laughing.

Heart thumping in his chest and gut wrenching with fear, Mick opened the back of his SUV and placed Baby Doe in the blanket on the floor. The child didn't move much and slept as he sipped occasionally on the bottle. The victory Mick felt in his progress with the child was overshadowed by the dismal situation at the camp.

"Where are they?" Mick groaned and pulled his revolver. He charged into the camper. "Chris! Tigger!"

The camper wasn't big and it was evident they weren't there. "Chris! Tigger!" Mick yelled louder when he stepped out of the camper.

He looked over to the area where the children had been playing. That was when he spotted a pair of legs. With a painful groan, Mick raced over, afraid to see the rest of the body.

It was a young man; his throat had been sliced. Mick saw this as he turned him over. He wasn't much older than Chris, and a heartbreaking pain shot through Mick. He lowered his head for a second then stood.

His body was huge and so was his voice, and with every ounce of strength and every bit of his lung capacity, Mick blasted out his loudest for his sons.

"CHRIS! TIGGER!"

His voice echoed in the woods around them.

There was no response

"Mick."

He jumped, startled when Ethan called. He didn't like the tone of Ethan's voice, and his heart dropped to his stomach. He pleaded in his mind *Please don't let it be about my sons.*

If anything had happened to them, Mick would never forgive himself. He was beating himself up over what had happened and he didn't even know what that was.

Why had he left? It was evident that the small camp had been raided. All of Mick's things that had sat outside his camper were gone. The bug out bag and sleeping roll were missing from the back seat of the SUV. There wasn't a single camper with a closed door and the supply shed was smoldering.

"Mick," Ethan called again.

Mick looked, and from around the corner, Ethan came walking with Madge. He seemed to be carrying her with her feet dragging as she held on to her stomach.

He rushed to them.

"She's been shot," Ethan said. "She's bleeding bad."

"Let me take a look." Mick pulled her hand and looked at the wound. "It's to the side and it went straight through, not a straight belly shot."

"I'm sorry," Madge whimpered. "I'm sorry. We tried. We tried to stop them. Liam got it first and then when me and Sara pulled weapons to get them to go, they just went haywire." Madge lowered her head and cried.

Mick swiped his hand down his face and tried to gain control. "Where are all the kids?"

Madge shook her head. "They got Bobby Miller. I think they thought he was older. He was the only one I saw them kill. I … I got shot right after."

"How many were there?" Mick asked.

Madge shook her head. "Six I think. Not sure." She winced. "But they took everything and I think they took the kids."

"Do you know what they look like? What they drove? How long ago they left? I know this is a lot of questions."

"It was about an hour ago, maybe less. And I can't tell you what they looked like, but I do know they were military."

Ethan locked eyes with Mick. "*Military?* Does that sound right?"

"Not at all," Mick responded.

"They were wearing military uniforms," Madge said.

"Okay, listen, Ethan," said Mick. "You got enough reserve gas in the truck. Take your mom and Baby Doe, get out of here and head to Lodi. Keep pressure on her wound and keep her lying down. Maybe have her hold Doe in the back."

"But Mick—"

Mick held up his hand. "Do not stop. Do not hesitate, hightail it. Take the highway south then head west. You can't miss the signs. Top speed will get you there in a couple of hours and your mom should be fine. Look for Lars Rayburn - he's a doctor - then tell him what happened." He walked toward the SUV, reached in the back, and picked up Baby Doe.

"What are you gonna do?" Ethan asked.

Mick looked up and around. "It hasn't been that long, they can't be all that far. I'll follow a trail. Something. But I guarantee this … I'm not stopping," Mick said, "until I find my kids."

* * *

Whispering, 'Go, go, go!' Chris urged everyone into the cabin and shut the door quietly. He hunched down and reached up to turn the lock.

"Jake, keep an eye out that window. Make sure no one is coming. Don't let them see you."

Jake hurried to the window and stood off to the side. "No one knows about the cabin. I think we're safe here."

"If there's a road here, they'll find it. We can't stay for long. We got to get what we can, rest for a second and head out." Chris set down the bug out bag and sleeping roll. "I'm just glad you knew about this place." He turned to Tigger. "Can you stop her from crying?"

"How?" Tigger tossed up his hands. "She's a baby! I ain't big enough to lift her." He looked at Emmie. "Hey! Stop crying. Now."

Emmie stifled her sobs, hyperventilating some.

"Hey, it worked," Tigger said.

The one room fishing cabin wasn't large. Chris grabbed the blanket from the cot and tossed it to the floor. He'd roll it up later.

"What all you looking for?" Jake asked.

"Some food to get us to the next stop, things to keep us warm. Maybe something we can use as a weapon."

"They have guns, Chris. I don't think we can compete with that."

"We're gonna try now, aren't we?"

Tigger said, "You know there's food in Mick's bag, right? And matches."

"I know."

"Maybe," Jake spoke up, "we shouldn't take anything important or a lot."

"Why do you say that?" Chris asked.

"Because if they find this place and it looks like stuff was taken, they may know it was us and come looking for us."

Chris stopped. Jake made perfect sense. "How'd you know to think about that?"

Jake bit his bottom lip. "When I was six, my dad kidnapped me. Well, he picked me up at school and said we were going away on a long vacation. We were running all the time."

"No way, that's a pretty cool story," Chris said then plopped to the floor.

Tigger asked. "You alright, Chris?"

Chris brought his knees toward his chest and lifted his hand. He sighed heavily. "Yeah, in a second. I just need a second."

And he did. His heart was still racing. He needed to catch his breath and his bearings. Everything was still so fresh. They had been running for nearly an hour. And they did so taking turns holding Emmie and covering her mouth. It had all happened so fast and Chris just followed his gut instincts to run. Run and hide, get away. He didn't have time to think or plan, and he needed to take time to do that before they got moving again.

The men who came to the camp weren't playing around and they were merciless. Certainly Chris hadn't expected it. No one had. He'd been playing around with Tigger when he heard the bang. The first sound wasn't a gunshot; Chris knew what they sounded like. It was more like a car crashing into something. But the second and third sounds were definitely shots.

He'd grabbed onto his little brother, who happened to be in the grips of Emmie at the time. When he lifted Tigger, Emmie dangled along, and Chris did his best to grab her as well. They were near the edge of the forest and Chris ran there. Just ducked inside to see if he could see what was happening.

He heard voices, men shouting. *'Grab that. Get this. Stop him.'*

Bang.

He crouched down on the grade, hand over Emmie's mouth, her toddler body tucked under his and urged them both to be quiet.

Tigger understood. With his free hand, Chris gathered leaves around them and then Jake slid down in a hurry.

"The soldiers just killed Bobby and shot Mr. Liam."

"Shhh," Chris hushed him and grabbed for him to get down. "Stay down."

"We have to run."

"Stay down!"

Chris listened, and heard one of the men shouting that he thought he saw more children. Another replied, "Keep looking."

Chris leaned his head toward Jake and spoke at the lowest whisper he could. "We do have to run."

"The cabin."

Chris nodded. He moistened his lips. He didn't know if it was bravery or stupidity, but he had to see what was going on. "Pull them back," he told Jake. "I'll be right with ya."

"Where you going?"

"I have to see what's happening. We don't know what we're running from."

Tigger whimpered, "Chris?"

"I'll be alright. Go with Jake. Just down the hill. On your belly. Okay?"

Tigger nodded.

Chris's hand still covered Emmie's mouth. "You got to keep her mouth covered, lift her and run quiet. Go straight but not too far," he told Jake. "I'll find you. Go!"

It was a switch of one hand to the other. No sooner had Chris removed his hand when Jake placed his over Emmie's mouth.

As slowly and as quietly as he could, Chris rose and belly crawled to the top of the grade. He peeked over. At first he didn't see much. He did see Bobby's body and he lowered his head for a second.

He watched the movement of the men. He could only see a few. They shouted out orders and moved quickly.

Then he noticed Mick's SUV. No one went near it. The men were concentrated over on the other side of the camp. Knowing that they had to run and make a getaway, Chris, in a low crouch run, ran to the SUV.

He ducked down, looking around. He caught a glimpse of one man. He was wearing a military uniform, but it was old, like the military used to wear in old movies. Quietly, Chris opened the door to the back seat.

On the outside chance they'd be stranded out in the woods for a while, Chris grabbed the bug out knapsack and thin sleeping roll. He slid them over to himself, made sure no one saw him, and then, in the same manner, crawled back and made his escape.

He found the others with ease. Tigger, Jake and Emmie hadn't gone too far down the hill. There, twenty or so feet from the campsite, they waited a few minutes and when the voices grew nearer they took off.

Jake lifted Emmie, Chris lifted Tigger and they ran at top speed.

The last thing Chris heard was someone shouting, "Down there! Look!"

But neither Chris nor Jake looked back; they focused and stayed the course.

* * *

"Found a map."

Jake's voice snapped Chris from this thoughts. He sat down next to Chris and slid the map his way.

"You're supposed to be on watch," Chris said.

Jake pointed to Tigger, who peered out the window. "He's better hidden than me. Besides, take a look."

It was like reading a foreign language. Chris had never seen a real map, let alone learned how to read one. "I have no idea what the heck to do with this," he said.

Jake grimaced. "Me either."

From the window, Tigger said. "Take watch. Let me look."

Jake produced a quirky smile. "How old is he again?"

"He's six, going on thirty. That's what Mick says."

"Who's Mick?" Jake asked.

"My stepdad."

"Hey, won't he come find us? We should just wait here."

"We could," Chris said. "But how do we know that they didn't get Mick and Ethan before they came to the camp? We don't. We gotta keep moving and figure out where to go."

Tigger squatted down, pointing back. "Take the window."

"God, pushy." Jake stood.

Tiger looked at the map.

"Tig, really, I know you wanna help but—"

"Look," Tigger said, "I may not know how to read this thing right, but I've seen *Dora the Explorer* enough to know we have to look for familiar things."

"Like?"

"There's a lake out that window, Chris. Ain't there water on this map?"

Common sense. Maybe his nerves were causing him to lose it, but Chris looked at the map. "We left Pittsburgh on a highway north." His finger trailed the map. "Has to be this highway here." He pointed. "We were headed to Lake Erie." He showed Tigger the lake. "So we have to be in this area..."

"Rosemont." Tigger's little finger pointed. "Does that say Rosemont?"

"Tig, you can read?"

"Yeah. Some words. Does it say that?"

"Yes. Yes!" Chris grinned. "Rosemont is twenty miles west of where we were, that's what Ethan told Mick." He moved his finger to the right, east, away from Rosemont.

"That little blue dot - water?" Tigger asked.

"Has to be. Go see if there's a pen in Mick's sack."

After Tigger stood, Chris continued to stare at the map. He had to learn it. What were roads, which way they would go, and how would they get to safety? But the real question was, where was safe?

He would think about it, but not for long. They couldn't stay at the cabin. They had to get moving. Aside from figuring out a direction to go, he had to figure out a way to let Mick know they were fine and moving forward on the outside chance that Mick would come looking for them.

JOURNAL ENTRY

I only have a minute to write, but I thought I should. Just in case something happens to us and this notebook is found.

Our camp was attacked by these guys in older military uniforms. I don't know how many, I only saw three of them. They killed a boy and other grownups in the camp.

Mick had left with Ethan to search for more kids in a town nearby.

I only hope Mick wasn't caught up by these guys on his way back. Not that Mick couldn't handle them, but what if he wasn't ready?

If he didn't, then I am glad Mick wasn't there when they came. Mick would have gone after these guys, like he always does, but they didn't care, there was no fair fight in these guys, they only shot.

I know Mick is out there and he'll look for us. But right now, we have to run. We're gonna head north to find the road and follow near that. But stay hidden on the way.

We got a baby with us. She ain't very old. At least she can walk, but she cries a lot and I don't know what to do with her.

Heck, I don't know what to do about anything.

For as much as Mick and my mom and dad taught me, no one said anything about running to save your life. No one taught me what I would need or should do.

I don't have a clue and I got three kids with me that I have to watch. No one said anything to me about how to survive if I am stranded. I guess no one thinks to teach their kids that.

I'll just have to do the best I can. If something should happen to me, I tried.

7. SMOKE AND MIRRORS

Tom didn't find Dan Hynes, the driver of one of his trucks; Dan found Tom.

Just about one mile outside of Wadsworth, the smoke was so thick Tom had to pull over. He didn't believe they could go any further.

His chest filled with a heaviness from the smoke, and even a cloth over his nose and mouth didn't help. He felt bad for the two men in the back of the truck, and for them and their safety, he couldn't go on.

"You sure you sent the trucks this way?" Rose asked.

"This is the way they would have gone. Big Bear Food Storage is just outside of Wadsworth. This was the last trip to unload the warehouse." Tom replied. "Son of a bitch."

Rose swiped her hand down her face. "Maybe they saw the fire and trouble and just stopped."

"We can hope." Tom shifted the truck into reverse and just as he tapped the gas, he heard a double bang against the rear of his truck. He hit the brakes. One of the men in the back of the truck pointed, and Dan Hynes smacked against the driver's side window.

His face was dirty and bloodied with brush burns.

"Jesus," Tom opened the truck door. "Dan!"

"Tom, thank God." Dan grabbed his chest.

"Get in." Tom got out, making room for Dan to get in the truck.

Dan struggled and grunted, holding on to his side as he climbed in, sitting next to Rose.

"Where are the others?" Tom asked as he got back inside.

Dan shook his head. "I don't know. We got separated. They were alive the last I saw, but we decided to separate so they didn't see us."

Tom turned the truck quickly and headed away from Wadsworth. "So who didn't see you?"

"Group of men. Big group. That's how I got hurt. They were speeding away, don't know if they saw me, but I dodged from their truck. Think I broke a rib."

Rose peered over Dan. "We can't leave the others, Tom, we have to look for them."

"I know, I know. But we can't see nothing with this smoke. Dan, which way were they? When did you separate?"

"Near the warehouse. We were pulling in," Dan said. "We saw the trucks; they beat us to the punch and were emptying it out. They had guns so we backed off. We ditched the trucks off to the side, but that was stupid on our part. They took them. Then we decided to split up. I went through Wadsworth."

"What happened there?" Rose questioned. "What's burning?"

"Everything," Dan answered. "I guess it wasn't supposed to be like that. When I arrived, they had a tanker and were emptying the gas station. They lit it up and it got out of control."

Tom twitched his head with a long blink. "Any idea who these guys were? Did they look like stragglers, a gang, something out of *Mad Max,* what?"

"No," Dan answered. "Soldiers." Rose looked quickly at him at the same time as Tom. "But not dressed like normal ones," Dan clarified. "Some were wearing black jackets. A lot looked like hunters."

"Yeah," Rose said. "Sounds like militia."

Tom asked, "Rose, you're part of Ohio Third aren't you?"

"No, Minuteman, but this doesn't sound like them. More like OFD … even then I can't see them burning Wadsworth."

"What are we gonna do?" Dan asked.

"Head back, organize and think," Tom answered. "Get on Henry to get back in touch with the government, see what they know. Rose, any thoughts about if we can find out if Minuteman or OFD is still operational?"

"Take a ride to their compound, it's not far. Buzz and I can take a ride out on the bikes."

Tom only nodded but didn't give his verbal agreement. His options were limited. He had to find out what was going on, because all of this was far too close to home. He hated the thought of sending Rose out with Buzz, but with Mick out of touch, what choice did he have?

* * *

<u>Las Vegas, NV</u>

He coughed his way through telling Lexi and Bill about there being rooms available in the hotel, and that at least a hundred people were there.

Cough. Cough.

He wasn't sure. He was just someone staying there. There were other people running it, and they were hoping to make it a stopping depot for those going east.

When Lexi asked why, he simply said, "Lots of people are going east. That's where the life is."

It made sense to her. After all, the flu had started on the West Coast and people on the East Coast had a chance to lock down, maybe stay out of circulation. They were able to prepare a better defense against the flu.

Bill asked the man, "How many have come through here?"

"'Bout a hundred pilgrims last week."

Cough. Cough.

Bill, in the middle of the conversation, wised up and stepped back. Lexi seemed to not care. They left him, and headed to find the lobby.

"What do you think is wrong with him?" Bill asked.

"I don't know. His coloring is odd. It's not just pale."

"You think it's our flu?"

Lexi shook her head. "No, not at all. First, with that cough, that stage of the flu, he'd be too ill to be playing a slot machine. Then again, he was drinking heavily. But I heard the cough. It rumbled, it was productive."

Bill chuckled. "Yeah, he had it productively on his chin."

"Exactly," Lexi said. "Did you notice the color?"

Bill snorted a laugh. "Uh, no. Well, yeah, but what does that matter?"

"Our flu didn't come with a productive cough. It was so thick it stuck in the chest. And also, when it was ejected, it was thick and brown. Remember? It was blood laced. This guy's phlegm was frothy. More than likely he may have pneumonia. But who knows?"

They followed the signs to the lobby and when they arrived, it wasn't what they expected. A wire cage fence was erected around the front desk, and a man wearing a dirty county police officer uniform stood up. His face was unshaven, hair wiry, and he had a shotgun draped over his shoulder.

"Welcome, folks." He stepped to the counter.

"Hi," Lexi said. "We're only passing through."

"Going east?"

"Yes."

"Isn't everybody?" He smiled.

Lexi returned the smile. "The man in the casino told us we can get a room for the night?"

"Ah, Charlie. He loves those slots. He doesn't even get up to take a piss. Has a bottle right next to him."

Bill winced. "Glad I missed that."

"I bet," the man said. "Well, we aren't a fancy resort, we're a stopping post. We ask that you don't cook anything in the rooms. Fire hazard, you know. You can do so outside or in designated areas of the hotel. Clean up after you leave. Sanitizer is in each room." He pulled a sheet of paper forward. "We're pretty secure. I have guys on watch. You can't see them, but they're there. Kind of defensive against trouble. Not that we have seen a lot of trouble. Folks are pretty good, just wanna go east. Glad I'm not there."

Lexi was curious. "Why not?"

"More people, more problems. Kind of like a reverse return to the Wild West now. Quiet, empty, and I like it. You can control what you have and what you need when you aren't fighting for scraps against a thousand starving people."

"Makes sense," Lexi agreed.

"So you're pretty protected here. One of the things we ask if that you check your weapons. We'll give them back when you leave."

Lexi looked at Bill.

Bill replied. "We have a knife."

"A knife?"

"We have an ax," Lexi said. "It's in the car. Tire iron? Does that count?"

"A knife, ax and tire iron?" the man said. "What kind of knife?"

Bill laid the six inch hunting knife on the counter.

The man pushed it back. "It's fine, you can hold on to that. Man," he shook his head and added with some sarcasm, "you guys are prepared."

Lexi smiled. "We try."

"I'm *joking*. What in the hell is wrong with you two?"

Lexi cocked back. "I'm sorry?"

"You're crossing the country with a knife, an ax and a tire iron. This isn't a Stephen King world. This isn't all the bad in one place, all the good in another. Good and bad are scattered about. More bad roam. Especially, I'm guessing, the further east you go."

"We discussed this," Lexi said. "We don't believe in guns."

"Well, you should. And if you change your mind, we have some you can barter for."

"Thank you," Lexi said.

"Okay, that's the rules. Now what do you have to barter for the room?"

Lexi peered up at Bill. "What do we have?"

"We have some food," Bill said. "Some water. Not much."

The man shook his head. "Food and water don't barter here. I'd take that knife, but I'd feel guilty leaving you defenseless." He sighed. "Any gold? Silver? Brass? Pennies? You got pennies, they melt down."

Lexi shook her head.

"What the heck, people?"

"What about skills?" Bill asked. "Can they be bartered?"

"Depends," he replied. "What's your skill?"

"Not me," Bill said. "Her." He pointed to Lexi. "She's a doctor."

Suddenly, the officer's entire demeanor changed. All expression dropped from his face and even his voice changed. "Are you serious?"

"Yes," Lexi said with a nod and swung her knapsack forward. "This is my bag. I have some stuff, not a lot. I really don't want to barter medicine if I don't have to." She grabbed a small billfold and put it on the counter. "Here's my ID."

"You still carry ID?"

"You never know."

He glanced down. "Alexandra Martin. You worked for

the CDC?"

"Lexi. Call me Lexi. And yes."

"And she's good," Bill added. "She's really good. I worked two outbreaks with her."

The man slid back the billfold.

"My skills won't get us a room?" Lexi asked with disappointment. "Surely, I can help someone? I mean slot machine guy …"

The man held up his hand, halting her. "You're a doctor. That skill will barter you more than just a room here. We have everything but a doctor. And lady, I can't tell you how glad I am to see you."

* * *

Mick took a second, because that was pretty much all he could spare. He took that second to acknowledge the pain in his gut and the feeling of being a complete failure.

All of his good intentions had gone right out the window. This was supposed to be a simple trip; a week, maybe more. The happy go lucky camp had seemed perfect after they stumbled upon it, and Mick hadn't given a thought to marauders rampaging through the camp. It hadn't even crossed his mind. How stupid was he?

He was responsible for the kids; he had promised Dylan he would take care of the boys, and now they were gone.

Were they hurt? Scared? Or had they been taken by those men? Mick couldn't figure out what the hell they'd want with the kids. He didn't trust that their intentions were good considering they had blasted through the defenseless campsite.

The car battery in his SUV was gone. In fact, any means of transportation had been dismantled or rendered useless.

There was still generator power to Ethan's trailer and while Mick scoured the camp for goods, he used that time to charge his phone. Not that he expected to make a call, but who knew if the phones would come back up? Mick was actually surprised they had gone down, especially since the struggling government was using them to communicate with Henry in Lodi.

Chris had his phone, he'd track that. Family GPS. Dylan had called that dumb, considering the boys never left Lodi. But Mick had called it a precaution in case their dad took off with them.

It was a cheaper phone, fewer bells and whistles, and therefore it kept the charge longer. For that Mick was grateful.

And Chris did have his phone. Mick checked the camper. Their coats and hats were gone, and so was the notebook Chris always wrote in.

Mick scoured the camp for clues as to what happened. It appeared the attackers had hit the gate to knock it open, and then shot a person right away, twice. A double tap.

They moved fast, in and out. They took commodities like gas, tires, things for cars. There didn't seem to be any dry goods left. And the box of deer jerky that Ethan told Mick about was gone.

More than anything, Mick looked for clues about the boys. If the people who raided the camp took the boys, surely they wouldn't have given them time to grab their things?

That indicate to Mick that likely they ran. Hopefully had run and gotten out of danger. The boys were smart, but there was a lot Mick never got a chance to teach them. Why would he? They lived in Lodi and he would always be there to protect them.

This time he wasn't able to, and he had to make up for that.

A few items were left behind. Mick wanted to travel light. He grabbed two bottles of water and a couple of small food items that were 'dropped' on the floor, probably as the men absconded with their supplies.

He had to figure out which direction they went. He ruled out the front gate, they were smarter than that. Logic dictated that they took off from the camper. Probably into the woods behind there. He focused on that direction until he crossed over the play area where he found Denny Dynamite.

Denny Dynamite was a cartoon and an action toy, and Tigger had cried for weeks to get those Denny Dynamite tennis shoes. They were close to a hundred dollars a pair, and Mick had gotten them and lied to Dylan about the price. The tennis shoe soles had Denny on them, and in the dirt before him now were repeated imprints of Denny.

Tigger had been was playing here. Was it from there that they had run? A wooded area was just a few feet from the play area. He followed Tigger's Denny shoe imprints. They moved, they stopped, they ... skidded.

Maybe Mick was looking a little more into it, he didn't know. But he moved to the wooded area. It was flat for a few feet, then there was a small grade.

And slide marks. Someone had slid down that hill.

Mick followed the sliding trail to where it ended behind a fallen tree. What he found wasn't much, but it was a tip of a shoe imprint. A Denny Dynamite shoe print.

Clenching his fist in gratitude, Mick could clearly see other footprints through the foliage. They crunched the leaves, splashed in the mud. They weren't big, they weren't man size. He didn't see any more of Tigger's footprints, but Mick figured that if they were running, then Chris was carrying Tigger.

By what he saw, Mick felt in his heart that the boys had taken off, they were on foot, and they were running.

They weren't that far ahead of him, and now he had a direction and a lead. He followed it.

* * *

Briggs made his second pass of the day into the small town of Damon. While he was able to receive radio signals at his base, Jon Wentworth was in Damon and that was who he needed to see.

Briggs arrived in town. He didn't drive; gas conservation was vital. He rode horseback. He didn't need security, or a team. That was why he was confused by the intimidation that people projected. They merely nodded as he rode in and stepped from his way. Not that there were many Damon townspeople remaining, and a lot of those in town were part of his team.

That would change. Damon, surrounded securely by a small mountain range, would serve as the capital in the newly governed post-flu world.

Briggs tied his horse to the bicycle stand in front of the former Walgreen's. The store had been emptied and organized, the windows painted black, and people were carrying items into the store.

On the pole outside was a hand written flyer: "Register at the municipal building for distribution and work."

Those flyers were posted everywhere. They were stockpiling things nicely and a surviving economics professor from a local college was coming with a list of jobs that needed to be filled, and planning for future tasks. But the system was simple. All hours worked earned rations for the week. Everyone received the same rations, even Briggs himself. Extras like alcohol were given on a first come first serve basis, weekly. That was the plan. Of course, they were still in the early stages.

Jon Wentworth wasn't an economist, politician, or farmer. He was an everyday guy who had worked for a wireless telephone company as a tower technician.

Briggs liked him. He was a reasonable man. Jon helped with radios and that was how Briggs learned of his skills.

Jon now sat inside the former McDonald's, sipping on a coffee when Briggs entered. Jon stood.

Briggs joined him at the booth. "How's it going?"

"Pretty good." The table was covered with papers. "I made radio contact and we should be getting towers one and three up. Those were your bounce points. Those were why we lost phones. It'll give limited coverage to the New York, Pennsylvania and Ohio areas, but enough for now."

"Excellent job. Any idea why they went down?"

"Tower three was damaged. We don't know how that happened, possibly a storm." Jon shrugged. "But once we get that up, I can network with the satellite to try to reach out to people all at once."

"You mean like those annoying little advertising text messages?" Briggs asked.

Jon nodded. "I need to find people to expand the network."

"Well, we only need to concern ourselves about our farmland right now for spring. I need that. *We* need that. We need to link up communities for this to work."

"And what if they don't want to link?" Jon asked.

"They must. If they don't, we'll have pockets of resistance. Really. Let's say ... Damon doesn't want to participate." Briggs shook his head. "Okay, we exclude them, they run out of food. They can't really farm here except private gardens. So ...they go after food. Where? They'll have to take from others." Briggs looked at the young man. "You don't seem convinced."

"It's just that ... people want to do their own thing. You'll have that to deal with."

"We will, but unless they are one hundred percent self-sufficient – producing their own food, livestock, resources – they can't survive without foraging. It's the same thing the government would do, if we had one."

"I guess that makes sense. And I heard ..." He trailed off.

"What? What did you hear?"

"My guy on tower three, the one from Ohio Minuteman? He said he thinks your group set fire to small town outside of Cleveland."

Briggs cocked back. "That's ridiculous. Why would he say that?"

"Your guys checked in with them on the way south to the warehouse, shortly after the fire broke out. Smoke could be seen as far as Cleveland. My guys saw it from the tower."

"And he thinks it was my men?"

"Yes. Only because that was the direction they went. And he said your men had … attitude."

"Attitude? Really? That group hasn't checked back in. I'll look into it." Briggs stood.

"Thanks and keep an eye on your cell phone. You'll be the first person I call."

Briggs shook Jon's hand. "I look forward to it."

"Jonah?"

"Yes?"

"You've given your men free reign on getting supplies, gathering survivors, that's a lot of power. You're not going to be able to negotiate with pockets of survivors and towns and get them to join you if your men run amok. If they did set fire to the town, who knows what else they have done?"

Briggs gave a jerky nod. "You sound convinced that I have them doing bad things."

"Maybe not on purpose." Jon lowered his head and lifted his coffee. "You speak often about structure; maybe a structured set of rules for these salvaging patrols is needed."

"I gave them rules. They're to get what they can find and pick up survivors. And most of all to protect themselves from those who try to harm them. I see no reason for them to deviate from that. What purpose would it serve to do harm?"

"There's no threat of law or punishment?"

"We have law. They are the first arm of law."

Jon tightly closed his mouth and raised his eyebrows.

"Do you know something else?"

Jon shook his head. "Just gut instinct stemming from a

lot of bad post-apocalypse books and movies."

"Acknowledged. I promise to look into it, but I highly doubt it is my men."

"Thank you."

"Thank you for your hard work."

Briggs shook his hand again and left. As he stepped into the sun, he saw one of his trucks pull slowly down the street. In the back were two women and a child. They had to be survivors that were picked up. The three of them were dirty, in disarray, and their faces had an unemotional glaze.

Briggs locked eyes with one woman as she passed. She looked scared. Had something happened? Was she trying to convey a message to him?

Briggs shifted his eyes to the men laughing in the cab of the truck. Such a contrast of demeanor from his men to the passengers. Immediately a sense of worry hit him. As the truck moved further away to the municipal building, Briggs shucked the worry and chalked it up to Wentworth's words stirring his imagination.

* * *

Tigger had the coolest shoes and Chris came up with the idea after he saw the muddy footprint on the floor of the cabin.

It took a little bit of time, but Chris hoped that it would work and keep him and the others safe and in the clear for a little longer.

There was a small gravel road about fifty yards from the cabin. Chris saw that when they were running. A bigger road was farther away and was just on the other side of the lake.

That main road led to a town. That was the one they would follow, not stay on it but off to the side. But before they went there, as quickly as they could, Chris and Tigger tromped hard and fast to the gravel road. Once they hit the road, Chris lifted Tigger into his arms, backtracked as carefully as he could in his own footsteps, then midway back, when he saw the opportunity and knew he wouldn't leave a footprint, he took the biggest jump he ever had before.

To him it was impressive, and it was far enough away from the trail of footprints he and Tigger left.

Plus, he had left a clue for Mick by leaving Tigger's footprint in the cabin. Only Mick would know what it meant. Chris felt confident, like he was doing his best thinking.

After leaving the fake trail, they carefully walked in the brush and leaves back to the cabin, where Emmie and Jake waited. Once they were all together, they followed the wooded area around the lake until they were far enough away from the cabin where any footprints wouldn't be seen.

Chris was proud of his idea and was certain his false set of footprints would keep the bad guys away and on the wrong trail long enough for Chris and the others to gain some distance.

8. A NEW PATH

As soon as Rose got back to Lodi, she wasted no time in grabbing Buzz, double checking the fuel on the bikes, and taking off on the 72 mile ride to the Minuteman headquarters.

Unfortunately, their trip proved futile, because when they arrived the place was locked tight and no one was around. But there was a note on the door that simply read, 'I'll be back'. It wasn't weather worn, but Rose didn't know when that would be.

She jotted a note of her own on the same piece of paper. She left her name, member number, and a landline number for her to be reached, along with a radio frequency. She asked that they please contact her and stated that it was urgent.

Then she and Buzz returned to Lodi.

She joined Tom at the clinic to deliver the news of her futile attempt.

"I feel fucking useless," Rose said.

"You tried," Tom said. "It's a wait and see."

"How's Dan?" Rose asked.

At that moment, Tom pointed as Lars emerged from the back.

"He's resting peacefully," Lars said. "Had two fractured ribs from the fall and a punctured lung. I had to insert a breathing tube, but that's temporary and he'll be fine. Do we know what happened in Wadsworth?"

Tom shook his head. "No."

"Well, they must be heading east, because if they weren't they would have been here by now."

Rose was about to ask her own question, when Buzz burst in the door, breathing hard.

Buzz was a burly man and he had to catch his breath. "Lars, we need you in town. It's an emergency. I'm heading to grab an ambulance from the EMT garage. Meet you there."

Without any further explanation, Buzz flew out.

"What the hell?" Lars blurted, and raced for the door.

Tom and Rose followed.

* * *

They had to drive in order to get there quickly. The Lodi Clinic was four blocks from the town center and when they arrived they saw the commotion. Buzz was already bringing the stretcher to a blue pickup truck.

Lars rushed to the truck with Tom and Rose right on his heels. "What happened?"

The man in his thirties, holding a baby, approached Lars. "Are you Lars? That big guy said he was getting Lars."

"I am and that child—"

"I'm Ethan. Mick sent us, and he said you can help him." Ethan handed Baby Doe to Lars. "My mom's been shot, too. The bleeding slowed down a lot, but she's real weak." He pointed to the stretcher as his mother was aided onto it by Buzz and another man. "Mick wasn't as worried about her, but this little guy, he's dehydrated, starving. We've been trying to give him fluids. He's better than he was, trust me, but he's still lethargic, if you can call it that in a baby."

"Whoa." Lars stared down to the baby. "You just rattled off a whole list. Mick? Our Mick?"

"Yes. He said to find you and tell you what happened."

"I have to get this baby and your mother to the clinic, these two will get you there and I'll talk to you then," Lars said.

"Thank you, sir."

Lars stepped away holding the child, and Tom moved forward.

"What happened?" he asked Ethan.

Rose added, "Mick sent you here?"

"Yes and yes. I didn't think I'd make it." His eyes shifted back and forth between Rose and Tom. "I had a camp. Six adults, eight kids. Mick and I went to a neighboring town to see if there were any children left behind and my camp was hit and raided. My mom was shot, and at least two others were killed."

Rose's hand shot to her mouth. "Where's Mick?"

"He stayed back. He had to." Ethan hesitated. "His sons are missing."

* * *

Mick located the small fishing cabin with relative ease. While the thicker foliage on the ground made footsteps nearly impossible to follow, the smell of the lake and sight of the cabin was welcoming.

He hoped with all his heart that the boys were in that cabin. As he approached he saw the footprints in the mud outside the door.

"Chris! Tigger!" Mick yelled and opened the door.

It wasn't locked and Mick's head dropped when he stepped inside and saw the cabin was empty.

He checked the cupboards and there was still food there. The boys didn't take anything, why not? The single cot didn't have bedding, but the pillow was covered in a case. That struck him as odd.

Just as he was about the leave the cabin, go back out and look for tracks, he spotted the single Dynamite footprint on the floor.

Not only that, but near it were two things. A snap snack, the tiny little crackers that Mick had placed in the bug out bag, and Chris had dropped his lucky double headed quarter. He loved it; it was a prank he had gotten out of a machine. He had used it so much, that everyone grew tired of it. *"Ha, ha, ha, Chris we get it."*

The thought of Chris and that coin made Mick smile. The boys had been there, they had thought enough to grab the bug out bag, there weren't any signs of blood, so they had to be fine.

They weren't staying put. Mick firmly believed in his heart that Chris had left that coin and snack bag as a sign that they had been there.

Mick picked up the coin and put it in his pocket. He walked back outside to look for footprints. He followed them around the back of the cabin and saw that they led up a hill. Two sets of prints, one was definitely Tigger's. They led to a gravel road and Mick didn't see any more prints after that.

But considering the prints had brought him to that road, Mick determined that the boys had to have taken that route.

And so did Mick. He started walking down the same road.

* * *

Las Vegas, NV

The man from the lobby finally gave his name; it was Matt and he had been a police officer for the county when everything started going crazy. He told his story while he waited for a replacement to come to the lobby so he could take Lexi and Bill to the floors above.

People were hit with the flu in Vegas, but the worst place to be was the airport. People got stranded. A lot of the residents of Vegas stayed, followed advice, hunkered down and beat the flu. But the tourists didn't really have that luxury. So many were stranded at the airport it was a flu zone like no other. The National Guard brought blankets and food and did the best they could to assist, and then they got sick and a lot of soldiers left their posts.

Matt was fortunate enough to have never even caught the flu. It surprised him because he was in the thick of things. He didn't have a wife or kids to run home to, so he helped out when and where he could.

Alaska hit the height of the flu the first week of September, Vegas was in full throttle before the second week.

"A lot of people died here," Matt explained. "These hotels on the strip and downtown were busy with tourists. When the flu hit, the airports shut down and there were no flights in or out. So they stayed. So many died. More than you would think. I believe the biggest problem we had were people who thought they beat the flu. They emerged and then got sick."

"Thereby starting the clock all over again," Lexi said.

"Exactly," Matt replied. "We had to burn the airport, flash fire it. There was no way we were getting bodies out. In fact, we're still working on body removal and it's been a month. We'll never get them all. We cleared out this hotel and the two next to us. Right now our primary focus is supplies."

"In this heat," Lexi said, "decomposition will be fast — they'll be mummified."

"Yep." Matt winked. "As sadistic as this sounds, it's actually a pretty cool thing to see."

Bill laughed. "That sounds like something I would say. Matt, how did you end up putting all this together?"

"It was simple at first. Out of the entire police force only four of us remained. Two of my men, well, they are just now starting to snap back from the loss of their families. We gathered a crew of survivors, grouped them into gatherers and clean up. Really, I was just focusing on what we could do for those who were stranded here. You're talking a lot of hotels, a lot of goods, supplies. If we kept one hotel powered up, we could keep the perishable stuff lasting for a while. My entire original intention was simple. The people of Vegas needed to know they could get food."

"But you became a depot?" Lexi asked.

"It was weird. Those in Vegas started to leave. We got word out that we would give supplies, and they were coming here for things to take with them, asking what they'd need, how to get gas." He shrugged. "We still had a lot of people staying though. Then about two weeks ago, you would think it was a holy pilgrimage. Like the gold rush. Like something was out east and suddenly everyone had to be there. People were pouring into town. Stopping in, moving on. The idea of a barter depot came when one man offered me a box of ammunition for two gallons of water and some Spam. And he said, 'this is like those places on the Oregon trail.' That's when it started. We organized. It works pretty well."

Lexi blinked several times. "How many people came through?"

"So far, close to a thousand. Yesterday we had … maybe twenty? We average now about twenty a day. Most come in, stay and leave. Every day a batch comes and goes."

It was about that point in the conversation that Matt's relief arrived.

"Sorry," he said. "I was held up. He really a doctor?"

"She," Matt corrected. "And yes. Yes she is."

"Holy cow, that's so great. You gonna give her one of the presidential suites?"

"Oh, you better believe it, and two steaks for these two as well."

"I'll make sure of it," the man said. "How long you staying?" he directed his question to Lexi.

Lexi really didn't know how to answer that, except to say, "Apparently there's a problem here, so I'll stay as long as you guys need us."

Matt grinned. "Thank you for that. Come this way."

He led them to a set of elevators, and as they stepped inside, he explained. "I'm making sure I separate them, because we don't know for sure what they have."

The second they stepped off the elevator, Lexi heard the coughing. It didn't sound like the hospital where an entire orchestration of infection took place, this was more like two or three people, all coughing uncontrollably.

"This way," Matt said. They walked past a few doors and he stopped at one, knocked once on it, then opened it up. "Mom?"

The woman coughed. "Matt?"

"You aren't gonna believe this. A doctor is in town."

"Oh, thank God," she said.

Lexi walked into the hotel room. It was one of the basic rooms and the woman of about seventy was in bed, propped up on two pillows. When Lexi saw her, she looked at Bill.

Their exchange of glances said that it was all too familiar.

"Ma'am," Lexi sat on the bed, "what is your name?"

"Lucy."

"Lucy, I like that name. What's going on with you?" she asked pleasantly.

"Fever…cold. My chest is full but I'm coughing good."

"That's good. That's good." Lexi patted her leg and took the stethoscope that Bill extended to her.

"This isn't the same as the flu. It doesn't feel the same."

Lexi placed the scope to her ears. "You had the flu?"

Lucy nodded. "I beat it. The cough stayed, annoyingly. But I felt better. I thought when the cough worsened again, that maybe I had gotten pneumonia."

"That could very well be." Lexi began to examine her. "Deep breath." She went through the lung and heart examination, removed the stethoscope and felt Lucy's glands. "When was the last time you took her temperature?" she asked Matt.

"Two hours ago. It hasn't moved from 101. I've been giving her ibuprofen every four hours. I would have given her antibiotics, but she's allergic to penicillin."

"There are many outside the penicillin family," Lexi said and stood up. She handed her stethoscope to Bill. "Her left lower lobe has fluid. It's not bronchial." Her eyes shifted to the nightstand and the wads of tissues. "Are these what you are using to blow your nose or spit?"

Almost embarrassed she answered. "Spit."

Lexi reached for her bag, and spoke as she rummaged through. "Any clue which one may be the freshest?" She grabbed a pair of gloves and placed them on.

Bill groaned and Lexi shot him a glare.

Lucy pointed to a tissue wad.

Lexi picked it up and unfolded it.

"Aw, geeze," Bill whined. "Warn me next time. I hate when you do that."

Lexi chuckled, and examined the used tissue. She reached inside and examined the expelled substance with her fingers.

Bill cleared his throat. "Lex, come on."

Lexi looked at him, then to Matt, who had turned away. "I would think that with what both of you saw during the outbreak, this would be nothing." She rolled the tissue and threw it away, then removed her gloves and tossed them in the trash as well. "The texture is good," she told Lucy. "So is the color. So I'm going confirm your diagnosis of pneumonia. Lots of fluids, we'll get a course of antibiotics in you, an expectorant, and in a few days you'll be good as new." She addressed Matt. "I'm also convinced that's what our boy Charlie the slot hero has as well."

Bill asked. "You can tell that without looking at his spit?"

"It was on his chin," Lexi winked. "Besides, the color of his skin lets me know his O2 levels are down." Again, she looked at Matt. "Did you clean out the hospital? Medfast places, things like that? Pharmacies?"

"Not all. We have a room of supplies," Matt replied. "If you can't find it there, there's still a ton left at the pharmacies and the hospital. But the hospital is a wreck, just so you know. We just didn't know what was viable to take and what wasn't."

Lexi nodded. "I can understand that. While I'm here, I can help."

"Excellent. Let's go to the next room." Matt said. "We have two more for you to look at, same as my mom." He bent down and kissed his mother on the forehead. "See, I told you I'd get you well." And then Matt walked to the door.

Bill reached out and grabbed Lexi's arm, pulling her back. "Wait, slot guy, this woman and two others. Is pneumonia contagious?"

Lexi shook her head. "No. But, I'm beginning to think, we may be seeing a delayed repercussion of our flu that we weren't expecting." She paused at the door. "Hopefully, that's all it is."

* * *

What Jon had told him stayed with Briggs throughout his lunch. He sipped a cup of broth, ate a cracker and thought about Jon's words; the things he'd conveyed about the Ohio search party, what his man in Ohio had told him. The look on the survivor's faces. His mind swirled. Then he thought about Jon. He was younger, but not only was he technologically smart, he seemed to represent both sides of reason, and Briggs liked that.

He had an idea of what he wanted to do with Jon, but first, he fired up the radio, and contacted Sergeant Nelson of the Ohio Minuteman.

"This is Commander Briggs of the United America

Army, how are you son?"

"Good," Sergeant Nelson replied. "What can I do for you, sir?"

"Hey, I know you guys are squarely in. Jon told me you sensed some problem with the guys I dispatched from Southern PA to clear warehouses."

"Well … shortly after I met with your guys, one of our towns burned to the ground. I just felt it ironic that they had recently been in the area."

"What were their attitudes?"

Silence.

"Sergeant?"

"Smug. Trying to act hard ass."

"I tried to reach them, no luck. Any chance you can send men out to look for them? I'll deploy some relief to you. I know you gentlemen are working hard in that area to organize."

"Sir, they said they were meeting up with another team in Pennsylvania, they're probably there by now. May be easier to dispatch from your end. But I can definitely use the help here."

"I'll get some men out to you, and I'll send out for the other group. Thank you, Sergeant."

Briggs ended the radio call, and like he had a dozen times in the previous two hours, he looked at his cell phone. Still no signal.

He downed the rest of his broth, and sought out Richards, one of his trusted men, one he had known long before the flu hit. He was in the troop dispatch center working on unloading trucks.

Briggs called for him and pulled him aside. "Richards, I'm heading back into Damon, and I need to speak to some incoming survivors and to Jon. What can you tell me about the teams from PA 149?"

Richards cocked back, seemingly surprised by the question. "149? Hold on." He grabbed a notebook and checked it quickly. "I haven't logged any into the computer yet. "

Briggs followed him to the small desk. "They contacted us when the flu was in full swing; we told them to hang tight and would give them a mission before they head up here."

"Yeah, I recall." Richards flipped through the notebook. "We don't really know much. Unorganized militia group. We don't know much about that group, but we accepted their help. Gave them three counties in Ohio and two in PA, they're to report back here in two days."

"So we know nothing about who they are?"

Richards shook his head. "The CO of the unit passed away from the flu. Seemed like a decent enough fellow. But, Jonah, we have to remember, we're taking all the help we can get. Are we having a problem with them?"

"Maybe. I tried to reach them."

"You won't be able to. They're probably out of range. We just gave them orders and you can talk to them when they get here. Unless, you know, they end up taking off with what they got. I mean, really, we gave them intel on food storage, weapons storage ... who knows?"

Briggs' eyes lifted. "I didn't think of that."

"It's a possibility with any of the unregulated units or those we don't know."

"Thank you," Briggs said. "I'll be back." He gave a swat to Richards' arm and headed to the stables.

He mounted his horse, and took a straight route into town. Upon arrival, he gave word to a guard to find Jon Wentworth, then Briggs headed to the municipal building where survivors were registered.

The young man behind the desk stood. "Sir."

"At ease," Briggs said. "Son, some survivors were brought in earlier. Do you know if they are still here?"

"Um ..." The young man scratched his head. "We brought in forty today."

"Really?" Briggs nodded, impressed. "This one was a

group of three. Two women and a child."

"Oh, yeah, a few hours ago." He went to the laptop. "They're over at the Med Center with Doc."

"Are they sick?"

"One of the women is. Doc is holding the other two for observation," he replied.

"What's wrong with them? Starvation, injury?"

"No, get this," he said. "Doc thinks it's the flu."

"Flu? Our flu?"

He shrugged.

Briggs lifted a hand. "I'll be back. If Wentworth gets here, tell him to stay put. I need to see what's going on."

Before the young man could acknowledge the request, Briggs had left the building.

* * *

Emmie hadn't spoken a single word since they fled camp, and now she was repeating over and over that she had to go potty.

This was another dilemma that Chris hadn't even thought about.

He thought he had it. They'd follow the lake then go straight. But somehow that road didn't seem as close as it had on the map.

"I have to go potty."

"I know, I know." Chris stared at the map. "Here's where I get confused. West is left. East is right. How do we know we're going east or west? Obviously, we didn't go straight."

"I have to go potty."

"I know you do," Chris looked at the little girl. "But there isn't a potty here, so you have to go behind the tree and pee."

"Potty."

"Oh my God." Chris closed his eyes.

"This is why I'm glad I'm a boy," Tigger said. "Don't

need anything special to pee. Just stand there and go."

"Potty."

Jake laughed and grabbed Emmie's hand. "Come on, we'll make you a potty."

"You sure?" Chris asked.

"I had two little sisters. I can do this."

"Cool. Thanks." Chris again returned to the map, then he noticed Tigger in a crouch next to him. "What's up, Tig?"

"Any idea where we're at?"

"That's what I'm trying to figure out. Road is north. Right there. But where is north?"

"Up."

Chris laughed. "That's funny. If my phone had service we could use the compass."

"Can't you use the sky like they do in the movies?" Tigger asked.

"Yeah, but it's cloudy. Where's the sun?"

Tigger stood and looked. "There."

Finally Chris saw it. It was lower than he expected, and just the tiniest speck of light. "Wow, it must be late. Sun sets in the west. We keep that sun to our left, we'll find the road. Good going, Tig."

"Done." Jake returned with Emmie.

Chris sniffed. "Why do I smell pee?"

"She's wet," Jake said. "I made her a potty but she still peed on herself. No big deal."

"Aw, geeze," Chris whined. "Between her and Tig, we'll leave a scent."

"Hey!" Tigger yelled. "I can't help it, I was peeing uphill."

Chris rolled up the map. "Let's go."

"You think you figured it out?" Jake asked.

"I think." Chris sighed. "I hope. It's getting late and these woods are the last place I want to spend the night." He grabbed Tigger's hand and Jake grabbed Emmie's, and they continued on.

9. WHERE NEXT?

"He's not two," Lars poured a drink at the bar, then walked around and joined Tom at a table. "My guess is about sixteen months. He doesn't talk yet, except one syllable words. Ethan referred to him as Baby Doe, my guess is he's a John Doe, so that's what I've been calling him. Doe."

"Will he be alright?"

"Yes. Yes, he will. Had Ethan and Mick not started fluids, even as little as they got into him, he would have died. Probably went three days without food. Last blood test his electrolytes were much, much better. Any idea what we're going to do with him? Anyone that can take him?"

"Ethan said Mick ...." Tom sighed, "that Mick took a liking to him. Maybe have Rose handle the baby till, you know, Mick gets back? What about the woman?"

"Fine. Bullet went straight through. No damage. Needs some rest but otherwise healthy as a horse." Lars reached over and laid a hand on Tom's arm. "How are you?"

Tom looked worse for wear. His face was drawn, shoulders slumped. "Dying inside, Lars, and there's nothing I can do. They're all I have left in this world. All I have. And I keep thinking, did these men grab them? Did they run? And Mick, he's looking for them. How? This isn't the old world."

"I understand, Tom, but I have faith in Mick. You know

that. If anyone can find them and bring them back Mick can. And he will."

"And then I will kick his ass for leaving them alone."

"I'm certain Mick already is kicking his own self."

The bell above the door dinged and Lars looked back to see a man of about forty wearing a camouflage jacket and pants walk in. He removed his cap.

"Can I help you, son?" Tom asked.

"My name is Craig Nelson of the Ohio Minuteman Militia. I'm looking for Rose Owens. Do you know where I can find her? I tried radio contact, but I don't know why I couldn't get through."

Lars questioned. "You came all the way down here to find her?"

"Yeah, I found that note she wrote and it seemed urgent. I thought … I thought there was trouble here like in Wadsworth."

Tom stood. "Do you know what happened in Wadsworth?"

"I have an idea. Not one hundred percent certain though."

Tom patted the seat next to him. "Sit down and tell us what you think."

* * *

Tom led the way up the walk to Rose's house. The front room lights were on and Tom paused as he passed her motorcycle. There was a sleeping roll tied to the back.

The front door was open, so Tom knocked once, opened the screen door, and walked in ahead of Lars and Nelson.

"Rose, you here?"

A single, 'Yep', carried to him and Tom followed the voice.

Rose stood in the sitting room; she was adding a few things to a backpack. A rifle sat next to it.

"Rose, what in the hell are you doing?" Tom asked.

"What the fuck does it look like I'm doing?" She zipped the pack. "I'm going after my son and grandchildren."

"Right now?"

"Should I wait? Huh, Tom? Wait until it's too fucking late and the trail is cold?"

"For crying out loud, woman," Tom barked. "It's gonna be dark in an hour. You can't be going out there. It's not safe."

"Well, I can't sit around waiting."

"I want them back as bad as you. I am sick with worry. You don't even know where to start."

"Ethan said his camp that was hit was right outside of Erie. Even circled it on the map. I'll find it. I'll start ..." she paused and leaned to the right, pointing to Nelson, "Who the fuck is this?"

Lars cleared his throat. "Considering you left urgent notes on this man's door, I'd think you know."

"Ma'am," Nelson extended his hand, "I'm Craig Nelson from the Minuteman Militia."

Rose cocked back. "I don't know you. I been a member for years."

"I know. I came from Ohio First Defense at the onset of the flu. When the military was breaking down, the militia was organizing for post-event. During the breakdown of the regular army, the militia is America's first line of defense, you know."

"Yeah, yeah," Tom waved out his hand. "Tell her what you think about Wadsworth."

"Well, considering she just mentioned a camp that was hit near Erie," Nelson shifted his eyes, "I'm pretty certain my suspicions are right."

Rose stopped packing and moving. "Go on."

"During the height of the flu, several organized and unorganized militia units were networking so as to come up with a viable plan after everything was said and done,"

Nelson explained. "We were contacted and stayed in touch, giving stats, we also were the link up to other Indiana and Ohio militias. Our mission was simple: to stay intact until the flu died out and then we would restructure."

Tom waved his hand. "Get to the point."

Lars closed his eyes for a second. "He is explaining so we don't ask questions, but I have a big question. I understand the restructuring, but isn't that the job of the government and our surviving president?"

"Where is he?" Nelson asked. "In a bunker? Waiting? You guys are only a couple weeks out of the flu, most of this country, finished well over a month ago. He didn't do anything, so we had to. We're getting pretty organized. We had a lot of units deployed to small towns like yours to help when the Army and National Guard pulled out. And then a lot of those soldiers started joining us over the last couple weeks. Anyhow… some militia units we avoided because we know they had rough edges. Some were rough and we didn't know. It's a gamble with unregistered militia. Unit 149, out of southern Pennsylvania, was deployed to this area for stockpile of abandoned supplies, survivor search, register towns for the United America Army, so all resources would be pulled, organized, shared. This unit is the one that I suspect burned Wadsworth. I didn't trust them, they seemed like trouble. When I spoke to headquarters about the signal tower, I mentioned it."

"What does this have to do with my son?" Rose asked.

"I'm getting to it." Nelson lifted a hand. "The commander contacted me about my report of this unit. He wanted me to find them to see if they were the ones responsible, but I told him I couldn't because they had to be long gone and were meeting up with another group from their unit in Pennsylvania. Last I heard … up near Erie."

Rose sat down.

"So the Wadsworth men and the other Pennsylvania men are from the same unit. 149?" Lars asked. "Chances are they're nothing but scavengers, not caring what they do or to who. And you think maybe these 149 people hit the Erie camp?"

"Birds of a feather," Nelson said. "Just ironic that we had trouble in Wadsworth, that's where the one unit went. And near Erie is where the others were at." He shrugged. "I think it's more than a coincidence."

Tom asked, "Were these the only two places they were given?"

"That I can't tell you because I don't know. I can try to speak to the commander again to see what orders they were given. Radio contact is sketchy at times. But cell phones will be back tomorrow. For sure. We've been working on the towers."

Lars said. "Gee, last I heard the government was working on it."

"They may be, but we'll make the progress," Nelson replied.

Tom snapped his finger. "Rose, Mick has that cell phone on him. All you got to do is leave a message, text him, something. Cause you know damn well he'll fire it up to look at pictures."

Lars added, "Then you can find out where he is and help him."

"Or," Nelson interjected, "and this is just a thought, what about telling him to head to the main base in southern New York State? They may be able to help him find his sons. Or he may find them there."

"That's if those 149 rebels show up. Our last report there were some kids taken by them." Lars said. "Really, they may have taken the supply information and are using it for their own benefit. Sure doesn't sound to me like they're team players."

"Ha!" Tom coughed. "No one is a team player. What gives this commander and base camp the right to come and steal from our warehouse?"

Nelson appeared humbled. "Begging your pardon sir, but whose warehouse was it? Who gave you the right to all that food? Would you feel the same way if it was the government?"

"Yep." Tom nodded. "I would. We laid squatters rights."

"And what happens when that supply runs out?" Nelson asked. "Have you thought of that? What next?"

"We're working on long term," Tom said.

"Will that include medical supplies, too?" Nelson asked. "This is why restructuring—"

"Can we leave the campaigning for militia restructuring out of this for the time being please?" Lars cut in. "Allow me to acknowledge that both of you have valid points, whether I heard them or not. Right now …" he faced Rose, "what are you going to do? Will you hold off packing and leaving like Rambo in the night?"

Rose turned to Nelson. "Phones will be up tomorrow?"

"Yes, Ma'am for sure. Parts of Indiana are already getting signals. Just need to cross towers and we believe that connection will be tomorrow."

"Okay. I'll wait. I'll call, wait until I hear back from Mick. But if he is still looking, then I am immediately heading out to help him."

* * *

Briggs wasn't a bad guy, or at least he never thought he was. He supposed people were intimidated because of his height. He never used it to push people around., but people did shrink out of his way when he approached.

It wasn't like he demanded respect, nor did people go out of their way to give it to him. His men respected him but didn't fear him. No one went out of the way to call him commander or say hello, they just stepped away when he walked by. The people of Damon and those who had joined up with his cause merely accepted what he was doing.

Doctor Fai Kiddi was wet behind the ears and finishing his residency at Allentown Memorial Hospital when the flu hit. Tossed in the throes of diseases, Fai, or Doc as everyone called him, was all they had as far as medical personnel went.

He was thirty, looked twelve to Briggs, and smoked a ton of cigarettes. When Doc first came to the town after the flu, everyone spoke loudly to him as if he were deaf, assuming he didn't understand English. But Fai was born and raised in Miami, Florida.

Briggs walked into the medical facility, which was a mere twenty bed hospital. He asked where Doc was and only received a point to the back room.

Someone should have told him the door was an optical illusion, and that he had to duck. Briggs assumed it was a step down and not a short door, and smacked his forehead on the arch as he opened the door and stepped through.

"Son of a bitch."

Laughter.

"Sorry," Doc said. "Shut the door will you? I don't want the smoke out there."

Briggs coughed and waved through the thick cloud. "You'll eventually run out of those things."

"Please, I have an in. Tobacco plants are growing a plenty. Plus I have a closet full of cartons. Last me two years, maybe. Then perhaps I'll quit."

"I doubt that."

"Me, too. What's up?" Doc asked. "Aside from that doozy of a red mark on your forehead."

"Fuck." Briggs rubbed his head. "Really?"

"Um, no. I'm kidding." He put out his cigarette.

"Good. It hurt. Anyhow, two women and a child were brought in. The woman was sick. You're holding the other two."

"Yep. What's up?"

"Do they have our flu?"

Doc coughed a laugh. "No, what in the world would make you think that?"

"Municipal said."

"They suck. No." Doc shook his head. "I'm detaining the other two in case it's something else, but I think it's more a case of the woman ate something bad. That's all. Stomach thing. They had a long journey. Your guys in Indiana found them and brought them here."

"Where did they come from?"

"Oregon, I think. Yeah," Doc said after a moment of thought.

Briggs whistled. "That's a hell of a journey."

"According to one woman, we'll be seeing a lot of that. Nothing is left out west. Population is here."

"I see. Well thanks ..." Briggs turned and stopped. "Hey, did they say if my men were decent to them? Any problems?"

"None that were brought up. They weren't scared of your guys if that's what you're worried about." When Briggs didn't reply, Doc asked, "You concerned about that?"

"No. No ..." Briggs paused. "Well, a little. Got a few crews out there I'm not familiar with and I worry, you know."

"I do. Well, no one brought in today showed any signs of fear or abuse if that helps."

"It does, thank you. And keep me posted on the health issues."

Doc gave a thumbs up then lit another cigarette.

"You just put one out," Briggs remarked.

"And I'm lighting another."

Briggs grumbled and started to leave.

"Hey, Jonah, duck so you don't get another red mark to match the big one on your head."

"So I have a red mark and you lied."

Doc smiled.

"Ass." With a shake of his head, Briggs walked out. He

remembered to duck.

He had intended to check on the survivors, but he took Doc at his word and opted against it. and instead returned to the municipal building to retrieve his horse. Wentworth was there waiting as he had instructed.

"You wanted to see me?" Jon asked. "Jonah, did you know you have a red mark on your head?"

"Yes." Briggs rubbed his head. "Doc threw something at me by accident. Anyhow …"

"No. Not yet. Tomorrow, I swear."

"What?" Briggs asked.

"You wanted to know about the phones."

"No, I didn't, but thanks. I wanted to ask you something else. You seem reasonable, Jon. I'm looking for a right hand man and would like you to be it."

"Really? Cool."

"Thanks."

"No."

"No what?"

"Um, as nice as the offer is, I'll pass. I don't want that much responsibility."

"You're in charge of getting communications back up, how is that not a big responsibility?" Jon shrugged. "Too bad." Briggs reached out and gave a swat to Jon's arm, sending him sailing sideways a foot. "I know you live in that one room at the police station. We'll have better housing for you at base." Briggs began to walk off.

"Don't I get a say so?" Jon asked.

"You do, but, Jon, you really have a voice of reason. You see a different side than I do. Like Richards, but Richards has other stuff I need him to do. I'd like you to be my right hand man. Please."

"Fine. But I guess I better get used to not being popular anymore if I work for you."

"Why is that?" Briggs asked.

"People don't like you. They fear you," Jon replied. "Not

that they have reason. But you can't be the nice guy all the time, Jonah. I wouldn't respect you as leader if you took the easy route."

"Appreciated." Brigs shook his hand. "Can you do me a favor? Doc just admitted a couple of survivors into the clinic. They came from the west. Keep an eye out on them. I have a weird feeling. Just check in with me tomorrow if there's a problem."

"You're not coming into town?" Jon asked.

"I hope to, but I have a team out there that I suspect may be causing problems on their runs. They're supposed to check in first thing in the morning, and if not, I'm going out looking for them."

"Don't you have men for that?"

"I do, but I sent these guys out. If they did bad, then it is my job to correct it." Briggs turned again to walk away.

"Jonah?" Jon called. Briggs stopped. "Yeah?"

"It'll be good being your right hand man."

After a wink and a nod of appreciation, Briggs sought his horse.

* * *

I'm an asshole, Mick thought. *I am the biggest asshole ever.*

He was angry and frustrated and couldn't believe he hadn't given Chris enough credit.

Mick had followed that gravel road for an hour until it led him to another set of fishing cabins. The boys weren't there; no footprints in sight, and certainly no Denny Dynamite prints.

Mick headed back down the gravel road. At first he wondered if he had gone the wrong way, assuming there was no way the boys would head back to the camp. He had followed that road until it brought him right back to the camp and it was there, internally beating himself up over his inability to find the boys, that he reached into his pocket and pulled out the coin.

Then he realized how much he had erred.

Chris hadn't dropped the coin next to the footprint and snack to say, 'Hey, we were here'. Chris had put that specific coin next to the footprint on purpose.

The coin was a trick; an illusion. A way to deceive.

Chris left the coin next to the footprint as a way to tell Mick the footprints were a trick. That had to be the message. If not, at his pace, Mick would have found the boys. Now, much time had been lost.

At a faster speed, Mick went back down to the fishing cabin again to start over. By then it was getting dark and the footprints were harder to see. He found a second set of tracks by the lake and followed them until they led into the woods. At that point, it was full dark and he couldn't see them anymore.

Mick had to stop; he'd start again at first light. The kids would stop for the night as well, he knew. As much as he wanted to keep going, the last thing Mick needed to do was lose more time by not following the correct trail again. He took heart in the fact that Chris was thinking ahead. That he was being diligent and smart.

He rested with his back against the cabin wall, and before he fell asleep, Mick said a prayer. He prayed that the next day he would have better luck and most importantly, that the boys were safe and well and stayed that way until Mick found them.

And he would.

* * *

<u>Las Vegas, NV</u>

Lexi returned from making one last round with her pneumonia patients. She washed up, changed, poured a drink, and shut the curtain in the hotel room. Not that it mattered much. It was dark outside and no other buildings were powered up. It was an eerie yet beautiful sight. She had always wanted to see Las Vegas; she just never thought that when she did it would be a dead city.

She wore a long tee shirt over a pair of shorts. The room was warm, though the air conditioning did help some. After sipping on her wine, she put the glass on the nightstand, propped her pillows and sat on the bed. She pulled only the sheet over her as she bought her legs up toward her.

Bill groaned in grogginess as he rolled over. He reached up and ran his hand down her leg. "Why don't you try to sleep? It's been a long day and tomorrow is another one."

"I know," she said softly.

"How are they?"

Her head bobbed from left to right. "Same. But I think I'll do better with intravenous antibiotics."

"That's what I thought. The hospital won't be easy. It may not be easy at all finding what you need."

Lexi nodded.

"You okay?" Bill asked.

She winced. "My stomach is bothering me some. I knew I shouldn't have eaten that steak."

"You didn't eat much."

"It's still red meat my body hasn't digested in while. I'll be fine," she said. "Go back to sleep. I wanna …" She reached to the nightstand and not only grabbed her wine, she lifted her phone. "I wanna check."

Bill slowly shook his head with closed eyes. "I can't believe you kept that."

"You never know. And did we know?" She lifted it. "Signal here in Vegas."

"That doesn't mean—"

"I know. But it's something to do until my stomach settles and I get sleepy."

"Okay. Goodnight. Wake me if you need me."

"I will." Lexi leaned down and gently kissed the top of

his head.

Bill rolled over.

She stared at him for a second. They had become close. They weren't lovers. She supposed in time they would be. But for the time being they were close, companions, best friends. They were together. She loved him and couldn't imagine life, especially the one at hand, without him.

After a moment, she returned to her phone. It was stupid, she knew it, and possibly a waste of time. But really, what would it hurt?

Following another sip, she set down her wine, and stared at her phone. She opened up her 'contact' folder. Over three hundred contacts. Did she even know three hundred people?

Lexi had a plan.

She started with the letter 'A', and the first person there. She chose, 'send message' and typed. 'This is Lexi Martin. It's October 16th. I am alive. I hope you are too.'

Send.

Next.

It wasn't much of a message, but one she would copy and send to every single person in her phone.

Twenty percent of the population was said to have survived the flu.

She didn't expect twenty percent of her contact list to get back to her, but she could hope that maybe one would reply. That's all she could do. Out of hopefulness, she spent the next two hours sending out messages.

JOURNAL ENTRY

I'm ready to sleep. It was a horrible day. We ran around the woods in circles and by the time we finally found the main road it started to get dark.

At least we found the main road.

We didn't see any cars or didn't come across any of those men who hit our camp. I'm glad.

We also haven't seen Mick. I keep looking over my shoulder, cause I keep thinking he's gonna be there. He has to be. It's Mick. He has to be okay.

According to the map, there's a town not far from here. If we get there, then I think I will know which way to go. Maybe someone there can help or give us a ride back to Lodi.

Jake thinks we should wait for Mick there. That if Mick is following us, he'll find us.

That might not be a bad idea.

But I'll leave another clue here, that we were here. Something to let Mick know which way we went.

For now, we're all tired. I can barely see to write. Tigger is asleep on my lap and Emmie took the blanket. She fell asleep on the way and we had to take turns carrying her.

We found a convenience store. There's nothing left in here, so I figured since it already was hit, it was safe.

I also think it's safe at night. Too dark for anyone to come out.

We have enough food. As soon as it gets light, I'll feed the kids and we'll get going.

I have to say I'm scared. I'm afraid I can't protect the babies if something goes wrong. I hope we find help soon. Or better yet, please let Mick find us.

10. BREAKTHROUGH

October 17th

At first light Mick was up and out looking for that trail of footprints by the lake. He followed to the edge, and watched as they veered off. He was hopeful until he realized that the kids were walking in circles. They had lost their direction, then after the tracks went back and forth in the same area, they started a steady course. When they hit the road, Mick knew they had lost a lot of time.

For sure he'd catch up, and he was certain of the direction because the Denny Dynamite tracks weaved a path of mud prints for a long time on that road.

After walking a half an hour, no cars passing him at all, Mick spotted a convenience store. The door was open and he trotted to it, calling out, "Chris! Tigger!"

There was no answer and Mick stepped inside.

The shelves were empty. Completely empty. Someone had come through and cleaned it out completely. He visually searched for clues, and when he heard the 'squeak' of a rodent, Mick spun around. On the bare second shelf, right above the sign for bread, a huge bold rat held a snap snack in its grip and nibbled on it.

By its feet were two more. Chris had left them on the shelf; surely he had to, he wouldn't have just dropped them there. The kids had been there at one point. Probably spent the night. Next to the rat, by the snap snacks, was an arrow written in the dust. It pointed to a word. Problem was, the rat's tail had erased a good bit of it.

"Are you kidding me? You got to be kidding me" Mick said out loud and reached out to smack the rat away.

The brave rodent wasn't giving in, but he did budge. Mick was able to make out the first letter, 'T' and a bit of the last letter. Using his best 'Hang Man' sense, he hoped Chris spelled out the word, 'Town'.

Arrow, word, it told Mick, hopefully they were heading straight ahead. He left the store and picked up the pace. Wearing down some, getting winded, Mick saw the first sign not ten minutes into this journey.

There was a town ahead, and it was only one mile away. It wasn't all that far - they had to be there. They *had* to be. The kids were walking, how far could they have gotten?

* * *

"Thanks, mister, for the ride, we appreciate it," Chris told the older man as they stood outside a small compact car.

The man emptied another huge canister of gas into the tank. "I'm not feeling right about doing this. You guys are so young."

"Yeah, but we're good, right?" Chris said. "We don't have but a few hours left of driving, ain't that what you said?"

"I know what I said, but you have two babies with you." He gestured to Tigger and Emmie, both the same size.

"I'm not a baby," Tigger claimed.

"Nah, he's just pint size," Chris added.

"Maybe you guys can travel with me a little further," he suggested. "We can find help, a radio, something."

"We can do this, mister, I'm certain." Chris said. "Heck, we trotted through the woods and ran for our lives."

The man stared at them.

Chris liked him. He thought immediately that the man had an honest face. He was the only one in the town when they got there, and the man was just pulling in as well. He had come in from another street. He was on his way to Maine to find his daughter and granddaughter. Last he'd spoken to them, they were alive and well.

He, like Chris, was surprised that no one was in the town. It looked as if everyone had just disappeared. Maybe they all went somewhere. Chris quickly learned they had. In the center of town, across from the really cool looking eyeglass place, was a memorial wall.

A brass soldier was the symbol and next to him was a flag, but the memorial wasn't what caught Chris' attention. It was the abundance of notes, messages, pictures of people. They covered the wall like wallpaper:

Have you seen her?

Mom, I went north.

Bill and Lacy Jones are in Damon, NY.

* * *

Survivors of the flu had plastered their whereabouts on the wall for anyone who might be looking for them.

The gas station in Cambridge was untouched. In fact, it had a 'help yourself' feel about it. Power was still on and the man filled his tank, then took cans from the store and filled them with gas. He drove with Chris, Jake and the kids until they hit the next town near the highway.

That town wasn't empty. There were people there, but they seemed like drones, not even realizing that a car had pulled in.

One woman did talk to them, and explained that those remaining in the town — and it wasn't many — were packing to leave and join a town of other survivors up north. Rumor had it that civilization was back in business in New

York.

She offered to take Chris and the kids there, but Chris declined. They had to get home.

That was Chris' main goal. He was certain that he'd make it home, he even tore a sheet of paper from his notebook and put it on the memorial wall in Cambridge. Triple outlined his letters that said, **'Mick Owens, we are fine and on our way home!'**

The man, his name was George, found a small car in the new town. It would do well on gas and hopefully be easy to drive, as he explained the basics to Chris.

"I'm leery," George told him. "Really, I am."

"No, really, we can do this." Chris was optimistic.

"Okay, remember what I told you. Not many cars if any on the road. Stay a steady speed, stay on the right, stay diligent and keep your eyes on the road."

"Yes sir."

"Buckle up."

Chris did so.

"Don't go too fast. Don't forget to put the car in gear if you stop. You know how to go and brake, right?"

"Yes, sir, I do."

"Stay on this road and in a few miles, you'll see the signs for Interstate 90. Take that west and it will take you right to Cleveland. Can't say if you'll run into roadblocks, but follow that map. I marked it for you."

"We got this, thank you."

"This is my telephone number. Should the cell lines go back up, will you call me and let me know you made it safely?"

Chris took the paper. "Absolutely."

"My daughter is going to kick my ass for doing this."

George buckled Tigger and Emmie in the back of the small car, told them to be still and be good, then waited until Chris and Jake got in.

"Thanks, again, mister." Chris said. "We owe you."

"Repayment is being safe. Godspeed."

"You said not to speed," Chris said. "I'm going slow."

"I mean .... Godspeed means be careful."

"Got it." Chris shut the car door and fixed his seatbelt. George helped him adjust the seat. He was certain he would be able to see over the steering wheel. After all he was as tall as his mother and she drove all the time.

He practiced like George suggested, touching the pedals. Right was gas, left was brake.

He turned over the ignition. It didn't sound like he did it right. So he tried again.

Grind.

George tapped the window and Chris wound it down. "What the heck was that sound? Is the car broke?"

"No, you restarted it. The car was already started. Look for light right there." George pointed to the dash. "That'll tell you it's on. Foot on the brake as you move it in gear."

Chris pushed down and shifted the car. His stomach twitched, he was nervous, really nervous but confident, and he would be super careful.

"Ease off the brake."

The car inched.

"We're moving."

"Good luck." George backed up.

At first, the car jerked when Chris hit the gas. It was touchy, but he got the feel of it pretty fast.

Jake had been looking out the back window. "He's in the distance now, still waving."

"Nice guy."

"Whew." Jake heaved out a breath. "You're rolling. I think you're going too fast."

Chris looked at the speedometer. "Says I'm going thirty."

"Maybe you ought to slow down. Just don't hit the gas all the time."

"Good idea," Chris said.

"You scared?" Jake asked.

"I am!" Tigger yelled from the back.

"Tig, shush, I got this."

"The baby peed her pants again," Tigger complained.

"So did you, and we ain't calling you out, are we?" Chris shook his head. "Kids."

Jake aimed his voice to the back seat. "Just sit still. We'll be in Ohio shortly." He looked at Chris. "We will, right?"

"Negative Nelly. That's what my pap would call you. Of course we will. Really. George said we'll have enough gas and will only have to use the little in the trunk." He shivered.

"And you're sure you can drive?"

"I'm doing it now, aren't I? Besides, I drove go carts all the time. And I don't think they'll be any wide fast bends with barrels in the middle of the road like on the go cart course. Might actually be easier. Just stay the course, stay on the road. Make it home." Chris smiled. "Piece of cake."

* * *

<u>Lodi, Ohio</u>

It wasn't what Lars expected to see when he walked into room 19 of the Lodi Hospital.

Betty Ann, the woman who had been the school nurse at the elementary school, and now was the only nurse at the hospital, told Lars that Baby Doe was doing remarkably. All levels were up, he'd eaten, and Henry had removed the intravenous drip before he left for the night shift.

It seemed a rather quick recovery, Lars thought, for a child so close to death, though stranger things had happened.

He wanted to see the child for himself and headed for his room. He didn't expect to hear Tom's voice, but heard him speaking soothingly and softly, and when Lars walked into the room he received the third surprise of the day. Tom was cuddling Doe, reading to him while the child nestled in his arms.

"Well, doesn't he look well, this morning?" Lars commented, reaching his hand out to the boy.

"He does," Tom replied. "You know, I came in here to check on him seeing how he is this prize possession of my son in law, and wouldn't you know it, the boy looked at me and held out his arms as if he has known me his entire life."

"That's amazing, Tom."

"Yeah, and he clung, Lars, he just reached his little arms to me and held on. Well, I couldn't put him down, I just couldn't."

"How long have you been here, Tom?" Lars asked.

"'Bout an hour, maybe more. Not sure." Tom hitched a breath. "I'm so damn worried about my grandkids, this was a shot of life I needed. I just started reading and he cuddled more. Look at him. When Dust … when Dustin was this age we spent hours like this." Tom cleared his throat.

"I remember."

"If it's all the same to you, Lars, I think I'd like to take this little one with me when he's ready to leave the hospital. I'll look after him until Mick decides what to do with him. I can take him with me everywhere. I'll make sure he eats and drinks."

"I think that's a great idea."

At a single knock on the archway, Ethan stepped into the room. "Hey, guys I just …" He trailed off and stared. "Wow, Doe looks great. I can't believe that's the same boy. Wait until Mick sees him."

"Amazing what a little watering will do," Lars said. "What's up?"

"Check this out," Ethan said. "Cell phones are back."

* * *

Rose was ready and on it.

She was packed and prepped to leave, but as she promised Tom, she'd wait to see if she got a hold of Mick when the phones went up.

Just about out of patience and ready to jump on her bike and go on a wild goose chase, Rose got word and then she looked at her phone.

She decided to give herself one hour to reach Mick and then she'd take off.

On her front porch, phone in hand, Rose dialed Mick. It went immediately to voice mail; she didn't leave a message. She hung up and tried again. She would do that continuously for one hour. After that, she'd try to reach Mick from the road.

* * *

Cambridge, PA

Mick dropped to his knees in defeat the second he stepped into Cambridge. It was a ghost town and he knew the boys weren't there. Where had he gone wrong? Where had he failed? The entire last leg of his journey was filled with hope of finding the boys. He thought of when they were born, all the Little League games, the times he'd stand up for them when they were in trouble and all the times he took the boys for overnights when Dylan was at the end of her rope.

Not that the boys didn't drive him nuts. They did. Tigger in his tiny tot body was years beyond his age in intelligence. He was sarcastic and funny and had more love and joy in his small body than a state full of people. Chris was always the antagonist, going against what Mick said, questioning him every step of the way. And Dustin … Dustin was the voice of reason, yelling at his little brother for questioning Mick, then turning right around and doing it himself.

Life would never be right without Dustin. Mick's heart broke every single time he thought of him.

The last thing he wanted was for anything to happen to Chris or Tigger. Where *were* they?

Maybe they were hiding in town ... maybe. He called out, but received no response. He'd search the town, after a moment of regrouping. It was when he was about to sit and rest that he spotted the memorial wall and all the flyers posted there.

Like a flashing red light, Mick saw his name. He believed he did and, hoping it wasn't his wishful imagination, Mick raced to the wall. Plastered over a stack of flyers was a note to him from Chris.

They were fine. More than fine. They were on their way home. Mick wasn't certain how that was; maybe they had run into someone in town. The note screamed relief at him and grabbing it, he pulled it to his chest and collapsed on the ground.

While the search was sort of over, his journey wasn't. Mick had to head back to Lodi, find a way there. He looked around the small town area and spotted a motorcycle in the open garage of a small gas station.

He fueled it up, but it wouldn't jump start right away. With a little work, Mick got it running. He strapped his belongings to the bike, and he was ready to ride. Before he did so, he did something else he had done many times on his search, he pulled out his phone.

He pressed the 'on' button, waited for the power cycle and the familiar face of Dylan to greet him. She was his wallpaper.

"Hey, baby," he said to her picture. "I know I failed you. But they left a note. They're on the—"

When his phone rang, it startled him to the point he nearly dropped it. He looked at the screen. Incoming call: *Mom.*

"Holy shit!" Mick quickly answered the phone. "Mom!"

"Mick, oh, God, thank God. Where are you?"

"Mom, I don't know if a man named Ethan arrived in town or not—"

"He did," Rose said. "He told us. Did you find them? Did you find the boys?"

"No, not yet. I followed their trail. They left me a note on a wall in this small town, said they were on their way home and they were fine."

"What do you think?"

"I think someone is bringing them home, not sure. I got a bike and I'm heading back to Lodi, hoping to get them on the way. We're only a few hours out."

"That's a good idea."

"Mom, did that little baby live?" Mick asked.

"Yes, he did. He is doing great. Is there anything you need me to do? Do you need help?"

"No," Mick answered quickly, then changed his mind. "You know what? Yes. We're really near 90 right now, and I'm gonna guess the boys took 90 and are coming in from Cleveland. Can you head out to meet them? You'll wanna take that route north toward Cleveland and then toward Erie."

"Absolutely, I'll leave now."

"Mom, there's that rest area, just where 90 junctions with 70. Outside Erie, remember? Meet me there if you don't find the boys. That's a halfway point. If neither of us have any luck, we'll go from there."

"I'm leaving now, Mick. Be careful."

"You too." Mick readied to end the call, but stopped when he heard his name.

"Mick?"

"Yeah?"

"I love ya."

"I love you too," Mick said, and hung up the phone. He was renewed, invigorated with hope and his adrenaline pumped. He mounted the bike, started it, and pulled from the service station onto Main.

Even though there wasn't any traffic, habit caused Mick to pause and look both ways. Had he not, he wouldn't have seen that in the direction he was heading, five trucks had pulled into the large gas station at the onset of town.

He could see supplies in the trucks and not only did men get out from the cabs, but they hopped from the back. Lots of men. Some wore camouflage, some wore black. They joked, laughed, hooted and hollered. Mick looked longer to make sure he didn't see the boys, and when he didn't, Mick, not wanting to wait around to see what they were up to, took off in the other direction.

11. DIFFERENT TURN

Briggs waited, and at eight a.m. he was ready to go searching for the missing men from unit 149. At the suggestion of his new right hand man, he'd waited two more hours, then headed toward Erie.

If they were coming they'd be coming up that way.

At ten on the nose, Briggs was out the door. He had one man in his jeep and four other highly trained men following in a Humvee, in case there was trouble.

They made it into Pennsylvania without incident, and Briggs didn't think they would run into any trouble. Most of the towns had been cleared out and the residents had moved to Damon.

Like he had a hundred times in the journey, Briggs looked to his phone to check for a signal. Then suddenly, he smiled.

"You're like a teenager, sir," his driver said.

"We have life in the phones again. Now why isn't he calling? He said he would call when the signal went back up."

"Why don't you call him?"

"What if we try to call at the same time?" Briggs asked. "Then that would be frustrating." I'll wait."

The driver glanced over at him. "Staring won't make it ring."

"Keep your eyes on the road, son. We have a six thousand pound vehicle tagging our ass, I don't want you to make a mistake and have them ram us."

"Yes, sir."

After a few moments, the phone rang. Excitedly, he answered it. "Briggs."

"You've been waiting to do that, I see," Jon said on the other end.

"I have. Feels good. Even though it hasn't been that long, it feels good. I thought you would have called right away, you were watching for the signal too."

"I would have but …listen, I got news," Jon said. "We got in touch with 149."

"Where are they?"

"You're not gonna like it. Seems they told us to stop bothering them unless we want to negotiate."

"Negotiate? What the hell does that mean?"

"It means they cornered off Pennsylvania near the lake across Erie. They said it's their territory now."

"Jon, how many men could that be? Ten? Fifteen tops? I mean, how much of a hold can they have on that corner?"

"From what I was told," Jon said, "they have more. They joined up with several other units that haven't checked in and I'm on that now figuring out who they are. They said they have survivors, and Jonah … I heard kids in the background. Crying kids."

Briggs snapped his finger to the driver, and signaled for him to stop. The driver held his hand out the window and slowed down before halting the vehicle.

Once the jeep stopped, Briggs stepped outside to have more privacy. "Tell me all you know."

* * *

"Aw man," Chris whined. "I knew it. I *knew* it." He hit the steering wheel as they passed a sign.

From the back seat, Tigger said. "I told you."

"Shut up, Tig," Chris barked. "We went East instead of West, didn't we?"

Jake held the map. "New York is north sort of, I don't know."

"We went east. We have to turn around." Chris said. "Let me see the map."

"Watch the road!" Tigger shouted.

"Tig, I'm only glancing. I'm good."

"You're gonna hit them."

"Hit what?" Chris asked, eyes shifting to the map and to the rearview mirror.

"Those cars."

Chris looked up.

Jake and Tigger screamed, and Chris, as he too screamed, hit the brakes. He wasn't going very fast, yet the car swerved some before coming to a screeching halt.

He breathed heavily. "Oh my God. Oh my God. Everyone alright?"

Jake nodded then his eyes grew wide.

"I'm fine, too!" Tigger yelled.

"Is Emmie …" When Chris turned around to check on Emmie, he saw Jake pointing.

Chris peered out the windshield. Walking toward the car was a very tall black man in uniform. In fact, he was the tallest man Chris had ever seen next to Mick.

"Holy shit." Chris whispered. "What do we do?"

"He has a gun," Jake said. "He looks mean. He's gonna kill us."

Tigger hollered. "Reverse! Reverse!. Get us out!"

"Good thinking, Tig." Nervously, Chris reached for the gear, shifted it, hit the gas, but the car was in neutral and only revved. He looked up the man grew closer. Hurriedly, Chris shifted again and hit the gas.

The car jerked forward.

Thump.

Chris watched as the front end of the car sent the man sailing to the left. He hit the brakes again and put the car in park. "Oh my god."

"You killed him!" Jake said. "You just killed a man."

"I didn't mean to. What do we do?"

"Go!" Tigger popped his body between the two front seats. "Go."

"I can't go, I can't." Chris shook his head and reached for the car door.

Jake grabbed his arm. "Chris, there are five other men. Just go."

Chris shook. His voice quivered. "I just committed vehicular homicide. I can't go anywhere. It just ain't right." He opened the door.

The second he got out, Tigger jumped into the driver's seat and grabbed the door, pulling it closed.

"What are you doing?" Jake asked.

"When they shoot Chris, we're getting out of here. I got this." Tigger's legs didn't even touch the floor, even though he slid all the way down. "I got this."

* * *

His insides trembled out of control, but Chris took in a brave breath and walked toward the five men who were standing above the man he had killed. He whimpered, scared, on the verge of crying. "I'm … I'm sorry. I'm sorry. I didn't mean to kill him. I don't drive. It was an accident."

The men parted like the red sea, exposing the man, who was sitting up. A trickle of blood rolled down his forehead. He wiped it and slowly brought himself to a stand, staring at Chris.

"Aw, geeze, aw geeze. You're big. Don't hurt me. Please, I didn't mean to almost kill you I swear. See? I could have ran. I didn't. I came back. Sorry."

The big man walked up to him. "Calm down. I'm not

gonna hurt you. You're all of what? Twelve?"

"Thirteen and a half," Chris corrected.

"Still too young to drive, and I'm sure you were nervous."

"I was, sir."

"Commander Briggs," one of the men called, "there are all kids in that car."

"You guys alright?" Briggs asked.

"Yes. We're just trying to make it home," Chris answered.

Briggs walked by Chris and to the car. He opened up the driver's door to see Tigger, who had slid all the way as far as he could on the driver's seat. Hand on the wheel, his head barely came to the bottom of the steering wheel as he diligently tried to reach the pedals.

"What the hell are you doing, little man?" Briggs asked.

"I got this," Tigger said, and then looked up. His eyes widened and he jumped quickly from the driver's seat onto Jake's lap. "I wasn't driving. I didn't hit you."

"I know."

Chris asked, "Are you okay, mister?"

"I'm fine. It takes a lot more than a Honda to kill me," Briggs said, then held out his hand to Chris after looking at the others in the car. "Jonah Briggs, and you are?"

"Chris Hughes. That little guy is my brother Tigger. Don't let his size fool you, he has a growing problem. And these guys, Jake and Emmie, we met at a camp. Our camp was hit by bad guys. Aw, geeze …" Chris stepped back in sudden realization. "You're wearing uniforms too."

"I'm not a bad guy, son. I know you don't have a reason to believe me, but I'm not. Where's home?"

"Lodi," Chris replied.

"Ohio?" Briggs shifted his eyes to his men. "You're going the wrong way."

"We were supposed to go west." Chris hung his head low. "We made a mistake."

"A good mistake. There's some trouble ahead. Chris, I want you guys to come with me, okay? I'll explain later. I want you to come, we'll get you fed, cleaned up and maybe try to contact Lodi to work out a way to get you back there."

"Do we have a choice?" Chris asked.

"Not really," Briggs said. "Trust me, it's for your own safety."

"We ain't under arrest for almost killing you, are we?" Briggs shook his head. "You said you wanna clean us up. Are we that dirty?"

Briggs closed one eye and shook his head. "Nah, but …" he dropped his voice low. "You guys kinda smell."

"Ah, geeze, those babies keep peeing their pants, that's why."

"You'll have that." Briggs placed a hand on Chris' back. "Let's go. Get your stuff and your gang."

Briggs stepped to one of his men by the Humvee. "We're gonna take these kids back to base. They were trying to get to Lodi, but since that's not possible, head west, see what's up. Do some reconnaissance, see what's going on, and get back to me. And by all means, if there are a lot of them, don't be a hero. Got it?"

The soldier nodded. "Yes, sir."

"Good luck." Briggs stepped way. "Check in. I mean it." He walked back to the car where Chris, Tigger, Jake and Emmie stood. He motioned his head for them to go to the jeep, then loaded them inside.

Briggs took a moment to watch the Humvee drive off, and then climbed in the jeep. He looked back at the group of kids. To him they looked scared, except the little guy. He looked completely unfazed and that made Briggs laugh. After telling them that everything was going to be all right, and hoping they believed him, they took off for Damon.

* * *

Las Vegas, NV

At a knock on her door at the crack of dawn, Lexi was greeted by Matt telling her that Palmer had taken a turn for the worst.

She gathered her bearings, got dressed, and went to see the man who was two doors down from Matt's mother. He had definitely gotten worse. His lungs had filled up even more and he wasn't responding to the antibiotics.

Matt's mother was the same, no improvement, and Charlie the slot machine guy didn't take his morning post at the video machines.

It was a tough strain of pneumonia, and though Lexi attributed it to remnants of the flu, she had to wonder if the deadly flu made the particular strain combative. Pneumonia after a bad case of flu was not uncommon, but this strain was stubborn.

It only reiterated to her that she needed to head to the medical center. While she was certain the flu epidemic had probably wiped out the hospital pharmacy, she was confident that other areas of the hospital would still have supplies.

It was a search and seize. She sent Bill with two of Matt's men to neighboring towns and communities to search for supplies. Bill knew what to get: intravenous supplies, antibiotics, chest tubes, suction devices.

She and Matt hit the hospital. A temporary fence was set up around the medical center with huge hand painted signs reading 'Closed'. The front area was filled with cots and tents and Lexi could only imagine what was inside. The bodies inside were baked in the sun like some old fashioned means of dehydration. Leathery, prune like arms extended from beneath blankets. Exposed faces were tanned and the eye sockets, cheekbones, and the areas under the necks were sunken in. Not one exposed body contained eyeballs. They had either popped out on their own or were carried away by one of the thousands of birds that seemed to take over Las Vegas after the epidemic.

The avian population survived the flu; they were the impervious and the dominant species in numbers now.

Lexi devised a search plan with Matt, and just as she was about to step into the hospital, she heard the ringing of her phone. At first she thought it was Bill until she looked down.

Henry Wilson.

She gasped out loud, asked Matt to wait, and answered her phone. Henry Wilson was the foremost authority on viruses. While Lexi was certain she knew what she was dealing with, it never hurt to get advice from a genius on the matter.

"Oh, thank God." Lexi said, then answered the phone. "Henry?"

"I got your text," Henry said.

"Henry, it is *so* good to hear your voice."

"You, too, Lexi, you too."

"Are you still in Lodi? Last I heard that's where you and Kirk were headed."

"We are. We made a home there," Henry answered. "Where are you?"

"You're not going to believe this," Lexi said. "We're in Vegas."

Henry laughed. "Getting in some gambling?"

"In a sense. It's weird. A lot of people – more than you would think – are on a pilgrimage east. Life's pretty dead and dry out this way."

"Well, it was first hit, least prepared. Why Vegas?"

"It's a major junction. A stop through. People on their way east stop here, rest, get supplies and move on. Just this morning, ten came in. They're headed to a place in New York. Do you know anything about it?"

"A little. Some new group trying to put civilization back together. Word reached there?"

"Yes, they're getting it through militia groups."

"So when should we expect you?"

"Bill and I will be here for a little bit. We're needed at the moment. Seems we have some serious post-flu cases of pneumonia. Four cases, tough strain. In fact, I'm at the medical center now rummaging for supplies. All of the patients said the cough never went away after the flu, and now they have these symptoms."

"I'd like to say we saw this one coming," Henry stated, "but unfortunately, we all brushed off that possibility."

"You seeing it on your end?"

"No. Are they residents there that are sick? Or pilgrims?"

"Residents."

"Don't dismiss the possibility that maybe a traveler brought something in."

"But they all have a common denominator," Lexi said. "They all lived here, and they all contracted and beat the flu."

"Just don't dismiss it, in case you find someone who doesn't fit that pattern. It could be something else."

"Like what?"

"Lots of things. Hanta virus out west is a big thing, lots of rodents."

"How do I check for that without proper equipment?"

"You're in a hospital now. Find a power scope. Vegas runs on the Hoover Dam. Right? You got power."

"We do. I'm gonna be honest, though. I rely heavily on programs to identify the organism. I'm a field doctor."

"Find a lab there. Find a scope. Take that and the monitor. Run a sputum sample and blood sample through for me and take pictures with the phone. Hopefully, Lars, Kirk, or I will be able to identify it. We're old school."

"I'll do that, thank you, Henry."

"Talk soon."

Lexi hung up the phone.

"Everything okay?" Matt asked.

"Yes. That was the head of the CDC, and he's with a top

virologist now. We've got other things to get aside from medical supplies. We're gonna try to transfer images of our pneumonia bacteria or virus, whichever it is, to them, and maybe they'll be able to tell me what course to take to beat this."

"That's excellent to hear."

There wasn't a smell of death. The decomposition smell had long since faded, and it had been replaced with old and musty. Some lights still flickered. The emergency room lobby was packed with bodies, but aside from the hum of the lights, there was another sound.

Coughing.

Lexi turned to Matt. Obviously someone was there, and not only were they coughing uncontrollably, they were dropping things. The cough was deep, rumbling and chesty. They followed the sound to the back hall, where they saw an open storage door.

The coughing clearly was coming from there. The back of the ER was dark; the lights didn't flicker. They barely worked and the only illumination was what little sunlight made its way through.

Lexi and Matt snapped on their flashlights.

"Hello?" Lexi called as she neared the storage room.

"We know someone's here," Matt said. "Do you need help? I have a doctor with me."

A long five second cough, and then a man replied with a choking, "Yes".

Lexi hurried to the closet. When she reached the doorway, her flashlight lit the face of the man. As soon as he saw her, her teetered and weakly slid to the floor. His face was gray, eyes dark, lips bloody and cracked.

"I've never been so sick in all my life," he said, then coughed again. "I can't breathe."

"We're gonna help you," Lexi told him, walked over to him and crouched down. "That's why we're here. We're getting more supplies. Can we take you with us where I am treating others?"

He coughed. "Others are sick too? Is it happening again?"

"No." Lexi smiled reassuringly. "What you and the others have is a repercussion of the flu. Sometimes the lungs don't clear after the flu, and pneumonia sets it. It's a tough strain, but we'll beat it."

"That's all well and fine." He choked on a cough and beat his chest. "But I didn't get the flu."

Immediately, Lexi looked up to Matt. He hadn't heard what Henry said, but Lexi did. Lexi wasn't only looking at another patient; she was looking at someone with the same symptoms, only he, unlike the others, was different. He didn't have the flu to blame.

JOURNAL ENTRY

Well, we aren't dead and we actually made it. Not home. Not yet. Soon. My last journal entry I was kind of scared. We were staying in a dark store and were walking.

I drove for the first time and I think I'll be good at it. I hit a big man, but he was fine. He is so big, I bet at one time he dreamed of being a professional wrestler. No one that big doesn't dream of stuff like that.

His name is Commander Jonah Briggs and he runs what he hopes to be the new Army in the US, he said something about how we have to defend ourselves.

I don't think he's with the bad guys that hit the camp because he kept making calls looking for them.

He seems nice enough, except he keeps saying he'll tell me why he can't take us back to Lodi.

He hasn't yet.

It didn't take long for me not to be scared. He gave us some chocolate for the ride. Emmie peed her pants again. I'm thinking all that potty training her mom did is probably out the window now.

That happens. I remember when Tigger got potty trained; we got a new video game and darned if that potty training didn't go right out the window.

Right now, I'm all showered and some doctor guy just took a look at me.

We rode through this small town; it looked a lot like Lodi.

People were moving about, acting normal, which is cool. Jonah told the doctor guy after he cleaned us up he wanted him to take a look at us.

I told Jonah I was healthy as a horse. He didn't believe me until the doc said I was healthy as a horse.

But Jonah was right, I think we all did smell. I didn't notice until I got out of the shower and got a whiff of Tigger. Man …. did he smell.

I'm waiting right now for the others to get bathed. Then we're meeting with Jonah. Hopefully, then we'll call home.

12. BATTING A THOUSAND

Las Vegas, NV

It reached the point of rushing. Lexi located not only the equipment she needed but also the supplies. Matt called for assistance to get the man to the main hotel, while he and Lexi loaded the items into his vehicle.

In Alaska at the onset of the outbreak, Bill had learned quickly how to insert an IV. Lexi had him start those on all of the pneumonia patients while she took specimens and samples.

"There's seems to be a new sense of urgency," Bill said to her. "What's going on?"

"I talked to Henry today," Lexi said, almost exasperated as she finished hooking up the computer to the microscope.

"That's good news."

"I asked him if he saw any post-flu cases of pneumonia. He hadn't and said not to rule out that it is something else. That maybe a pilgrim brought it in."

"Like what?"

"I don't know."

"But we have a common factor - all of our patients previously had the flu."

"Until the latest one," Lexi said. "He said he never

caught it."

"Yeah, but so did Charlie the slot guy. We found out that was a lie."

"Well, hopefully I am overreacting, but better safe than sorry."

"True, but Lex," Bill laid his hands on her shoulder, "what are the chances and where would these pilgrims get it to bring it in?"

"I know, but them bringing it here isn't my concern," Lexi told him. "It's the ability they have to take it with them that's the problem. What if there's a three to ten day incubation period?"

"You're getting ahead if yourself," Bill said. "Do your tests, send your pictures to Henry. I'll take care of the patients."

"Thank you." Lexi tiptoed up and kissed him on the cheek.

A knock came on the newly made lab door, and Lexi saw Matt standing in the doorway.

"I got six guys ready to go. What is it exactly we're looking for?" he asked.

"Sickness of any kind. Flu, cold, stomach virus, anything," Lexi informed him. "Go from hotel to hotel, camps, pilgrims, houses, door to door — I need to know if anyone else is sick in this town. They may be and since they don't know about me yet, they may be staying inside."

"We're on it." Matt turned and left.

Bill looked down to Lexi. "What do you think they'll find?"

"If all goes well, absolutely nothing," Lexi said. "For that … let's hope."

* * *

Damon, NY

Chris, Tigger, Jake and Emmie sat alone in what looked like a small cafeteria, with seats attached to the tables. They each had been given a bowl of soup, a hunk of bread and a candy bar.

Tigger ate his soup slowly, Emmie played in hers, but Chris thought it was awesome. It had a tomato taste to it like his grandmother used to make. He wiped the bread around the bowl to get the last drop.

Jake pushed his bowl to Chris. "I'm finished if you want the rest of mine,"

"No, I'm good."

"When's that big guy coming back?" Tigger asked. "The one you tried to kill."

"I didn't try to kill him on purpose. I don't think I could though, he's awfully big."

"Bigger than Mick," Tigger said.

"He's not bigger than Mick. Close, but not bigger than Mick," Chris said in Mick's defense.

"Mick's wider."

"True," Chris conceded. As he finished the last drop of his soup, he saw Briggs walking in.

"How's lunch?" Briggs asked as he joined them at the table. He looked at Tigger, who was staring at his legs. "What's wrong?"

"Was just seeing how you fit on that little seat," Tigger said.

Briggs smiled. "Well, you guys look good and clean. I have a woman in town, Doc's girlfriend, and she said she'd watch Emmie for a little bit to give you boys a break."

"She can't keep her, though, 'cause I am taking her with me home to Lodi," Chris said.

"I realize that. How are the clothes?"

"Army like," Chris said. "You aren't making me be a soldier are you?"

"No." Briggs shook his head.

"'Cause I don't want to be a soldier. When I'm older

maybe, but not now."

"I'm not."

"You have me dressed like one."

"That's because it's all we had on hand, Chris."

" A whole town at your disposal and this is all you had to fit me?" Chris asked, gesturing to the camouflage pants and tan tee shirt he was wearing.

"On hand, yes. I didn't go into town. Trust me Chris, it's only clothes."

"Good. 'Cause I ain't ready to be a soldier yet."

"I am!" Tigger exclaimed. "You can make me one."

"Now, why are you going and talking like you can be a soldier?" Chris said. "You have to be a certain height."

Tigger sulked.

Briggs laid his hand on Tiger's head. "You'd make a great little soldier."

"Great little militant," Chris corrected. "He's a tyrant."

"I am not," Tigger argued. "I don't know what that is, but I know I am not."

Jake added, "It's because he's small. Small guys have that."

"Enough," Briggs held up his hand. "Before we start fighting, Chris, our cell phone signals are back up. Is there a grown up you can call? I'd like to speak to them."

Chris grew bright and then slumped. "My phone's in that car. I don't know numbers by heart. I just press the name."

Surprising them all, Tigger spoke up. "330-hot vids."

Chris turned to him. "What?"

"Pap's video store. 330-hot-vids. That's what Patrick told me, easy number to remember."

"It is!" Chris said. "Oh, wow, I can't believe I forgot."

Jake asked. "But will your pap be at the store? Isn't it closed down?"

"Oh, no, my pap will always be at that store. People always wanna watch movies." He looked at Briggs." Can we call him? Can we call our pap?"

"Absolutely. That's what I was hoping for." Briggs handed the phone to Chris.

* * *

Lodi Ohio

Even though Tom had the high chair behind the counter with him, he held on to Doe. Or rather, Doe held on to him. Tom lifted movie cases and showed the baby. "And this one is about zombies. Yeah." Tom picked up another. "This is about wrestling. Your new brothers love wrestling and I'm sure you'll be brainwashed into that as well."

He looked up at the ding of the bell to see Lars walking in.

"Making house calls?" Tom asked.

"Store calls." Lars walked closer. "How is he?"

"He's good. He's been taking a bottle and I soaked some Ritz Crackers in Carnation sweetened milk, he ate them right up."

Lars smiled. "Good. You do know you can put him down, right?"

"Well … I figure he is needing some love and a pair of arms to hold him for a spell. No one's arms need filling more than mine."

"Are you feeling any better about Chris and Tigger?"

"Nope. Not until I see them. They're smart boys but they aren't survival smart. While other boys were camping and in the Scouts, they were watching wrestling and playing video games."

Lars gave Tom a quirky look when the phone rang. "Someone is calling?"

"Been calling all morning. For some damn reason *Mad Max* is in demand and Ross has it." Tom reached over and grabbed the phone. "Afternoon, Hit and Run Video."

"Pap!"

The phone nearly dropped from Tom's hand as he stood. His heart raced, his ears filled with blood and he immediately wanted to cry. "Chris?"

Lars hurried over. "Chris?"

Tom nodded.

"Aw, geeze, Pap it is so good to hear your voice," Chris said.

"Are you guys okay?" Tom asked. "Really?"

"Oh, sure, we're fine," Chris said. "I drove you know. Hit some man, but he's fine. Probably because he's big. That's where we are."

Tom shook his head. "You hit a man with a car and you're with him?"

"Yeah, some little town in New York. We went the wrong way. He got us. He's an Army guy, you know. Have you heard from Mick? I'm worried about Mick, Pap."

"Mick is fine. He found your note."

"Oh, good."

"Chris, where exactly in New York are you?"

"I don't know, but there's a problem getting us home."

"Chris, give me a clue. You don't have to say out loud, a simple yes or no will do. Are you kidnapped by militants?"

Chris snorted in his laugh then replied. "No. Geeze. Here. He wants to talk to you. I love you, Pap. I'll call you again."

Before Tom could say anything, a deep male voice came on the other line.

"Mr. Roberts? This is Commander Jonah Briggs of the United America Army."

"The United what?"

"America Army."

"What in blazes is that?"

"It a large organization of merged militia groups along with military personnel to restructure and rebuild America."

"Okay. Can I have my boys back?"

"Sir, there is nothing more that I would like to do than to see these kids get home. But right now, a situation pretty close to you is making that a dangerous thing to do."

"What do you mean?"

"It appears — and I am waiting for confirmation — that a band of independents have set up a blockade in the Erie, Pennsylvania area. They're reportedly dangerous."

"Take them out."

Briggs paused. "I'm sorry, did you say take them out?"

"Yeah. If they're bad news and you're this new army, take them the hell out. Or can't you?"

"We could, but we believe there are civilians there and we don't want to put them in harm's way. And that is why, until the situation is safe, I think it's best that the kids remain here for a little bit. I'll keep them fed and safe and in constant contact with you. But as you can imagine, if I took them south and looped around, it would be a risk and a long haul with four children."

"Four? I only have two grandchildren with you."

"Chris said they're all going to Lodi."

"Well, I'm sure my grandson has all good intentions with his newfound friends and we'll take them in, of course, but only two are my grandsons. Chris and the little guy."

"The one aged six going on thirty?"

"That's the one."

"I like him."

"He's an acquired taste." Tom breathed out heavily. "Not much of a choice, then? Where are you located?"

"Damon, New York. And I promise you I will take care of them, keep them safe and bring them home safely."

"Well, you better. Not that I'm a man who likes to threaten those in authority, but if anything happens to those kids, you not only have to contend with me, but with their father, and that's a big force."

"Would this be the same man that Chris wants to see me wrestle?"

Tom laughed. "That would be the one."

"Then you have my word and my promise, and now I'll give you numbers so you can stay in touch."

Tom grabbed a pen and wrote down the three numbers that Briggs had given to him. He ended the call, and stared outward as he tried to hang up the phone and kept missing the base.

Lars reached over and aided him. "So the boys are fine?"

"Safe, fine, and in good spirits enough that Chris is planning the return of wrestling with Mick and this guy."

"That is good to hear. Very good to hear."

"Yep, and I know now where to send Mick. Seems there's a divide and a blockade of bad up near Erie."

Lars cocked back. "That's where Mick and Rose are meeting."

"Not gonna meet, cause neither one of them can get through. I better give them a heads up." Tom lifted the phone again.

"How are you feeling now?" Lars asked.

"Better, but now since I know the boys are fine, I am pissed as hell at Mick for losing them." He started to dial. "I might just encourage this wrestling match to take place."

Lars laughed and then he took Baby Doe while Tom made his phone calls.

* * *

Outskirts, Erie, PA

Rose had no idea her phone was even ringing. She spotted the rest area and when she saw Mick wasn't there, she figured she'd ride ahead just a little.

It was only a few miles and Rose slowed down her bike and then turned it off. Something was happening ahead. She saw men moving cars on the highway and across, forming a blockade of sorts.

They must have heard her motorcycle because a few of them stepped away to look.

Rose was fast. She moved her bike quietly to the side of the road, walked it a little bit then when she was at a safe enough distance, jumped back on and rode to the rest area.

It was quiet there and didn't appear to have been touched or visited in some time. She removed her helmet, kept the bike idling, and reached around to her pack.

When she pulled out her phone she saw she had missed calls. Two from Mick and three from Tom.

Opting to return Mick's call first, Rose readied to dial when it rang.

"Tom," she answered. "Hey, can I call you right back? I want to get a hold of Mick. I'm supposed to meet him and something is going on in Erie."

"That's why you need to talk to me. Erie is taken over. Don't know much more than that except it's a dangerous situation. I got a call from Chris. He and Tigger are fine. They went the wrong way and are in some small town in New York. And it's that takeover that's making it tough for them to get home."

"What the fuck do we do?"

"You head back here. Especially since we know they're fine. And I'm thinking, unless Mick decides to take on those guys in Erie, we send him for the boys. I got the name of the town."

"You wanna call him or should I?"

"I tried, he's not answering. Probably can't hear the phone. But head on back, and I'll keep trying."

"That sounds good." Rose ended the call, stowed the phone back in her pack and was grabbing a bottle of water when she saw the truck pull into the lot.

They pulled up fifteen feet from her and stopped. Her hand stayed inside the bag, yet instead of a water bottle, she held a knife, concealed in her grip, and slowly removed her hand. She didn't think reaching for her rifle, strapped on her bike, was all that good of an idea.

Four men stepped from the trucks. They all were armed and looked more like a pack of wayward hunters than anything else.

"Well it's a broad," one said. "Saw you riding. Thought for sure you were a man." He stepped closer. "Kind of look like a man. What you doing out here all alone, Grandma?"

Rose had a grip on one handle bar and didn't answer. She sized up the men. Two stayed back while two walked closer to her.

"You may want to get off that bike," the same one said. "That's a commodity we want."

"You're not getting my fucking bike," Rose said calmly.

He laughed, hyena style and mockingly. "Listen to the mouth on Grandma." He aimed his weapon at her. "Off the bike, lady."

The kickstand was down and Rose slowly dismounted, not moving far from the bike.

The other men laughed as if the intimidation tactics of the front guy were the funniest thing.

Bullies.

They just seemed like dimwitted bullies to Rose. The last thing she wanted to do was show any reaction to them.

Stay cool. Calm.

The first man stepped even closer, his friend right at his side. He reached out and touched Rose's face. "You think you're a tough broad. Look at you. Still not bad looking for an old lady. You can be my cougar."

"Don't touch me again," Rose warned.

The man brought this fist to his mouth, laughing at her. "Feisty. I like it. You're gonna come with us. We can …" he dropped his voice some, "we can have a good time. I like feisty."

"No."

"No?" he scoffed. "Really? *No.*" He reached for her.

Rose swatted his hand away. "I told you, don't touch me

again."

"Look, lady…" He stopped face to face with Rose. "You'll come with us or I will fuck you up."

Cool, calm, and staring into his eyes. Rose whispered. "How about I fuck you up instead?"

He laughed loudly and obnoxiously. He looked over his shoulder to the two men hanging back and said, "Did you hear her? She said she's gonna fuck me up. Now how does she figure?"

No sooner did he turn back to look at Rose, than she said, "Like this." Then reared back and gave a short quick head butt to the man. He stumbled, not much, but enough for Rose to jab hard and fast to his nose. He flew backwards to the ground.

The other man lunged for her and with a pivot of her body and the ejection of her knife, she swung out hard and in one motion, slit his throat.

Her adrenaline pumped fiercely and Rose didn't have time to comprehend any pain she was in from the head to head connection. She jumped on her bike, gave it a kick start, and peeled out of the parking lot. Her heart beat out of control and she could barely catch her breath.

She heard the gun shots and prayed they wouldn't hit her.

They didn't.

They hit her bike instead.

At full speed, her tire gave in and the bike spun out of control to the right. Despite her attempts to steer, she was unable to control the bike and it flew off the road. The second it went over the grade it toppled, sending Rose sailing high in the air. She landed hard against the grassy surface and all went black. Her limp body rolled until she came to an abrupt halt, deep in the woods.

* * *

West of Erie, PA

At the two miles to Erie sign, Mick's motorcycle gave out. It fluttered its last bit of energy and just died.

He opted against fixing it, because he wasn't all that far from Erie. He could smell the lake, saw that the trees were bending. He was close, and decided he'd walk.

After grabbing his gear, he reached for his phone. He figured he'd call his mother to tell her he was on his way. He tried and it went to voice mail. He then did the next best thing. He called Tom. He conveyed to Tom his battery was beeping, and only heard Tom say Rose was headed back to Lodi. He didn't hear why. The phone died.

"You gotta be fucking shitting me," he shook his head. He longed for the day of cheap, no nonsense phones that held a charge. It had been twenty-four hours since he charged his phone. He should have known better.

About a mile into his walk, he realized how lucky he was that he wasn't riding on a noisy bike.

Cars lined the road and a huge crane lifted more cars on top of each other.

Someone had built a wall across the highway. Who? And why would they have done that? It concerned Mick mainly because if the boys headed in the direction of Erie, then they had run into that blockade as well.

He dodged to the side of the road. He had to get a look to see what was happening and how he could get to the other side. He stayed low and as he neared the blockade, he belly crawled to stay out of sight.

Arm over arm, he inched his way closer to the road, and just as he reached it, a foot slammed to his back and he felt the cold steel of a gun to his head.

A voice whispered, "Don't move. Don't make a sound. Inch back. They'll shoot you if they see you."

"How do you know I'm not with them?" Mick asked in a low voice.

"Because you wouldn't be sneaking a peek, now would you? Get back."

On his stomach, Mick crawled backwards. He felt vulnerable unable to see who was aiming at his head. Once a distance from the road, the man ordered him to turn around.

Ready to fight, to take the man down, Mick flipped over.

A steady aim was held on him, not by one man, but by three. All three were dressed in some sort of black and green camouflage outfits.

Mick plopped back in defeat.

"What are you doing sneaking around in the woods?"

"My bike broke down," Mick said. "I saw the blockade. I wanted to see if there was any way around. I'm just heading home. What are you—"

The quick footsteps drew Mick's attention and another man, dressed the same way, slid down and joined the others.

"Who's he?" the newest member asked.

The other guy said, "Trying to get through. What do you have?"

"Not good, Dexter. They created a barricade around the tourist section of town. They spread out but the outer areas aren't that guarded.

"How many men?" Dexter asked.

"A lot. At least a hundred."

"Shit. Armed?"

"Yes. Very."

Mick sat up. "Who are you guys?"

Dexter indicated his men. "We're from the United America Army. My name is Dexter Green, this is my unit. We were sent here to surveil this area and report back to the commander."

Mick's head spun. *Commander? United America Army?* What had he missed? Had he been so focused on Lodi that he never even noticed what had evolved in the country around him?

Dexter asked his spotter, "Did you see civilians?"

"I saw them bringing a couple in. I heard kids."

"Shit," Mick said, and started to stand.

Dexter guided him back down. "What the hell are you doing?"

"The kids. I have to see if my kids are in there," Mick replied.

"You can't go rushing in there. Didn't you hear? There's a lot of men and they are armed. Why do you think your kids are there?"

"We were at a camp. I left with another guy to search a town and—"

"You left your kids alone?" Dexter interrupted.

"They weren't alone, there were other adults there, but yeah, I'm an asshole." Mick rubbed his head. "I've been following their trail. They got ahead of me because they found some sort of ride back to Lodi and I'm afraid they are in there. I gotta get them out."

"Did you say Lodi?" Dexter asked.

"Yeah."

"One of the kids named Chris?"

Mick's eyes widened and he sat up. "You seen him?"

"Yeah, about thirteen years old. He was driving a car with three other kids. He hit the commander."

"Are they alright? Was there a little boy there? He looks like a toddler, but he's not."

"Yeah. Blonde haired boy." Dexter laughed then caught himself. "Sorry, but he tried to drive the car after Chris got out to check on the commander after he hit him."

"That's sounds like Tigger. Where are they?"

"We picked them up. They were headed the wrong way, which was a good thing now. They're fine, back at our base."

Mick exhaled a breath as big as his huge frame. "Oh my God. Thank you. You don't know what that means. They aren't going anywhere, right?"

Dexter shook his head. "No. They'll still be there and you're welcome to come with us. But we have to finish up here first, and we parked a ways back."

There was no question on what Mick would do. Of course he would go with the men. Rose was safely headed back home and Mick would go to the boys. He was abundantly relieved to hear the kids were safe, and Mick could rest a little easier. He could think beyond finding his children. His mind swirled with questions while waiting. He wanted to find out not only who these people barricading Erie and holding civilians were, but also who the hell were these men calling themselves the United America Army?

JOURNAL ENTRY

I'm not sure if I should call him 'Commander' or 'Jonah', but he's a pretty cool guy, and I told him all about our town and the people there. He seemed to know it from the news. I threw down the challenge again for him to take on Mick in a wrestling match.

I told him it would be a great way to show the world that we're coming back and yet entertain. I mean, who wouldn't want to see the two biggest guys in the apocalypse fight it out?

Mick would win. I have to say Mick would win.

Speaking of Mick, my pap said Mick got our note. I'm glad. I was worried about him. I'm sure he was scared for us kids, but think about it: he lost us. Not on purpose, mind you, but he had to be blaming himself. I think I'll tease him about that when I see him.

Jonah Briggs said he was instituting rules in town for the kids. Doc's girlfriend has a weird name. It's Mary. I told Jonah that it was a weird name. I mean not that Mary sounds like it's unusual, but no one under the age of eighty is named Mary and I don't think I ever met a Mary.

Anyhow, Mary was the kindergarten teacher in Damon and Jonah wants to start school again. Back to the one room schoolhouse days until he gets more teachers. There are too many kids for them to go every day. Doc volunteered to teach science one day a week, that's what Jonah said. I like Doc. He's funny and doesn't look like a Doc.

As odd as it sounds, I like the idea of school starting again. I hope Lodi does that. But there aren't that many kids left. Not that there are all that many in Damon, but there's at least a hundred and that is way more than Lodi.

Every afternoon is movie day at the theater for kids only. That's when I realized there were a hundred, cause I counted the kids in the seats. It was an old cowboy movie but it was fun. Me, Tigger and Jake got our popcorn cup and were told to bring it each day. Man, it wasn't a lot of popcorn, but it was sure good. I ate one piece at a time really slow so it would last.

Me, Tig and Jake are at the library now waiting on Jonah. Him and that other guy had to speak to Doc about something. The library is cool.

Tig is having fun. Even though it's not too bad here, I can't wait to go home.

13. DARK TURN

Las Vegas, NV

"Anything?" Bill asked as he walked into the new lab, which was the laundry room at the hotel at one time.

Lexi bit her bottom lip. "I think I failed in the picture."

"Let me see. I *was* an award winning photographer you know." He held out his hand for her phone.

"I don't think anyone takes good phone pictures." She gave him the phone.

"You've got a good phone, you should …" Bill paused. "Scratch that. This is the worst picture I have ever seen. Do you need glasses?"

Lexi playfully slapped Bill on the arm.

"They aren't gonna be able to figure this out," he said.

"See I think they will," she said. "You're under the misconception that they'll look at the microbe and know what it is instantaneously."

"Won't they?"

"No, it's not that easy."

"However, picture taking with an expensive phone is," Bill said sarcastically. "And you failed that. Get it up on the screen again please."

With a few clicks, Lexi pulled up the images. Using the phone, Bill snapped a few pictures. He reviewed them.

"There. They're good." He handed back the phone.

"Thank you."

He took in the screen shot of the microbe and remarked how it reminded him of an alien. "Do you have any clue what this is?"

"It looks familiar," Lexi said. "Like I should know it. And when and if they figure it out, I'll probably get mad for not knowing it."

"I have no idea what it is," Bill said. "In case you were asking me."

Lexi laughed, and her smile dropped when Matt walked in the room. "Hey, you look upset. I was just with your mom. She's doing well."

Matt shook his head. "Not her. Are our other people okay?"

Lexi nodded. "Stable. Why?"

"Can you guys come with me? We found some sick people. And you were right, they didn't come here because they had no clue we had a doctor."

"You didn't bring them in?" Lexi asked.

"No, and I don't think I should." Matt gave a wave of his hand. "Come with me."

Lexi walked across the room for her bag. She added a few things back into it, zipped it and asked Bill, "I wonder what's up?"

"Would you think I was overreacting to say I just got a twitch of fear about this?"

"Not at all." Lexi tossed her bag over her shoulder and left with Bill.

She had no idea what they were going to see, but like Bill, she was fearful.

* * *

Damon, NY

Doc held out his hand to halt Briggs from opening the

door. He had led the commander to the top floor of the hospital and to the far back set of rooms, stopping at the glass wall. "I can't let you go in there."

"Why not? You said it was about the patient that came in from out west."

"Yes."

"That's her, right?" Briggs pointed to the window and the lone occupant of the room, a woman in a hospital bed.

"It is and that's why I can't let you in there. The flu pretty much wiped out all the quarantine stuff and bio hazard suits. What we have left is minimal and we need it for our workers until you can find us more."

Brigs gave an inquisitive look. "What's going on?"

"I asked her when she left the west. She said eight days ago, give or take a day. She said they stopped twice overnight, once in Vegas, the next day in Indiana, and that's where our guys got her. So it's falling in the incubation period. The child and another woman with her are showing symptoms. I need those men who brought them in. I need them here and away from everyone for two weeks."

Briggs closed his eyes with a tense expression.

"They went back out?" Doc asked.

Briggs nodded. "Not for a run though, to head home. They're taking the long route because of that insurgent blockade. Hopefully, they won't run into them and get captured."

"No, actually, if they've got this, hopefully they *will* get captured by this problem camp."

Briggs seemed offended. "That's heartless for our men."

"Well, if this band of merry mercenaries clocked Erie and burned a town, who knows what else they can do? It would be an easy elimination of them."

"What the hell does this woman have?" Briggs asked.

"I can't confirm, I can only guess. I don't have the means to really test."

"The guess?" Briggs folded his arms.

Doc exhaled. "I saw it when I was a kid. Not here in America, and that's why it doesn't make sense. It has to be something else, because I can't figure out how she got it."

Briggs huffed in frustration. "What? Tell me what to prepare for."

Doc nodded as an indication to the woman. "Look at her face. Her eyes, her ears, her nose. Look closely."

Briggs did and he whispered, "Are they… bleeding?"

"They are, and she's been vomiting blood as well," Doc said. "She's dying, Jonah. From something that doesn't happen here in America. I think – no I'm almost positive – " Doc faced Briggs, "that she has Ebola."

* * *

Las Vegas, NV

Vegas wasn't an easy place to get around. The only thing in its favor, post-flu world, was that it was flat, easy on gas.

Walking was out of the question; they *had* to drive. The heat was unbearable, the wind was fierce, like a high heat blow dryer basting wave after wave of dirt and sand, and starving birds grew bold and brave, swooping down occasionally at the solo walkers.

Matt managed to put up tents that stretched across some of the property for those who ventured outside, but it was best to stay indoors. He even told Bill to move the car to an indoor garage, which Bill did. Even though it was under the awning of the casino drop off, it was getting buried in sand.

They took Matt's car. Four blocks down was the Stay Rite Motel. Nothing fancy, basic, cheap accommodations for the thrifty Vegas tourist who wanted to stay on The Strip.

Admittedly, Matt didn't have a full grasp on how many people lived in his new stopping post town. There could have been some that passed trough. A few still lived in houses on the outskirts, but most of them made their way inward. While his men kept track of those they saw stroll into to town and where they settled, it was hard to do an accurate count when they didn't enter into barter or need anything.

So Matt and his men cruised slowly, looking for signs that people were staying in a building. Places they recorded as stops pilgrims made, one of which was the Stay Rite Motel. Four blocks away from the Matt-age, as everyone joked.

"We knew they pulled in about a week ago, haven't heard from them," Matt told Lexi as they drove there.

"You didn't check on them?"

"No, why would we? We probably would have inquired this week, because of this …" Matt pointed to the three motorcycles in front of the motel, all of them covered with sand that came mid-bike. "They haven't moved."

"What about from our hotel to here. Anyone?"

"No one reported anything. We'll try again, especially after this."

"Are they dead?" Bill asked. "Is that why you didn't bring them?"

"Worse," Matt answered.

Bill looked at Lexi. "Worse than dead?"

She crinkled her face in confusion.

Matt stopped the car. "Got your gloves and mask?""Yeah," Lexi answered. "But—"

"Put them on." Matt reached to the center console of the car and pulled out a pair of gloves and paper thin respirator mask.

Lexi did as instructed and so did Bill. Matt opened the car door. Toting her bag, Lexi followed Bill to room 7.

Matt knocked. "Mr. Randal? Hey, it's Matt again. I brought the doctor for you guys."

The man's voice was raspy and nasal as he replied from the other side. "Thank God."

The door opened. Lexi stood in shock. Matt looked at her

with a 'see, I told you' nod.

The man looked engorged, but he wasn't. It was just an illusion brought on by the red swollen and puss filled bumps that covered every square inch of his face, neck, and exposed arms. Even his eyelids had them.

"Wanna confirm what I think this is?" Matt asked Lexi.

She didn't say, but Bill did. He didn't need to be a scientist, viral specialist or doctor to know what Mr. Randal had.

It was clearly … smallpox.

* * *

"Sorry, gentlemen, I got hung up," Lars said as he entered the laboratory portion of the clinic.

Henry and Kurt sat there waiting.

"Everything okay?" Henry asked.

"Well, our bullet wound victim is doing well, thank you. Minuteman Nelson sent a man to us this morning who was sick. Fever, malaise, body aches, stomach ailment," Lars said. "I've just drawn blood and not done a work up yet."

"Waterborne illness?" Henry suggested.

"That's what I think. When water is not filtered, purified, this happens. And seeing how we are the top medical community, we're going to get them," Lars said. "Speaking of which, since phones are up, have you spoken to our Commander in Chief?"

"I called," Henry said. "He didn't answer."

"The president didn't answer." Lars rubbed his chin. "Odd. Is he alive?"

Kurt laughed. "He's just busy, putting a country back together."

"I think he'll be surprised to learn people have been doing that. Alright gentlemen, what do you have?" Lars asked with a single clap of his hands.

"This." Kurt spun the computer screen to face Lars. "Lexi

Martin sent these from Vegas. Four patients all with the same symptoms. Her first couple of photos sucked, then she sent this one."

"Oh, wow. Unreal," Lars said. "Wow."

"Wow?" Henry asked. "Are you going to tell me you know what this is? Because we have some guesses, and thought we could brainstorm."

"I know what it is, no guessing here," Lars said.

"Just like that?" Kurt asked.

"Yes," Lars said. "You two ought to be ashamed of yourselves for not knowing. Then again, why would you think it? It's an odd one. Plus, you know, I *am* Lars Rayburn."

Henry shook his head. "Okay, Great One, what is it?"

"Simple. Well, not simple, it's deadly. However ..." Lars hesitated, "it's SARS."

14. UNCOVERING TRUTH

Erie, PA

When Rose first started coming to, she found it hard to believe she wasn't dead. The last thing she recalled was flying off the side of the road, her body airborne.

Then nothing.

She wasn't wearing a helmet: How in the world had she lived? And for sure she wasn't dead. She as in far too much pain to not be alive. Her head throbbed and her body felt as if it weighed a thousand pounds. She actually was afraid to move.

Her eyes were still closed and she was certain that she was somewhere outside. It was cold and she could feel a wetness against her face. She had probably landed by a creek and her face was in mud.

She moved, and in doing so, a hard, sharp, stabbing pain filled her side. It felt as if something was stuck inside of her. Perhaps she was impaled. The pain was horrendous and she opened her eyes.

It was dark but not dark enough to conceal the fact that she wasn't outside.

She had to move, find out what was going on. She lifted her head and it throbbed even worse. Shifting her eyes down, she saw she had been laying on a canvas tarp. It was covered in blood, fresh blood. Was it hers? She had been face down and it took everything to turn over some. The pain was tremendous. Every part of her hurt.

Surely her ribs were broken, maybe even her leg. She brought her fingers to her face, felt around, it was drenched. Where was she bleeding from? Fingers probing, she found a few spots that could be the culprits.

Above her eye, her chin, and the side of her head held a gash so big, she could feel the separation of skin.

Where was she? She blinked several times to clear her blurred vision and lifted her head the best she could. What looked like old mail was scattered about the floor and that was when she saw the lettering on the canvas sack: USPS.

She groaned softly, thinking, *What the fuck am I doing in a post office?* And as she attempted to get up, a pair of legs slid into her view.

"No, no," the young female voice pressed. "Close your eyes and lay back down. They're waiting for you to wake up to hurt you."

"Are you shitting me?" Rose asked, her voice rough, raspy. She cleared her throat.

The young woman had to be no older than eighteen. Her long dark hair was tangled and messy, she tucked it behind her ears. She had dark circles under her eyes and a huge bruise on her cheek. Her bottom lip was cut and bleeding.

"I'm not sure," she said. "They keep coming in, looking at you, then leaving. They'll be back in again. Please," she begged, "lay down."

"I'm not afraid," Rose said.

"No, but you're hurt. Bad too," she told Rose. "Just lay still. If they bring me water, I'll give you some, okay?" She looked over shoulder, so frightened. "Lay still." With that she scurried away.

Lay still? That wasn't too hard of a request considering every movement caused her agony. The pain in her side was beyond bad. It was almost too difficult to breathe, which was why Rose couldn't talk. Through shallow breaths, Rose whispered. "Do you have a towel? Something, I can press against my side?"

Rose was lying on the painful side, but knew, if the rib was broken – and she was sure it was – that was the best way to lay and put some pressure on it.

"A towel isn't going to help your side," the girl said, her eyes constantly shifting toward the window.

"Please, something," Rose pleaded.

The girl huffed a breath and quickly, in a crouched position, hurried across the room, grabbed another canvas sack and brought it to Rose. "Do you need it bunched up?"

"Yes, thanks."

The girl brought her bottom lip into her mouth, rolled the bag and looked over her shoulder. It was evident to Rose that she was terrified. "Here." She gave it to Rose without looking, then hurried away.

It would have to do, and Rose would have to use her energy to hoist up enough to tuck the bag under her. When she did, she saw why the girl told her the bag wouldn't help. As soon as she pulled from the ground, even a little, Rose realized it wasn't the head or eye that caused the wet canvas, it was her side.

Blood poured out from her side. The question of whether or not her rib was broken was answered when she saw the bone protruding from the open wound.

Rose wasn't just injured, she was pretty sure she was dying.

* * *

Las Vegas, NV

Lexi didn't have a clue what do to. She'd studied smallpox but was never fortunate enough to work in the field with the cases. It honestly tumbled her back and scared her.

She did the best she could, examining them, but the sight of the bloodied and yellow stained sheets made her stomach turn.

Smallpox. It was not only highly contagious, but those who survived were never the same physically.

The three people in the hotel room felt horrible and they conveyed that when they started to 'spot' they were pretty sure they knew what it could be, so they'd stayed away from others.

Lexi told them she wasn't sure how to handle it, but would find out. She promised. She examined them, took their information and said she'd be back.

As soon as she left the hotel, she told Matt. "They can't leave. I also need your men, to be cautious and check the area for more cases." She scrubbed her hands with sanitizer.

"Is that what I think it is?" Matt asked.

"Oh, yeah."

Bill ran his hand down his face. "What the hell, Lexi? Can our people at the hotel have early symptoms? I saw a documentary once and it said that it starts out like the flu."

"I don't know, but I will find out. Maybe Henry had a chance to review those pictures we sent. If not, this may give him a lead." Lexi pulled out her phone and dialed. It took only two rings and Henry answered.

"Lexi, I'm glad you called. We were just about to call you," Henry said.

"Oh, Henry, I have to tell you something."

"We have to tell you something too, but Lars Rayburn wants to be the one."

"Lars … Lars wants to speak to me?"

"Yeah, he was the one who figured it out. Hold on, he's down the hall. It'll take me a minute."

Lexi's eyes widened and she turned to Bill. "*Lars Rayburn* wants to speak to me. *Me*. Oh my God." She laid a hand on her chest. "I am so not worthy."

"What the hell?" Bill laughed then blinked several times. "Okay, you mentioned his name before. He's just a doctor, why are you so excited?"

"It's Lars Rayburn. *Lars Rayburn.* Only the most brilliant mind in all of virology, *and* he saved Lodi, sort of. Lars ..." she gasped. "Wow. I get to speak to Lars Rayburn. He also penned a dozen romance novels under a pseudonym, too."

"A sensitive virologist. Hmm. No wonder you're acting like he's some sort of Donny Osmond."

"Who?" Lexi asked.

Bill waved her off.

Suddenly, Lexi spun. "Yes, Lars, I am here."

"So wonderful to speak to you," Lars said. "And I heard wonderful things about you. Good job."

"Thank you. It's an honor."

"I have news for you, Lexi. I looked at your virus photos."

"I have news too. Scary news."

"Please, go first," Lars said.

"Three more sick people were found. Holed up in an old motel. Lars, they ... they have smallpox."

"Smallpox, you say? Well, my dear, you seem to be in a pickle in your Sin City depot stop. Aside from your three smallpox patients," Lars paused for dramatic effect, "you have four people with SARS."

Lexi dropped the phone.

* * *

Even though the lady Mary seemed nice enough, Jake told Chris he felt better staying with Emmie. Mary invited Chris and Tigger to stay with her, but Chris declined. Her apartment was small and Jonah Briggs gave Chris and Tigger their own small room to share. Plus, Chris liked the big eating room they had at the base. Not to mention, he felt safer there.

He thought it was cool that Jonah Briggs was hanging out with them. He made a lot of calls and people came in a lot, but Jonah told Chris he enjoyed their company. And, he would need him to call his grandfather in a little bit.

Something was up. Chris knew it. He couldn't figure it out, and was hoping for a clue when Jon came in the room and pulled Jonah Briggs aside.

Chris hushed Tigger so he could listen. Jon didn't say much. He whispered that two Indiana men had a flat tire and were hanging back as instructed a few days.

Jonah sighed.

Chris wondered why a flat tire was a good thing.

Then Jon told him that 'they still couldn't get through' and that's when Chris' interest was piqued.

Jonah Briggs replied, "Keep trying. If no luck, we'll have Chris to try his grandfather."

Jon left and Briggs went back to the card game.

"Something happen in Lodi?" Chris asked.

"No. No," Briggs replied. "Why?"

"Well you told Jon that I could call my pap."

"We're watching a situation," Briggs winked. "No worries. Take your turn."

"It's my turn, thank you." Tigger laid his card down. "Don't give Chris my turn. He cheats as it is."

"Now why would you say that?" Chris asked.

"You do illegal stuff," Tigger replied. "Like driving a car without a license."

"I drove 'cause I had to," Chris said in his defense. "I did good too, even if I hit him." He pointed to Briggs. "Your head okay?"

"Yeah, it's fine. I'm tough."

"You thinking anymore about taking on my stepfather in a return to wrestling match?" Chris asked before he took his turn.

Briggs laughed. "You're obsessed with this."

"It's for my brother," Chris said sadly. "He loved wrestling. We both did. It was our 'thing'."

Slowly Briggs raised his eyes. "Well, maybe then for that reason."

Tigger spoke up. "You'll win."

Chris gasped. "I can't believe you said that! Mick is tough. Didn't he protect our whole town? Just because Mick is getting old and got a big stomach doesn't mean he can't maneuver in the ring."

"This Mick," Briggs said, "he sounds like a good guy."

"He is," Chris said. "He's great. Been in our lives our whole lives, even if he wasn't married to our mom. He's always been around."

"He's emotional," Tigger added.

Briggs coughed out a laugh. "You use big words, little man."

"I'm smart. I have to be. I'm too little to be anything else."

"But, he's right," Christ stated. "Mick *is* emotional. Cries all the time and stuff."

"I'm telling," Tigger snickered.

"Go on, I'll tell him you said he can't fight."

"I didn't say he can't fight. I said Jonah Briggs will beat him."

"Jonah Briggs is big but I don't know if he can beat Mick." Chris turned to Briggs. "No offense, Jonah Briggs."

Jonah smiled. "Pick a name guys. Jonah. Or Briggs. Or Skip."

Both Chris and Tigger burst into laughter.

"What?" Jonah asked. "That was my nickname growing up.

"Skip?" Chris fluttered his lips. "Oh, I wouldn't be telling people you had a nickname like Skip. They may pick on you." He paused when Briggs merely raised an eyebrow. "Okay, maybe they wouldn't."

"Jonah?" Jon said as he stepped into the room.

Briggs held up his hand to the boys and stood. "What's up?"

"Erie guys are back and said they really need to speak to you." Jon said. "And …" he shifted his eyes. "There's this really big biker looking guy here saying he wants his kids."

Before Briggs could question, before anything came from his mouth, a loud shriek from both Chris and Tigger rang out as they shouted "Mick!"

They jumped to their feet and as they did, Mick rushed into the room, passed Jon and Briggs and didn't make it two feet before he was blasted bodily by the boys.

* * *

Mick dropped to his knees and took both boys into his arms. "Oh my God," he said, his voice gravelly with emotion. He held them tight, wanting to just absorb them into his body, being and soul. He could barely breathe his chest felt so full. His throat closed and tensed, making it even harder to talk. There he was, holding them, feeling them, when he thought he had lost them. "Oh my God, I am so glad to see you boys. I was scared I'd never see you again. So scared."

His hand grasped the back of Chris' head and his other arm had Tigger tight to him. He kissed Chris, then Tigger, then repeated kissing them again. "Thank God. Thank God."

"I … can't … breathe," Tigger gasped. "You're strangling … me."

Mick laughed and released his hold. "I'm sorry."

"It's good to see you too, Mick." Chris grinned. "Boy we missed you."

"And I missed that." Mick touched Chris' smile. "I was so worried." He kissed Chris again then turned to Tigger. "And you." He put both his hands to Tigger's face, and plastered him with kisses.

Tigger accepted the kisses, but not for long. He crinkled

his face, shook his head and said. "Enough please."

"Sorry." Mick sniffed and ran the back of his hand under his nose.

"You okay, Mick?" Chris asked.

Mick nodded.

"You crying, Mick?" Tigger asked. "We're okay, we aren't hurt. We're good. Why are you crying?"

Chris gave a light backhand to Tigger. "Knock it off, he ain't crying. You can't be saying Mick's crying. Not in front of…" He motioned his head upward.

In the midst of the reunion, Mick didn't see or notice the other man in the room. How he missed him, he didn't know. Mick stood up and extended his hand. "Mick Owens."

"I figured as much," Briggs shook his hand. "Jonah Briggs."

"Thank you." Mick held firm to his hand for another moment. "Thank you so much for taking care of them. For finding them."

Briggs shook his head. "They found me."

Tigger added. "Chris hit him with the car."

"What?" Mick looked down to Chris.

Nonchalantly, Chris waved his hand. "It was not real bad. I was driving and I hit him. He's okay, though. See? He don't go down easily. Not that if you guys were to square off that he wouldn't go down."

Mick looked to Briggs. "He really hit you?"

"Yeah, but it was my fault," Briggs replied. "I was standing in the road. Your boys speak often and very highly of you."

Mick looked at Chris and Tigger. "They're my world."

"And you're theirs," Briggs said. "Well, if you'll excuse me. You must be hungry and thirsty. Help yourself. I need to talk to Wentworth and I'll be right back." He shook Mick's hand again. "Glad you guys are reunited. Chris, show him where the food is."

"Yes, sir, Jonah Briggs." Chris lifted his hand as Briggs

left. He rambled on to Mick in typical Chris fashion. "He's a nice guy, Mick. Didn't hurt us, yell or anything. Been real good to us. Fed us, got us clean. I'm not joining the army or anything, I'm dressed like this cause that's all he had. My clothes smelled 'cause Tigger kept peeing his pants."

"I didn't pee my pants, Mick. I missed," Tigger argued.

"It's fine, Tig. I'm just so glad you guys are okay. That this guy had you."

"Say, Mick?" Chris said coyly. "He's almost as big as you."

"Okay..." Mick was curious. "Why is that important?"

"Do you think, not now, but maybe some time in the future, not too far in the future, but some time before both of you guys get too old, that you can maybe bring back wrestling against each other for one match?" Chris cocked an eyebrow. "Maybe?"

Mick opened his mouth to speak. What would he say? His heart was full and his head was spinning far too much to playfully give Chris a hard time. He was still absorbing the gratefulness over the fact that the boys were right there. Mick smiled, murmured a passive, "Maybe", and grabbed onto the boys, bringing them into him one more time

15. DARK

Lodi, Ohio

Henry grew restless and a bit agitated over the fact that he had tried to reach the President of the United States. He felt like a pain in the rear for as many times as he called. But he knew the phone lines had to be up or the president's line wouldn't ring.

He was positive it was a cell phone, because the president had previously told him he wasn't getting a signal in the bunker. Last Henry had heard, they had since moved topside and the President, Secretary of State, Assistant Director of Homeland Security and a general from Washington were working on restructuring.

That was October 3rd.

The flu had been declared over everywhere but Lodi, and perhaps a few little towns. Two weeks had passed and still no word.

Well, nothing from the government.

Finally, Henry broke down and in his frustration sent a text: *This is ridiculous. If you aren't dead, call us now.*

"Really?" Kurt asked with a laugh when Henry told him. "Very teenage of you."

Henry grumbled. "I'm not used to the government shit. You're the one who was government."

"Isn't that funny, though?" Kurt said. "I was head of the CDC and people still think you were the one."

"That's because I ran the epi center when you guys toppled."

"I was there."

"You were, the whole time," Henry stated. "Now, we have this bastard of a problem." He rubbed his chin. "And we can't start to tackle it or come up with a plan until we get all the facts from Lexi and a course of action. Meaning, we have to speak to the president to find out what he has in the works."

Kurt tsked. "Nothing."

"Why do you say that?"

"You have wayward groups of men burning out towns, wiping out warehouses and blocking themselves into Erie, I'm betting with our missing men from the food run. You have some new force calling themselves the United Army of America—"

"Something like that, but close."

"They have every on the board militia group hooked up, linked up and working together, as Nelson said. With a lot of reserve soldiers and active duty. The president has little, if anything, to work with. Maybe he needs to work with what's out there."

"Or maybe he is and is busy, that is why he hasn't called," Henry suggested.

"You believe that?"

Henry tightly closed his mouth and widened his eyes to Kurt. The *bleep* of his phone caused him to look down. "You have to be goddamn kidding me."

"What?"

"He can text, but he can't call? Now who's teenage?"

"What's it say?" Kurt asked.

"Simple, *call you in a few*." Henry tossed down the phone. "Really? *Really*?"

Kurt laughed. "That tells me he has nothing. And it's time to do what you do best."

"And that is?" Henry asked.

"Like you did with the flu," Kurt said. "Take control."

* * *

Erie, PA

"How long …" Rose had to cough, but couldn't. She forced out a peep, winced, and held tight to her side. "How long have you been here?" she asked the young girl.

Her name was Lola, and she told Rose she was just getting ready to go into her senior year when the flu hit. She'd lived in Maryland, and was the only remaining member of her entire family.

"How long have I been in Erie or how have I been with this group?"

"I wouldn't say you're in this group. Held by them, is more like it," Rose remarked. "How long?"

"Over a week. Maybe a little longer."

"Why didn't you try to escape?" Rose asked.

"I haven't always been in this post office. Only a couple days ago when things got crazy and Ace went really off."

"It's like bad fiction." Rose adjusted her position. "They just ransack and loot. It's odd. With all the death, I wouldn't have thought it."

"Neither would I. I didn't think it started out that way," Lola said. "I headed out of home to DC, I thought maybe there things were getting back on the ground. I ran into Ace – that's his nickname. He worked with the president and left. Was joining up with some others that were gonna put the country back together. He was gonna help. That's what he told me. When the guy in charge was doing well, getting lots of stuff, I think Ace snapped. He didn't like someone else having control," Lola whispered. "That's what he kept saying. 'No one is going have control over my life or my food.'"

"What about this … this other person?"

"Last I heard he was moving on things and Ace wants to stop him. Ace got others to join him, start a separate society from this guy."

"Societies?" Rose asked. "This other guy has to be the one …" She struggled to breathe. "…the one my friend Nelson was talking about. He said … he said he joined forces with some guy."

"Is Nelson nice?"

"He's … he's good people." Rose immediately was putting two and two together. Nelson had joined forces with the guy in New York, and the fire starters had to be the Ace guy's group. "Why are you now a prisoner?"

Lola shrugged sadly. "I opened my mouth. We got in fight, because they were making people come here against their will and …" her head quickly turned at the sound of voices. "Lay down. Hurry. They're coming back again."

Lola had told Rose over and over that she didn't think they were coming to make sure she was okay or hope that she was getting better.

Rose realized they had other intentions as soon as they walked in.

She assumed her earlier position, lying still.

"She's still sleeping," Lola said to them.

"She moved," one male voice replied. "She's laying different."

"Yeah, I saw that, but she didn't wake up." Lola's voice had a quiver.

Rose could tell the girl was scared, she heard the voice step near her and didn't expect what happened next. Her eyes were closed and the slam of the boot into her body took her by surprise.

Lola screamed.

The cruel first kick took everything Rose had to remain silent and in her pretend 'coma' state, but the second kick was far too much.

Rose didn't have the strength to fight, to yell or scream.

She only grunted her agony.

Lola defended her by yelling at the two men, "Why you gotta be so mean to her?"

A 'shut your mouth' and slap to the face was their response and they walked out laughing.

Lola cried when they left; Rose didn't. There was no more fear of them walking in, and she didn't have to play 'comatose'. Rose had to think of helping herself or she would die right there on the floor of that post office.

She took a moment, breathing through the waves of pain. "I had higher hopes for humanity," Rose seeped out after they left, and dropped her head to the floor.

"Me, too," said Lola.

* * *

Damon, NY

Are you kidding me? was Briggs's first inward response, but he felt it too unprofessional to blurt out. His returning men from Erie told of what they found.

Men, too many to count. Their vehicles, three gas tanks, huge tractor trailers that Briggs could only assume were his missing warehouse items. Weapons.

"East, West, South," Jon told him. "And they contacted us when you were at the clinic."

Briggs inhaled hard through his nose. "Why didn't you get me?"

"They gave a short message and didn't want to talk to you."

"That's absurd. How did they get this many men?"

"We've been at this for weeks, Jonah, and apparently so have they. Up until recently they were working for us."

"And they barricaded themselves in Erie, Pennsylvania?" Briggs had a sense of sarcasm. "How ridiculous is that? Really. We're working with people who can farm further south and out west. What does Erie have? It's cold."

"Fresh water fishing, Ohio farm land, Amish country …"

"Wait. Wait." Briggs held up his hand. "Those are our territories. We spoke to people. We have men and women there."

"I think they plan on branching out."

"Branching out as in taking them?" Briggs shook his head. "This is unreal. Really unreal. How fucking hard is it to get everyone on the same page? I spoke to these people. What made them defect to this group?"

"The New Republic."

"Oh, they have a name now? Swell." Briggs shook his head. "This is not what we need right now. We have other things to deal with."

"Like the clinic?"

"Yeah. It's not good. Doc is trying like hell to reach Lodi, they have doctors there. Scientists," he growled in frustration.

"Jonah, as your newly designated right hand man, may I?"

Briggs lifted an eyebrow.

"You started putting things in motion when others weren't even thinking about it. You had people hacking up a lung while giving their thumbs up to you. You pulled it together. In a perfect world, everyone would have followed your plan, done their part, the wheels would have rolled smoothly, and people would be singing happy songs while skipping across your new fields of grain."

"Was that necessary?"

"Yeah, it is to give you an idea of how ridiculous a notion it was to believe that everyone would want to do this."

"People need structure and order or else they panic and have chaos."

"Yes." Jon nodded. "But they want their own structure and order. Your plan was good. Too good. It came together perfectly, until someone else decided why should the UAA have it all? Why should they follow your law and order?" Jon held up his hand in defense. "I'm playing devil's advocate here."

"I understand. So, right now, we have a dangerous wedge between us and the west."

"Done on purpose, I am thinking. If returning units can't reach you … well, they might as well stop there. And they have civilians."

Briggs rubbed his head. "What exactly was the message?"

"Short and to the point," Jon said. "They said they'd be in touch with their demands and we'd be wise not attack or confront because they hold an ace."

Briggs squinted in thought. "What the fuck is the ace supposed to mean?"

"I'm thinking kids. According to that boy, Jake, the men who raided their camp took kids."

Briggs grimaced. "Do you have a name? Maybe it's someone we contacted, or if they're from the 149."

"Yeah, Shane Drummond."

Briggs' eyes slowly widened in revelation. "What? He from the 149? Do you recognize the name?" Jon asked.

"Oh, I recognize the name alright. That makes me worried now about that Ace. He's not from the 149th." Briggs exhaled. "He was government. Homeland Security."

* * *

Lodi, Ohio

Tom wanted to kick himself for being so insensitive. With Baby Doe his new and self-proclaimed responsibility, Tom needed help with the store. People came in regularly, grabbed a movie then returned it. It was like the public library.

He had gone over to Joey's house. Hit and Run Video

had two employees aside from Tom before the flu, his daughter Dylan and Joey, a teenager.

Tom went to Joey's to see if he wanted to come back to the store, something to do, and was surprised that the seventeen year old boy was living alone. His parents had both died of the flu.

He asked if they boy had eaten, if he was okay. Joey was glad Tom stopped by and quickly accepted the offer. Then Tom made another. He told Joey that since he had the baby, he could use help at the house.

The teenager would pack his bags and move in with Tom, after he worked his shift, of course.

Tom put Joey on the three to seven shift. Dylan had hated that shift. Of course, she hated all shifts. Tom's mind wasn't on the business. He had tried to get a hold of Rose and she wasn't answering. He wanted to see if anyone would volunteer to take a trip. He couldn't get a hold of Mick, and Baby Doe seemed to be constantly hungry and fussy.

Tom's mood worsened by the hour. At least he knew his grandsons were safe, but they hadn't called, and Tom wanted to speak to them. Before he settled for dinner or called Nelson to see if he could do a search party for Rose, Tom stopped at the video store, Baby Doe perched on his hip.

"Hey, afternoon, Mr. Roberts, how's it going?" Joey asked.

"It's going," Tom answered. "How are things here?"

"Weird."

"How so?"

"Well, aside from it being busy, the phone keeps ringing."

"The phones are ringing?" Tom asked. "Are you answering it?"

"Dude, of course. But that's not what's weird. I keep getting a wrong number."

"What are you talking about?"

"Some guy keeps calling here, saying his name is Doctor Kitty. You know, like little kiddy or kitty cat, and he keeps on asking for our virologist. Something like that. I told him it was the wrong number, we only had movies. But he called back. He thinks I'm falling for his joke." Joey shook his head. "Kitty."

Tom took a second, trying to remain calm, keeping in mind all the boy had been through. "Joey, did it dawn on you, in a post-pandemic world, maybe folks wouldn't be playing prank calls?"

"Yeah."

"And?"

Joey shrugged.

Tom grabbed the phone and turned the base. He clicked through the list of numbers that had called into the store. "Three times? Was he the last one that called?"

"Yes, sir."

Tom handed Baby Doe to Joey, grabbed a rental slip and wrote down the number. "Watch him." Tom walked toward the door. "Don't drop him. Be nice. I'll be back."

"Okay."

Tom paused at the door, looked down at the paper. "Wrong number," he grumbled with a shake of his head and walked out.

* * *

Erie, PA

"I can't!" Lola cried, shaking her head.

"You have to," Rose insisted.

"I can't. I'm sorry."

"Listen to me." Rose grabbed her wrist. "If you don't, then you're going to have to deal with my dead body in here. I have to stop this bleeding and block this lung."

"It's going to hurt you."

"It will, but it will feel better after, I promise." Rose stared her in the eyes. "Please, Lola."

"Okay," Lola said reluctantly.

Rose had taken the draw strings from several canvas sacks. She found a small sack, folded it to make a binding wrap, and had it partially on her abdomen, with two drawstrings wedged within her fingers. After Lola agreed to help, Rose gripped one end of the binding.

The plan was simple. Push, wrap and tie. However, Rose couldn't do it alone.

"No matter what," Rose told her, "I'll try not to scream. When I inhale, you push that bone in place as best as you can. Try to get it back into the injury."

Lola shuddered.

"Baby, I know this is tough. I need your help, okay?"

Lola sniffled and nodded.

"Ready?" When she got the agreement, Rose inhaled.

She groaned and cried as Lola pushed the rib back into place. She was too gentle and Rose urged her to be forceful.

The pain was tremendous and Rose didn't need to see when the bone made it back in. When Lola succeeded, she held it in place, then brought the binding over, still keeping her hand hard and with pressure to the fractured area.

"Hold it. Hold it," Rose instructed and brought the first drawstring over. She tied it. "See if you can make the binding tighter.

Lola did and Rose secured the second drawstring.

She had done the same to her leg, but that wasn't broken, just badly bruised. Once her ribs were bound, Rose exhaled fully. "That actually feels better."

Lola wiped her hand under her nose. "You sure?"

"Positive. I can actually ..." Rose took small breath, "... inhale without that dagger feeling." She extended her hand to Lola. "Help me stand."

"Maybe you should rest."

"No. I need to stand. Get my blood circulating. I don't want a blood clot." She wiggled her fingers.

Lola grabbed her hand and pulled.

It took some struggling but with a grunt, Rose managed to get to her feet. At first she was half bent and then slowly she stood upright, holding on to her side. "Thank you."

A new noise caught their attention. A slow, loud, clapping.

Clap. Clap. Clap. Clap.

Rose looked over her shoulder.

A man stood there. He wore jeans and a sweatshirt. He was impeccably clean, and his gray hair was buzzed so close to the scalp, in the right light he would have looked bald.

"You are impressively resilient," he said.

"That's Ace," Lola whispered.

"Ace?" Rose looked at Lola then to the man. "This is him? He doesn't look all that tough. I would have run away from him in a heartbeat. How'd you get stuck here?"

Ace laughed. "You're feisty and she didn't run away because where would she go?" He lifted his hands. "She has nothing. We feed her. She, unlike you, doesn't have resources."

"I don't have resources," Rose said.

"Yeah, you do. And obviously, you're resourceful." He pointed to her makeshift bandages.

"I don't have a choice now do I?" Rose asked. "Obviously, you don't want me dead or you would have done it. And if you keep me around longer, waiting on killing me, I might as well have my strength up. I won't go down alone."

"I believe that." He folded his arms.

"What's your game here?" Rose asked. "I'm obviously some sort of prisoner."

"You are. You inured one of my men and killed another."

"Your men are bastards," Rose spat. "They threatened me and the other ones out there burning towns, well, if they represent your little group here, then you're all bastards. So, I'm, a prisoner. Sentence me, kill me or let me go."

"Can't do any of that. And I can't kill you just yet."

"Why is that?"

"People are commodities."

Rose coughed and laughed. "That's a fake compassionate response."

He smirked. "You think I'm being a humanitarian about people being commodities? No. Right now, people are bargaining chips. For things I need. After I get them, they'll be useful for work and will need what I have."

"Get your head out of your ass. Hitler tried it once, you saw how it worked out for him."

Ace laughed. "Yeah, well, he gained a lot in the process, now didn't he? He just made mistakes."

"I have nothing of value and I'm an old lady that no one wants to barter or bargain for."

"I wager differently," he said. "Where are you from?"

"Nowhere. Everywhere. I was just roaming the country."

"I call that bull. You're in good condition, other than the accident. Not starving, not dirty. Your bike was in good repair and you had limited supplies. You're local. Cleveland ...maybe a pocket of civilization that we missed, or the golden town of hope. Lodi."

"Lodi?" Rose scoffed. "Last I heard, Lodi went under."

"Last I heard from the president, Lodi was spared pretty good from the major losses and they stockpiled heavily. I was wondering where everything from the warehouses went. When we got there, maybe a quarter was left."

"I don't know about the warehouses. I don't know about Lodi."

"We'll see," Ace said arrogantly. "I was hoping you'd talk. But I see, you're not ready. When you are, let me know. I'll get you some water and fresh bandages so your wounds don't get infected. Have a good evening ladies."

Rose held back the waves of pain and fought tooth and

nail not to show how hurt she actually was, but when he left, she folded. Lola helped her to sit. It hurt with every step she took, every word she spoke.

She wondered what his purpose was for stopping in. To see if she was dead? Ready to talk? Did he actually think he would get information from her? He probably didn't realize he gave her more information than she had given him. Or had he done that on purpose? Maybe a way to scare her, make her concerned for her town. If that indeed was his intent, despite what she showed or conveyed, Rose was scared. She was scared to death for Lodi.

* * *

<u>Las Vegas, NV</u>

They were all getting worse, and after getting the diagnosis from Lars regarding their 'coughing' patients, Lexi realized why. She wasn't treating them correctly. And in actuality, there wasn't an effective treatment for SARS at all. Antiviral medications in studies were somewhat effective, but the defense was time, oxygen and fluids in conjunction with any medication that Lexi could give. But she was limited; there was very little of anything remaining.

Those who were infected wasn't what worried her, it was the fact they were dealing with something as contagious as their flu. Though not as deadly, it spread just as easily. She was certain more cases would pop up over the course of the next several days, and that didn't include those who passed through Vegas. How many of those took the virus with them?

There were no other cases of smallpox, but another illness appeared in the suburbs of Vegas. Matt's team discovered that not long after.

Things had quickly become a mess in Vegas.

Matt conveyed his gratefulness to her because had Lexi

not shown up they would not have known what they were dealing with.

Lexi still didn't know how it was occurring. How all of a sudden, these severe illnesses were appearing. Had civilization and technology really kept them at bay?

Her visit with Slot Machine Charlie was depressing. He was the worst. He barely moved. The oxygen flowed into him but Lexi was certain he had gone into respiratory failure.

They retried a respirator from the hospital, actually several, but it may have been a little too late.

A rush of nerves caused her not to sleep the night before and she had been going all day long. She was beat and took a break. Bottle of water in hand, heart heavy, Lexi walked outside. It was hot, but it felt good.

"Someone said they saw you come out," Bill said as he walked up to her where she sat on a bus stop bench. "Can I join you?"

"Please."

"What's wrong?"

She sipped her water and didn't answer him.

"Okay, that was a bad question."

"Oh, Bill." She leaned over and rested her head on his arm. "What the hell is going on? Haven't we seen enough death and suffering? This is going to get bad. People aren't the only things that spread this."

"I know. But we're gonna face this and fight it, just like we did with the flu."

"What if we get sick?" she asked. "What if everyone gets sick?"

"Lex, this isn't like you to be talking like this. You're tough, strong and smart. You'll figure out what to do."

She pulled away and hung her head. "I'm just so tired of death."

"We all are, but this doesn't mean these people are dying. They're just sick. Sick with a couple of odd diseases. But still sick."

"And now the new cases."

"You heard Matt, they aren't using the city's water purification system. Could be that."

"With our luck it's cholera or hemorrhagic fever."

"How the heck are we getting this soup pot of sicknesses?" Bill asked. "Look at all these birds, I'd say they found a general store and are flying the germs in here."

Lexi's head sprang up. "Oh my God."

"What?"

She stood. "When is our telephone call?"

Bill looked at his watch. "Fifteen minutes. Why?"

She reached down and grabbed his hand. "Come on."

"Where we going?"

"To find a map," she said. "I think I know what this is."

* * *

<u>Lodi, OH</u>

Henry watched Lars while he was on the phone, as did Kurt and Tom. Lars didn't say much, he wrote down more than he spoke. He ended the call simply and said, "We have a telephone meeting in a few minutes. Hang tight. I'll call you back."

Lars hung up.

Henry said, "I take it the video store boy was wrong and it wasn't a wrong number."

"Not at all," Lars replied "Seems their commander remembered your store number, Tom, and he gave it to Dr. Kiddi."

"It's easy," Tom said. "That's why I picked it."

Kurt asked, "So what's going on? Something is up."

"On the positive front," Lars said, "Mick couldn't get by Erie either. Seems he met up with some men from the UAA."

"Tell me he is with the boys," Tom said hopefully.

"He's with the boys."

"Hot dog." Tom smiled.

"But not so fast, that wasn't the point of the call," Lars said. "They have three cases of what this doctor believes to be hemorrhagic fever."

"W-what?" Henry stuttered. "How is that possible? That's *not* possible. He has to be wrong."

Kurt added, "It has to be something else. They just developed symptoms of hemorrhagic fever? Can't happen."

Lars shook his head. "No. They arrived with it. Travelers from west to east. It's a big thing now, you know, going east. Well, at least for those not going through Erie. This is strange." Lars leaned back. "If there were enough readers left alive, I'd write a book."

Tom chuckled. "Probably end up one of them gay erotica novels you write."

"I wrote romance," Lars corrected. "Romantic comedy. I resent that."

"Lots of people said it," Tom replied. "Called that one book gay erotica."

Lars shook his head. "One scene. One paragraph and I'm scorned with quips from right wing fanatics."

"Rose called it that," Tom said. "You think she's right wing?"

All them, Lars, Henry, and Kurt responded at the same time. "Yes."

"She ain't right wing, she swears too much," Tom argued. "And I'm worried about her. Nelson said he was sending a party out for her and he'd get back. Something is wrong." He looked down when his phone rang and he lifted it. "Maybe not. There is a bright spot." He grinned.

"Rose?" Lars asked.

"Yep." Tom pressed a button and brought the phone to his ear. "Rose, damn it. Where the hell are you? You should have been back in Lodi hours ago. We're worried."

Henry watched Tom's face. The smile dropped instantaneously and suddenly his expression was drawn.

Lars stood, as did Kurt, and they watched Tom.

Tom said nothing. The five second conversation was over and Tom's arm dropped.

"What's wrong?" Henry asked. "What is it?"

"We got more problems," Tom said then pursed his lips. "They have Rose."

* * *

<u>Erie, PA</u>

The bottle of water dropped on the floor and rolled toward Rose, followed by a bag of bandages. Rose looked at them.

"That's a start. We'll see what happens next …" he paused, "*Rose*."

Slowly, Rose lifted her eyes to Ace.

"I said I'd bring you water and bandages when you were ready to talk. Because I am a kind and generous man … here they are."

"I didn't say anything."

"No, but your belongings did. Actually, your phone. It survived the accident and you had several missed calls." Ace said. "Actually, I didn't expect the person that answered to spew out everything I needed to know."

"No one would give you information," Rose snapped.

"Oh, but they did. They answered the phone calling for you and saying you should have been home hours ago … in Lodi."

Rose closed her eyes.

"Yeah, Lodi." Ace grinned. "I'll be calling them back."

"Lodi has nothing you want," Rose said.

"You're kidding right?" Ace laughed. "Apparently, you must have been so busy in that town that you missed the news. Oh, yeah, coverage galore about how Lodi was spared. How Lodi's chief of police put an iron wall of bikes around the town, quarantining it from the world. And how the government, in an attempt to save them, dumped tons of medical supplies in there. Medical supplies that would save the town should they get the flu. Along with weapons."

"It didn't work," Rose said, her voice weakening.

"Yes it did," Ace argued. "Let's look at Erie, this town. Population pre-flu was 100,000 people. The mayor, who by the way is a good friend since our securing his town and feeding his people, says maybe ten percent remained. Ten percent? That's not including how many of the survivors died from starvation, other ailments, chaos. Any city over 100,000 burned itself out and is lucky to have five percent remaining after all was said and done. They're still dying. Smaller towns fared better, keeping about twenty to thirty percent alive. But Lodi .... how many did you lose? Thirty percent? That's nothing. Not in the scheme of everything. It was the golden child. Why was Lodi so special?"

Rose shook her head. "I don't know."

"I do and that's why you are special to me. The best bargaining chip ever."

"I'm not important enough for Lodi to bargain."

Ace fluttered his lips. "It's Lodi, every person there is a bargaining chip. I had to hear about that down in the bunker. I was locked in. Against my will. I couldn't get out of that government bunker. I had to hear praises about Lodi, stories about it while my family died without me there."

"That's not our fault."

"Really? Because my wife didn't catch the flu until after supplies were sent to Lodi," Ace said. "If I remember correctly, without treatment you stood a 99 percent chance of dying if you caught the flu. With the treatment, your odds of dying were a quarter of that. It pissed me off and I resent that."

"So why bargain? If you hate Lodi and resent it so much,

do what you need to do. Try."

"I will. After I get what I want."

Rose shook her head. "There's nothing in Lodi you can't get elsewhere."

"I beg to differ. There's something very special in Lodi." He turned and walked to the door.

Lola, who had remained silent, hurried to stop him. "Ace, she's needs more than bandages. She's got a fever. An infection. She's in pain. She needs a doctor."

Ace titled his head with smug look. "I don't have one … yet." He opened the door and, after a smile to Rose, he walked out.

* * *

Las Vegas, NV

A map was spread out across the counter and Lexi's phone, on speaker was in the center of it. Bill stood across from her.

She had a hint of excitement to her, and rightfully so; she believed she had figured out the source of the illnesses and a way to end and anticipate any further outbreaks.

"Currently," she said, in a speakerphone conversation to Lars, Henry and Kurt, "there are fourteen BSL-4 facilities in the United States."

Bill asked. "BSL?"

"Biosafety Level Four," Lexi explained. "They hold the world's deadliest and biggest threats. There are fourteen in the United States. These are known facilities. There are several private ones that may carry but are unauthorized to hold BSL-4 viruses, the bulk of which are in the east. In Virginia, Boston, Georgia and Maryland. Fort Detrick, to be exact, has five labs there, because as we know, it's US Army Medical Command."

Henry cut in, "That is federally run and houses the

weapons research."

"Yes," Lexi stated. "The other labs; two are in Texas, one in Kansas, Montana, Ohio and the newest facility is in California. I believe that is where our diseases here are coming from. If you recall, the Centers for Disease Control were one of two places in the world that had smallpox, until this California facility was approved."

Lars said, "Which would explain our pilgrims having hemorrhagic fever. Animals, birds, food, water, you name it. Dr. Martin, how did you find the facilities and locations so quickly?"

"I knew them," Lexi replied. "Kurt may remember that he gave snap quizzes on this stuff all the time to the field workers."

"You snap quizzed your workers?" Lars asked, turning to Kurt. "How anal."

"Guilty," Kurt said. "But it works out now. So, Lexi, basically, this facility went hot."

"It had to. Power went out, safeguards went down, sealants no longer worked, and the germs are seeping into the air and ground and anything and everything passing through will carry it. It is a hot zone right now."

"Wait a second," Bill interrupted. "These places carry dangerous shit, why aren't safeguards put in for this? Don't they have a self destruct button or something?"

"The failsafe mode has to be initiated," Kurt answered. "I recall we did that at both Georgia buildings and Vermont. I know specifically because I flipped the switch. By now the labs are extinguished, and I am a hundred percent certain that those two are sealed."

Henry added, "I can vouch for Virginia. Kurt and I pulled the kill switch on the viruses before we left. But we were working closely at the end. I don't know about the others."

Lexi said, "Apparently the California facility went hot, which leaves me to worry, what about the others? Are they hot as well, or on their way? Would the president have received notice?"

"If the computers were up and running," Lars said, "Homeland Security would have recovered the alert on what labs were put into failsafe mode. Again, if the computers were up and running."

"Wait," Henry interrupted. "The Assistant Director is with the President. He may know."

"If he remembers," Kurt said. "He may not recall which labs sent alerts if they don't have access to that info."

"Why wouldn't they?" Bill asked. "I would think that's some vital info to remember. Heck, to even think about right away."

Lexi nodded. "I agree. But then, did we … yes, Henry and Kurt shut things down, but after, did you worry if the others did? You may have assumed, but the problem is we were all consumed with the flu."

"Assume, consume," Lars said. "We should assume none of the remaining labs hit failsafe and consume ourselves with fixing this. Now, a lot of our remaining soldiers have joined forces with our diligent militia who have been putting things together."

"I heard about that," Lexi commented. "Pilgrims said a division over this side of the country was encouraging people to go east. Keep everyone together to work together."

Henry suggested, "Maybe we can get the groups to work with us to shut these down."

"We have Matt," Lexi said. "He'll get some men, they can handle the California labs, Montana and Kansas."

"That could be dangerous," Lars noted. "California is a hot zone, probably a good mile circumference. They all could be."

"Then they suit up before going in. I'll instruct them on precautions and what to do. Get them in, report a breach if there is one and burn it out."

"In the meantime," Kurt said, "since you have a soup of

sickness, try to keep them apart. The last thing we need is for these viruses to marry into one super bug."

"Oh my God," Henry uttered.

Lexi looked at Bill. There was something about his tone. "What?" she asked.

"There *is* a superbug," Henry replied. "We all know it. Think. Lexi you probably don't, but Lars does. Kurt does too. Hell, you signed the petition and were the first one."

"Holy shit, I forgot!" Kurt gasped. "The MHS."

Lars groaned. "They already married them to create a super weapon. It's a married virus of three types. It was created to be climate controlled. It's a surface and particle weapon. Release it, it attatches, breeds and remains on surfaces. Victims that don't inhale it upon release can aspire it from any surface. The fault was, it didn't work in hot environments, the bug would burn out in higher temperatures. Starting at eighty degrees, it lost potency. It can be burned out, but the colder it is the longer its stays alive on surfaces. The colder it is, the longer it lives. Days, weeks, months."

"Fortunately," Henry added, "there is supposed to be an antidote."

"Yeah, but you read the specs," Kurt said. "If given within two hours of exposure. After that, forget it. This is deadly, no treatment, no cure. Theoretically it shouldn't be an extinction bug. It's a weapon. Ground zero victims die immediately. Those exposed take a couple of days to get sick and they aren't even contagious until a day before symptoms appear. And when they do, it's an internal time bomb. Our biggest concern is someone getting this weapon."

"Who would want it?" Bill asked. "It's a dead world already. Who would want a biological weapon?"

"Crackpots like those that built the wedge in Erie," Henry answered. "Who knows? This has to be top priority. Whoever we send to Maryland not only has to go in there, they have to find this bug, confirm it's there and guarantee it is destroyed."

Lexi made a huge circle over Maryland. "I'll work on my end to get people out there ASAP."

"We'll start organizing on this end," Henry said. "And we'll touch base in the morning. Let's try to get our first team out by then."

"Oh, I'll have a team out," Lexi said. "Rest assured, I'm on this now."

The conversation ended and Lexi sighed, looking to Bill. "This is a nightmare."

"I know. I want to go."

Her eyes widened. "You can't."

"No, Lex, I can and I will," Bill retorted. "I know how the suits work, hell, how many people did you and I suit up? Plus," he closed one eye, "I want to make sure this is done. I want to be certain this can't be a threat and I'll not know it, if I'm not there."

"All this can be done in a couple of days," Lexis said. "Are you sure?"

"Yes, yes, I am."

"I hate sending you, but I don't think I'd feel secure about it if you didn't go. I trust you."

Bill slipped his hand behind her head, brought Lexi close, and placed his lips gently to her head. "It'll get done. All of the facilities. I feel it. Then after, let's make a pact."

"What's that?"

"That we do our best to make sure this world never gets this bad again. We have a chance. A fresh start. After this is done, let's do it right."

Lexi smiled gently at him, stood on her tiptoes, and kissed him, then she settled into Bill's embrace.

* * *

Damon, NY

Tigger fell fast asleep on Mick's lap and Chris wasn't far behind. Mick knew they had been going for days and probably felt safe enough to rest finally.

Chris wrote in his journal as he rested against Mick. Occasionally Mick took a peek and he saw his name. There was nothing better than his reunion with the boys. After Mick cleaned up, they ate supper and hung out by themselves.

He'd be lying if he said he didn't shed tears of gratefulness as he took a shower. He spoke to Dylan, out loud, telling her he was sorry that he lost the boys and would do whatever he could to make the future as best as he could.

Watching Chris write, Mick thought back to their conversation, only because he saw the words 'double headed coin' written in the notebook.

"It was really smart of me, wasn't it Mick?" Chris asked.

"Yeah, yeah it was. Actually brilliant."

"Then how come you didn't find us right away? Did you get lost in the woods, too?"

"No. No I didn't. I followed the gravel road."

"But I left you an awesome clue saying *not* to follow that trail."

"I know. I didn't give you enough credit."

"So you actually thought I just accidently dropped my coin?"

"I did."

"Well, next time you'll get it right."

"Let's hope there s never a next time." He kissed Chris and laughed when Chris made a comment about him always kissing them.

They talked and then grew tired.

Chris yawned and that made Mick pull from his thoughts. "You okay?"

"Yeah, tired. That's all. Long day."

"Why don't you go to sleep? I'm gonna go catch a

smoke," Mick said. "And find Briggs, see if I can work with him about getting us a way to get home." Risking ridicule, Mick bent down and kissed Chris again. He slid out from under Chris, stood, then bent down and lifted Tigger, placing him in bed. "Why don't you get in bed before you pass out on the floor?"

"Okay."

Mick started to walk out.

"Mick?"

"Yeah?"

"Glad we're back together. I love you."

"I love you too." Mick winked. He walked down the corridor, pulling out his pack of cigarettes. He took the side door out, not wanting to be too far from the boys.

When he stepped outside and lit up, he saw Briggs sitting by the truck, a phone in his hand. He looked as if he were sending a message. Mick walked toward him.

"Evening."

"Evening." Briggs stood. "You guys okay?"

"Oh, yeah, we're fine. Thank you. Tigger is asleep and Chris is just about there."

"They have to be exhausted. They had a hell of a day."

"They did. I have a question for you," Mick said. "Do you have anything you can give us so we can make the trip back home?"

"I'm sure we can get together something. When are you wanting to go?" Briggs asked.

"Tomorrow. Maybe one more day of rest."

"You're joking right?" Briggs asked.

"Why would I joke? We can't stay here."

"Why not?" Briggs questioned.

"This isn't our home. We have a home. We have family in Lodi."

Briggs nodded. "I understand that and I'm not saying to stay here long term. I'm saying to wait."

"For what?"

Briggs took a moment, he moistened his lips. "You came with my scout crew from Erie. You obviously know there's a wedge of hostiles set up in the middle of your path."

"Yeah, I do, I'll go south and around."

"Just to be sure, you'd have to go to Maryland."

"What's the issue with this?" Mick asked coldly. "I want to take my boys home."

"Then take them when it's safe."

Mick laughed.

"You think that's funny?"

"When exactly will it be safe?" Mick questioned with sarcasm.

"My men and I plan—"

"Oh, that's right." Mick cut him off. "Your men."

Briggs shook his head. "What is your problem?"

"You're not seeing it because you're on the inside. Take a look around. Look at what you have. Made civilization into a militaristic society."

"You think? Have you been to Damon? Harrisburg? Philadelphia. Damon isn't the only pocket in our control. They aren't military installations. They are towns."

"There it is. The word. Control," Mick said. "Control is the exact reason you have that wedge in Erie. How did they get there? Do you know who they are?"

"Yes."

"And I'm willing to bet they were part of this all." Mick's arm swung out. "You can't project a dictatorship without someone wanting to be the bigger guy on the block."

"You think that's what this is?" Briggs asked with an edge. "You think this is a dictatorship? A monarchy?"

"I think you saw the end of the world as an opportunity."

"Fuck you." Briggs said with an 'up' motion of his chin. "You think this is an ego thing? A rule the world thing? Think again. You wanna do this? Go ahead. I'll gladly step aside and put you in charge. Go on. It's yours. You put together protection from the assholes who will band together out there. You work with people to rebuild farming and feed, clothe, house and meet the medical needs to fifty thousand people. Because that's what we had at last count. Fifty thousand. We're working on a structure so we can all work together."

"No one asked you to do it."

"And nobody stepped to the plate. Someone had to."

"And that person just so happened to be you."

Briggs growled his frustration. "You're not getting it are you? No, of course you wouldn't. Because you don't know. You were locked away safe and sound."

"I kept my people that way."

"*Your people,*" Briggs said. "What is so different from what you did, and what I'm doing? I'm just doing it on a larger scale. You don't know what's out here. If you did, you wouldn't have taken your boys on a road trip and you certainly wouldn't be bringing them the long, uncertain route back home to a place close to the hostiles." Briggs stepped closer to him. "You think three days out here is enough to give you an idea of what happened to the world? While you were informing your town of this flu – which we all watched on the news – we were caring for our sick. When the government brought you in supplies to test a cure, we were burying our dead. And while you waited for the flu to pass, we were already rebuilding. It started long before the world ended. We had the insight to plan ahead." Briggs tossed up his hands. "Only thing was, we kind of thought we'd hear from you. From Lodi. But we got nothing."

"That's because this isn't right. Not at all," Mick argued. "Guns, soldiers, tanks. Going from town to town, gathering people, making them think you're the answer."

"We are."

Mick shook his head. "You're the answer because you took all the food."

"It was organizing the food until this country got back on

its feet to grow its own again. Organizing so everyone got and no one was without."

"It was not for you to do. We have a president. We have a government."

Briggs lifted his hands. "Where are they? Last I heard they were in a bunker ordering your town everything it needed and now nothing. No word."

Mick laughed. "You left them nothing to restructure with."

"They have a whole country. They should have been rebuilding before things fell too far apart. You have another answer?"

"Yes. Yes," Mick squeaked. "Let it alone. Leave it be. Let towns be towns and be on their own. If the government broke down then let the towns take care of their own."

"That's your answer? What about when you run out of food for your town? Go to the next one? Take from them? Who will they take from?" Again, Briggs shook his head. "I'm not going to argue with you about what I built here. I'll give you what you need to get back to Lodi. Just ... just get them boys back safe." Briggs turned and started to walk.

"Briggs." Briggs stopped.

"I'm not an asshole. I'm really not," Mick said softly. "I'm grateful for what you have done for my sons. I understand what you're saying about all this ..." he waved about his hand. "It's not for me. It's not for my town. I really can take care of my own."

Briggs nodded. "I believe that."

"I won't come to you for help. But know Lodi is there if you need anything. Just leave us out of this all."

Another nod, and Briggs continued to walk.

Out of the darkness a voice carried to them. "Lodi already is a part of this all."

Both Mick and Briggs turned.

Doc walked up the path, his lit cigarette illuminating his face. "I didn't want to interrupt you two in the middle of your pissing contest."

"Excuse me?" Mick asked. "They what?" He raised an eyebrow.

"Hold on big guy," Doc lifted his hand. "No worries. Lodi didn't join the cause in your absence. They just got suckered in." He approached them both. "Egos aside guys, I just got off the phone with Lodi. We have a big problem."

JOURNAL ENTRY

It feels good to be with Mick. I know we were safe and all, and I was the cool kid driving, even though I hit Jonah Briggs. But it was still awesome to see Mick. He really looked for us and didn't give up.

I thought it was funny and I'll tell him when he calms down, that I couldn't believe he didn't get my clue with the two headed coin.

He seems uptight. Probably nervous because of all the military around here. I know something is bothering him because he is smoking again. My mom always hated when he smoked, but it don't bother me none.

I heard him and Jonah arguing about something. At first I thought they were gonna duke it out and I didn't want to miss it, so I jumped out of bed and ran to the window. They were standing a good distance apart. They weren't really screaming, just talking loud. I guess when you're big like that your voice is big too.

I don't know when we're leaving to go home, but I hope that Mick waits until the bad guys are taken care of. Not that I don't think we're safe with Mick and all. But he's only one man. And for as cool as Mick is, they have a lot of guns and they don't hesitate to shoot. I know. I saw.

Heading back to sleep. Mick still didn't come back yet. Man, he must be smoking a lot.

16. PREPARATIONS

Lodi, OH

The Lodi Diner was set up like a war room. Since it wasn't open, Henry and Kurt moved the tables together to create one big one. A large map of the United States was center, along with three phones.

"Did you tell the president he can't do that?" Kurt asked.

"He doesn't have the manpower anyhow. Reserve units he was able to get in touch with are far west. A few south," Henry replied.

Nelson was on hand. "We got in touch with them last night after your call. They're ready. Militia units we can move out whenever. Reserve units not committed to anything are waiting on word from the president. Gotta get the president to give word to allow them to give my units down in Texas access to the bio suits. I have men who are willing to do that once they get instructions."

"I'll get on that," Henry said, "get clearance. I will personally instruct each grouping. I want men paired in teams for the mission."

"Did the president say if the homeland director remembered anyone sending failsafe alerts?" asked Kurt.

"He wouldn't know. Homeland guy went AWOL.

"Shit," Kurt exclaimed. "Probably looking for family."

"Nelson," Henry said, "we know we have reserve units

waiting on executive orders. Do we know their locations?"

"Further south. Louisiana, Mississippi, Florida, Texas. I got a handle and am in good connection with what remained in Kentucky, Ohio and Indiana."

"How many still remain? I know some were going east," Henry said.

"A lot, actually," Nelson replied. "We weren't sending everyone. We have to have people here to help. Cleveland isn't dead. They have tens of thousands remaining."

Kurt swiped his hand down his face. "If the Kentucky location goes hot, this is another nightmare, worse than the flu, because we don't have resources to handle it."

Henry grimaced. "There's no power there. It probably already is hot, and our best chance is to burn it out, do an inventory of what remains first."

Nelson asked, "I know Briggs needs men to head toward Erie once he comes up with a plan."

"And that can't be the president," Kurt added. "He wants to just storm it and burn it. I'm guessing there are civilians and Erie residents."

Nelson touched the map with his finger. "From what I was told they barricaded here." He pointed. "One spot. But I am gonna guess they branched south with men and probably will head East and West."

"We need some of your men on our town access routes," Henry said.

"I'll pull them in, ASAP. What about Kent? We need volunteers to go, manpower might be strained in this area and we want to shut down that lab right away. It could take days to pull someone in to do Kent."

Ethan's voice entered the room. "I've been listening, I'm sorry." He stepped closer. "I know you guys are trying to keep things from upsetting the residents, but with all the activity on the street, it's hard not to know what's going on. So, I'd like to volunteer for anything. This Kent thing you're talking about. I'll do it."

Henry looked at him. "Son, to be very honest, it's a lab. A Biosafety level four lab. It needs to be shut down, contents identified and burned out. It could be dangerous."

"Any more dangerous than if it doesn't get shut down right away?" Ethan asked.

"Just delayed," Henry answered.

"Then I'll go. You may wanna put me with someone that knows how to burn a place out." Ethan smiled. "I probably won't know that."

"We can handle that," Henry assured him. "As soon as Lars gets back with the logistics of it all, we'll get you prepped. Thank you." He rubbed the back of his neck. "Speaking of which, where is Lars?"

* * *

Tom poured Lars another cup of coffee in Tom's kitchen. Lars was certain he didn't look his usual confident self. In fact, he looked and felt as distraught as if he had been hit by a truck. His hands were folded in a prayer fashion, covering his nose, and he breathed heavily outward when the coffee clicked against the table.

"Thank you, Tom." Lars brought down his hands.

"I wanted to tell you alone," Tom said, joining him at the kitchen table. "When I called you to come over, I had just heard from them. No one but you and I are aware of the deal. They're giving us a few minutes and then they're calling back."

"There really is no choice."

"Yeah, there is. I told them we need to speak to Rose when they call back. They want you, but I haven't spoken to Rose. We'll see what she says."

"Why me?" Lars asked,

"Well, you *are* Lars Rayburn."

"But I have this reputation in Lodi, within the infectious disease community. Not the world. And certainly not in

Erie, Pennsylvania."

"I got a theory on that. We were all over the news when the flu was in full swing. Only town not hit. We're the town where the Rayburn therapy for the flu was gonna be tested. You have a reputation as being a brilliant doctor. Now, if they got to know you like we do, they'd realize it's a façade."

Lars gave Tim a quirky look. "Your attempt at humor is appreciated. But again, why me?"

"They need a doctor, maybe?"

"But if they watched the news, as you suggested, then they know there are three here. Why *me*?" Lars jumped when the phone rang.

Tom lifted a hand then picked up the phone. "Hello?" He waited. "Not talking to you anymore until we speak to Rose. I want to talk, then Lars." There was a pause and Tom's face lit up, but only briefly. "Rose, what in God's name …? You sound … how are you? I thought you were dead." Another pause and Tom closed his eyes. "Did they tell you? Okay, then Lars needs to speak to you. Rose, Mick's fine. When I speak to him what do you want me to tell him?" Tom waited. "Absolutely, I will do that. Here's Lars." He handed the phone over.

"Rose?"

Her voice was crackly and weak, not the typically boisterous Rose. "Lars, I'm here."

"What happened, Rose? Can you tell me why you sound sick?"

"Got in a cycle accident. Broken rib. It's a compound and it punctured out. I'm thinking another punctured in. I'm not doing good, Lars."

"I know they're listening, Rose, but do you know why they want me there?"

"No I don't. Other than a doctor, and it's an exchange so you aren't for me. Lars …" She paused and strained a cough out, "don't do it. I am not worth your life. You are too valuable to—"

"Rose?"

"Enough talk," said the man on the other side who took over the conversation. "We meet at the rest area just outside the interchange of 79 and 90."

"No," Lars said. "I'll meet you at your barricade. I need to get some medical supplies together. I want to work on Rose, examine her and then she can leave. I don't trust anyone else."

"Suit yourself."

"And one more thing, I will not be treated as a prisoner there. I am a prestigious virologist and I will be treated with respect. I am sure you and your thugs can accomplish that. Because I promise you, if I am not treated as a guest or am treated with anything but respect, you and your men will not know if that is penicillin or poison that you ingest when you're ill. Got that?"

"Deal," the man said after a brief pause. "You have four hours."

Lars handed the phone to Tom.

"Lars, what the hell are you doing?" Tom asked sharply. "You heard Rose. She's bad."

"It's Rose," Lars said. "Mick sacrificed for this town, the least I can do is sacrifice for Mick. I couldn't save his wife, let me try to save his mother."

Tom closed his eyes hard. He choked on his emotions. "Henry and Kurt—"

"Are not to know," Lars said firmly.

Tom opened his eyes. "What?"

"Only you. I go alone. I go with no one knowing. I don't want anyone trying to stop me or follow or try to rescue me." Lars sipped the coffee, stood and then picked up the cup again. "I'm gonna take this with me. I have supplies to grab from the clinic."

"Did Rose say she needs you?"

"Actually, she said not to come."

"Then maybe —"

"No." Lars shook his head. "There's no question. Other than Rose, there is one valuable reason for me to go."

"What's that?" Tom asked.

"Eventually, there is going to be a clash. Them against us or them against that new army. Hell, I believe they'll come into this town, but before they do, they need an insider. I'm going to be that insider."

"Oh, that's just like you, trying to make another name for yourself." Tom stood and spoke with sadness laced sarcasm. "The new post-flu generation will raise their children to say, 'you wanna grow up to be like Lars, don't you?'

Lars smiled sadly. "I pray the post-flu generation has children." He grabbed on to Tom's arm. "You are my friend, Tom. I appreciate the concern. But I'm going in there, I will help Rose, and I will find out about this place and what all they are doing."

"How will you get us this information?" Tom asked. "They'll be listening, you know."

"I have ideas." Lars winked. "Oh ye of little faith. After all, I am Lars Rayburn."

"That you are."

Lars looked at Tom deeply, trying to convey that he had it under control and that everything would be alright. Then he left. He had far too much to get ready and too little time.

* * *

<u>Damon, NY</u>

Chris stood in the doorway of the small church. It was the place they were using as a school. He didn't go in, he watched. It was chilly out, but he didn't mind, he was too engrossed. He'd smile when Tigger raised his hand to answer a question and cringed when Tigger got it wrong.

Tigger looked happy, even anxious. Chris watched for a

while, holding Emmie's hand even though she clutched tightly to his leg for security.

It wasn't her hand that Chris felt touch upon his back. He knew the touch and he looked up to see Mick. "Hey."

"Hey, Chris. What are you doing?"

"Watching. They're having school. Look at Tig. Don't he look happy? Man … it's pretty cool, though. You know, them having school."

"I bet you miss it."

"I do, and I miss my friends."

"Why don't you go in?" Mick cupped his head.

"I will. Ain't the older kids' time yet. You don't mind, do you?"

"Oh my God, not at all. I'll probably stand here and watch you. Who's your girlfriend?"

Chris snorted a laugh. "This is Emmie. Say hi to Mick, Emmie."

Emmie buried herself further into Chris.

"She came with us from the camp. Was running with us. Did real good too, huh, Emmie? Except she peed her pants a lot."

Mick smiled.

"I predict in twenty years her and Tigger are gonna be married. You wait and see. He can't be her boyfriend now, though. She's half his age and that's illegal or something. She's gonna come with us to Lodi, Mick, if that's okay?"

"Chris, I think —"

"She don't have a family. I can take care of her if you don't want to."

"Chris—"

"I really like her, Mick. We can't leave her behind." Chris crinkled his brow. "You don't want her?"

"What? No. I was gonna tell you I think that's a good idea. I'd like that."

"Whew," Chris said in relief. "Good. 'Cause I already told her about Pap. If you are alright with me bringing her home, what is it? You have that look on your face."

"That look?"

"Yeah, you can't hide things Mick. Really, Mom even said so. Said your face reads like a book."

"What are you reading, Chris?"

"Worry." Chris gasped. "Oh, no!"

"Oh no what?"

"My friend, Jake. It's my friend Jake, isn't it? He died?"

"What? Who's Jake?"

"The boy that came with us," Chris said. "You're here to tell me about him 'cause he got sick last night and Doc is keeping him at the clinic."

"I don't know about Jake, but I wanna talk to you. Walk with me over there." Mick pointed to a bench.

"Okay." Chris lifted Emmie and carried her with him to the bench.

"That's pretty cool, Chris," Mick said. "I'm awfully proud of you right now."

"Someone is dying."

Mick winced. "Why are you talking like that?"

"Because I know that look. That look scares me."

"You're also pretty perceptive. But I'm not here to tell you about anyone dying. I wanna talk to you on a grown-up level."

"I can handle that, Mick, I drove a car."

Mick put his hand on the back of Chris' head. "That you did, and you even managed to hit a man without killing him." He cleared his throat. "Chris, you know about the bad guys that put up the blockade right?"

"The ones in Erie?"

"Yep. I was on my way through there, and I was meeting my mom. Seems – and this all I know – it seems these guys got ahold of her first."

Chris' eyes widened. "Oh no, they got Rose?"

Mick nodded.

"Whew, thank goodness Rose is strong. Bet she took out

a couple of them bad guys. Your mom is tough."

"That she is, but as you can guess, I'm pretty worried."

"I would be too. I am," Chris said. "I'm sorry. You're gonna go get her, right Mick? You're gonna go get your mom and help her? That's what you wanna talk to me about?" he rattled. "You wanna leave to get her and that's fine. We're safe here."

"I want to get her, yes, but we don't know enough about the blockade, who all is there, what they have and how many innocent people are there. It's gonna take some planning. But we'll get her. In the meantime, there's something else."

"Whoa." Chris sat back. "What?"

"The flu that wiped out most of the world escaped accidentally from a lab. That lab was remote and it got out long before everyone caught it. Problem is, there are lots of these labs in the country, and they have more than one deadly disease. The diseases are contained and safe unless the power goes out. Then there's a chance these viruses will leak out. Birds, other animals, people moving by the buildings, all of them can catch it. This happened in one lab already."

Chris jaw dropped. "We're all gonna die from deadly viruses?"

"Not if I can help it. There will be an effort today and tomorrow where people are pairing off, going to these labs, making sure all the viruses are still in the cases and then we're gonna burn them out so they never threaten anyone again."

"You said we…"

"That's what I want to talk to you about. Five of these labs are in Maryland, on a base I know well. I want to go because I want to see for myself that these things are destroyed. For you and your brother, I have to know that they are. Especially Maryland, because there's a germ there that's worse than anything we've ever seen."

"Are you asking me for permission?" Chris asked.

"Actually, Chris, I am. You tell me you don't want me to go, I won't go. No problem."

"You want to do this?"

"I kind of have to do this."

Chris closed his mouth tight and gave a proud look. "Then you go. You won't be gone long, right?"

"I'll leave in the morning and be back before you go to sleep."

"Then you do it, so we can be even more proud of you."

Mick pulled Chris into him and kissed him.

"Then you gotta get Rose back, Mick. You have to. Emmie needs her and Rose ain't never had a daughter."

"We'll get her back. Then all of us, we head back to Lodi and live life as normally as we can."

Chris pulled back. "Say, Mick? When you told us you wanted to take us away from Lodi for a change, did you ever think it'd get this crazy?"

"Absolutely, not. I definitely got more than I bargained for."

"And a daughter."

Mick smiled, taking in the moment, holding Chris and Emmie close to him for a while.

* * *

Las Vegas, NV

The sun was barely up. Lexi stood with Bill and one of Matt's men by the car they would take on the trek to California.

Lexi was nervous. She hated to be away from Bill and it would be the first time in almost two months that she was.

"You got the suits and the extra duct tape?" Lexi asked him as she fiddled with the collar of his shirt. "I told you where you would find the lab —"

"Lexi." Bill grabbed her hand. "We went through this. I know what to do, I know where to look, and we have this under control. I promise."

"You'll be out of radio range and I don't think the cell signals will be up out there."

"Then we'll discuss everything when I get back. You have a lot here to keep your mind occupied. You have some pretty sick people who need tending to."

"It's going to be hard to concentrate, Bill. Unlike the others, *you* are going into a hot zone."

"I'll be fine."

"Please, please be careful out there. You're all I have left in this world."

"And you're all I have, too. No worries." He placed his forehead to hers.

"You two are the first warriors in the battle. You know that."

"And we'll kick ass. We'll be back tomorrow." He stepped back, grabbing her hands and bringing them to his lips. Just as he walked to the car, he halted, turned and went back to Lexi.

"What is it?"

Bill shook his head and without further words, leaned down to Lexi and kissed her. Really kissed her for the first time ever. He pulled back. "I love you."

Her lips quivered and, scared to death that she'd never see him again, she whispered that she loved him as well. She would have said it louder but her throat tensed up.

She stood there watching as they got in the car and pulled away. It was much more than going off to clean the lab. It wasn't the old world where they could stop for gas, call for help if they needed it.

The world had transformed and it wasn't for the better.

Hopefully, sealing the labs and destroying them was one step to changing all that for the future.

* * *

Lodi, OH

Henry looked at his watch. He couldn't wait any longer. Nelson had an explosives expert from the Ohio National Guard come into Lodi and prepare for the trip with Ethan. Lars was nowhere to be found and the Kent trip needed to be completed. It would be, of all the lab missions, the first to be taken out, even if they weren't the first to leave.

After an hour, the president finally gave his orders and the units in Texas prepared. All of them were given the same instructions.

"Remember to suit up two miles before Kent," Henry told Ethan. "Do the buddy system. Check each other's suits. Duct tape the vulnerable areas. Sleeves, legs, all that."

"Got it," Ethan nodded.

"The suits are heavy and will be awkward to move in so be careful. You got two hours in the tanks, and should be able to communicate with each other. Check for power outages, then signs of a breach, dead animals, birds, stuff like that. You may have trouble getting through the secure doors if power is on."

"If that happens we'll power down. We have this. We'll be back before dark."

"Be careful and good luck," Henry said.

"Will you watch my mom? Check on her?" Ethan asked. "I'm worried since she's only one of a few patients at the hospital and Lars never showed up."

"I'm sure she's fine, I'll check on her."

Henry wished him luck once more, then watched them walk away. He didn't want to let on that he was worried. Something had to be happening at the clinic for Lars to have stayed away. He'd missed the early morning briefing and had never answered the phone.

After the jeep had rolled off for the mission, Henry

spotted Kurt coming his way.

"You missed the send off as well," Henry said.

"Sorry, I was at the clinic, checking on the patients."

"Is Lars having problems?"

"Lars isn't there," Kurt said.

"Have you checked his home?"

Kurt nodded. "Not there either."

"For crying out loud, I hope he isn't dead or something. What about Tom, where's he?"

"I'm guessing at the store."

"This is odd." Henry started to walk.

"Where are you going?"

"To the video store. Tom runs this town, why wasn't he at the meeting? I'm telling you, something is up."

* * *

Tom looked up only briefly when the bell on his door dinged and Henry walked in. "Hey, Henry." He returned to skimming an old magazine. His stomach twitched as if he were in trouble.

"Tom." Henry walked to the counter.

"Ross didn't return that Tom Cruise film if that's what you're wondering," Tom said, keeping his eyes on the magazine.

"That's not why I'm here. Do you know where Lars is?"

"Nope."

"He didn't show at the clinic, he's not home."

"You don't say?"

"He didn't show for the meeting," Henry said. "And neither did you. It was a strategy briefing."

"Was that this morning?" Tom shook his head. "I must have slept in. Having a teenager living at the house stirred things up."

"Tom, come on. Where's Lars?"

Tom put down the magazine. He was ready to say he

didn't know, but his head dropped.

"What?"

"I can't lie. I can't. I was supposed to wait until tonight, but I can't."

"Where is he?" Henry pressed.

"About right now," Tom looked at his watch, "he's in Erie."

* * *

<u>Erie, PA</u>

He arrived at the barricade and set the bar of expectations the second he stepped from the car. "My name is Lars Rayburn. Do not point those guns at me. Get whoever it is that is in charge, they are expecting me."

The men didn't respond. They looked at him mockingly. There were only six of them and Lars made a mental note of that.

"Are we done being juvenile? I will tell you one more time, inform whomever it is that controls you people that I have arrived. I assure you that any further delay will result in more than likely some sort of vile consequence and not by my hand."

One of the men lifted his radio, asked for Lars's name again, then whispered something to the others. Within minutes a man who identified himself as Ace arrived.

Lars outwardly projected the attitude that he couldn't care less. They patted him down for weapons and opened his large duffle bag. He told Ace, "I will gladly remove all items from this bag, but I'd prefer you and your men's filthy hands not to touch or contaminate my sterile items."

Ace informed his two men to stop their search.

"Take me to Rose, then we'll talk."

"You're awfully demanding," Ace remarked.

"You have one of my friends here, you want to barter her

for me. I'd say you are the one who is demanding. Where is Rose?"

Ace huffed and waved his hand. He instructed Lars to get into the car and he drove him about four blocks into the thick of things.

Lars spotted very few civilians. Most of those who hung around sat in front of abandoned stores, drinking, smoking and talking.

Another mental note.

They pulled in front of a Breast Care medical office with an old 'Flu Aid Center' sign still posted on the front. At the door, Lars paused. "Is she here?"

"Inside, yes," Ace said, and opened the door.

"Do you have any children here that you have found?"

Ace shook his head.

"Let's try this again. There is a woman in my town who says that a band of men, not far from here, shot her and took children from her camp. Do … you … have children here?"

"I'll check on that."

"Once you do, I would like to see them." Lars walked in the door. As soon as he did, he saw Rose on an examining bed sitting in the middle of what once was a lobby of the building. He rushed toward her, setting down his bag next to her.

"Rose."

She managed a gasp. "Lars! Lars, what are you doing here? I told you not to come!"

"And when do I listen to anyone?" He gripped her hand and turned his head to Ace. "She's not going anywhere and neither am I. Can we have privacy please? I'd like to examine her."

Ace gave them a disgruntled look, but he complied and left the room.

Rose leaned her head forward. "You should have stayed back, Lars. It's bad here. These men aren't good."

"I kind of figured that." He stood upright. "My

goodness, Rose. What kind of mess have you gotten yourself into?" He pulled down the sheet and looked at the seeping bandages. "Who did the bandages?"

"I did, and a young girl named Lola."

"They're still seeping."

"It's bad."

"Oh, you're probably exaggerating. I know you." He slowly removed the bandage from her side and drew a sharp breath. The wound was still open and he could clearly see the broken rib as it partially protruded. It seeped a yellowish pus and around it, her whole body was black from retained blood and bruising. He tried, with everything he had he tried not to show a facial reaction, but Lars failed.

"Lars?"

"I'm not gonna lie to you, Rose, this … this is bad." Lars had known Rose for many years. He knew her as a tough woman who could handle anything. It was apparent she was handling her injuries valiantly. What threw Lars for a loop was when Rose nodded and then began to sob.

"Rose?" Lars dropped to one knee to be close to her, face to face. He grabbed her hand again.

"I'm never gonna see my son again. I'm never gonna see my grandbabies am I?"

"Rose …"

"I'm sorry," she sobbed. "I'm sorry, nothing scares me more than never seeing them again."

"That's not gonna happen, Rose." Lars stood up straight. "That's why I came. If I have anything to do with it, you'll be driving us all crazy again in Lodi, including teaching them boys to have the same foul mouth."

"You said it was bad..."

"It is. But hey, I'm Lars Rayburn. I can fix this."

"Do *not* tell anyone I was crying. I swear to God, if you get me better and tell people, I'll fucking kill you." She wiped her eyes.

"Never. Well," Lars tilted his head, "I'll hold it over your head and use it as blackmail." He squeezed her hand firmly and spoke with seriousness. "We'll get through this, Rose. I'm here now, and I'm not leaving until you are well enough to fight your way out of this door. And you will be, you will."

Rose sniffed and nodded and Lars released her hand.

It was the best front Lars had ever put on in his life. He portrayed optimistic and arrogant, when Lars actually was worried and insecure about it. Her rib was so far out of place he was certain she had a punctured lung and possibly other internal injuries. Not to mention it was infected, and Rose was more than likely septic.

But Lars wasn't a quitter, he had battled worse, that was for sure.

He wasn't giving up. He couldn't.

* * *

Glenn Grove, CA

Sixteen miles before his destination, Bill spotted the first body on the road. Another mile further, there were three more. They had apparently set up camp off the side of the road. It looked to Bill as if they'd pulled over because they were ill. All three were dead, their bodies decimated by disease and decomposition.

He found their target site with relative ease. It was like following a trial. Carcasses of animals, birds and several human beings paved a pathway. Unfortunately, the laboratory was located only a few miles east of a small town.

Anyone that had survived the flu in that small town didn't survive the breach.

It was absolutely, without a doubt, a hot zone. Bill found it difficult to maneuver in the suit, worse than the one he wore when he battled the flu. Even though he never needed to wear one, it made others feel as if they were protected –

from him.

Several times he had to stop and check to see if he had torn his suit. He hadn't, but his delays ate up time. Perhaps he was just being neurotic, but it was better to be neurotic and safe than complacent and dead.

With time running out on their tanks, Bill and the other man set the C-4 explosives in the lab. They burned out what remained in the lab, the containers, the holding units and everything else, but what had already escaped into the air was too far beyond them.

It was the best they could do. They stayed until their tanks neared empty to make sure there was no flash fire that could get out of control, and then they left the town.

* * *

Damon, NY

"Jake is going to be just fine, it's just a stomach flu, that's all," Mick told Chris.

"Then why can't I see him? You don't think he has one of them viruses that escaped, do you?"

"To be honest, Doc probably thought that," Mick said, "but he doesn't now." He placed a plate of food at the table before Chris and then one before Tigger.

The table came to Tigger's nose.

"You want me to make you a booster?" Mick asked.

"I'm not a baby," Tigger said. "I drove a car."

"What?" Chris laughed. "You tried to get away." He turned to Mick. "When I hit Jonah Briggs, Tigger tried to leave me there. Good thing his pint sized body couldn't reach the pedals or see over the steering wheel or I would have been abandoned."

"I gave it my best shot," Tigger replied as he adjusted to kneel on the bench. "How come you made eggs, Mick?"

"That's what I wanted to make."

Chris sniffed the food. "Smells good. Jonah Briggs said we could have anything. There's beef in a can, you know."

"I know. I wanted eggs." Mick sat down at the table.

"You always make us eggs," Chris said with a peaceful smile. "I remember when you used to come over in the morning, get us ready for school, and make us breakfast."

"That's because your mom used to think Ho Ho's were a healthy meal."

"I got more than that," Tigger said. "You guys would leave for school and me and Mick would have a really cool lunch. We'd go to Medina a lot for lunch."

"No way, that's cheating." Chris said. "Wasn't that cheating, Mick?"

"Spoiling is more like it. Besides, your mom hated to cook."

Chris paused with his fork to his mouth. "I miss her. I miss her and Dustin and Gram. I miss them so much, Mick."

Mick reached over and grabbed Chris' arm. "I miss them too. We will for a very long time."

"Do you think about them a lot?"

"Every day, a hundred times a day. Everything and anything makes me think of them."

"Me, too," Chris said. "One day we'll see them again, though."

"Yes. But not for a long time." Mick retracted his hand and started to eat.

Briggs' voice entered the cafeteria before he did. "We have a man in," he said. His boots squeaked as he skidded to a stop. "I'm sorry, you're eating."

Mick waved him to the table. "Join us. There's plenty, grab a plate. Food's on that counter."

"I think I will." Briggs took a look at the plates and walked to the counter to retrieve a meal. "Bacon and eggs. Nice. We had beef in a can you know."

Chris lifted his hand. "That's what I was telling him, Jonah Briggs. But he insisted on cooking a Mick meal. It's good though, don't worry, Mick can cook some eggs."

Briggs joined them at the table. "It smells great. Thank you."

"You were saying something?" Mick said. "About a man in?"

"Ah, yes," Briggs said. "I spoke to Tom." He looked at Chris. "You need to call your pap before you go to bed. He was saying that."

Chris gave a thumbs up as he ate.

"Anyhow," Briggs continued, "thought you'd want to hear the update. Tom's a bit frazzled, seems he took in a teenager named Joey and a baby that you found."

Mick sat back with a relief filled expression. "Ah, yes, Baby Doe. He must be doing well. Joey has to be the teenager that worked with him."

"Don't know," Briggs said. "He couldn't talk long, but long enough to say, 'We have a man in there'. The 'Rebels', as I like to call them, wanted to barter for your mom. Seems she was in a motorcycle accident and was hurt, but will be okay, from what Tom said, because Lars is there."

Mick dropped his fork. "My mother was in an accident?"

Briggs nodded. "I'm sorry. But this Lars is inside the rebel camp with her."

"Lars is a famous doctor," Chris said. "He's the reason most of us in Lodi beat the flu. You know Rose will be fine if he's there."

"I'm sure …" Mick faltered, " I'm sure he will take care of her." He looked at Briggs. "Lars Rayburn was the trade?"

"Yes. Tom said he'll get us the information we need about that camp. He may code it, but he'll get it to us."

"They aren't gonna let him contact us."

"He already checked in to say he was with your mom, so that's hopeful."

"That *is* very hopeful," Mick agreed. "Knowing that Lars is there makes me feel better until we can get in there. But Lars... why was he the trade?"

Chris answered that. "He's the big celebrity, Mick. You know that. Everyone wants Lars. Maybe they have a sickness that no one can cure but him."

Out of the mouths of babes, Mick thought. To Briggs he said, "Or something else."

"Exactly," Briggs said.

"What?" Chris asked. "Why are you guys looking at each other like that?"

"Sizing each other up," Tigger said knowingly.

Briggs laughed. "That kid cracks me up. The vocabulary he has."

"Wait until he swears," Chris said. "You won't be laughing then."

Mick looked at Tigger. "And we're not sizing each other up. Christ. You boys..."

"I think you two should," Chris said. "Really, think about it. It would boost morale, having wrestling come back."

"Chris," Briggs said, "I don't really think people are that concerned about it like you are."

"Not yet, but tease them with the idea," Chris said. "They'll be rallying."

"Well they aren't rallying around us, Chris," Mick said. "We're not young men. We aren't trained. We'll both have a heart attack if we attempt to wrestle."

"Aw," Chris whined. "Fine. I was looking forward to it too."

"They could arm wrestle without a heart attack," Tigger suggested. "Can't they?"

Chris' eyes grew wide. "Yeah! Can you?"

"Chris, no," Mick replied.

"Why? You scared, Mick? It's okay if you're scared of Jonah Briggs."

"I'm not scared, Chris."

"I won't ask you again, if you're scared."

"Chris," Mick snapped, "I'm not scared. God."

"Then you'll do it?" Chris asked excitedly. "Oh, come on Mick, please? For me. I need this. I'll commentate, Tigger will cheer. Please. Do this. Please!"

Briggs looked across the table to Mick, then to Chris. "If we do this, Chris, will you stop bringing it up?"

"Yeah," Chris tilted his head. "Maybe. Yes. Yes. I will."

"Mick?" Briggs asked.

Mick huffed. "Fine. Fine."

"Yes!" Chris jumped to his feet. "You two know the rules." He watched Mick lift his arm. "And Mick, it's okay if you lose, I won't think less of you."

"Chris, what the hell?" Mick snapped.

"Just saying..." Chris looked at Briggs. "And Jonah Briggs, if you lose we won't think any less of you either. All in fun. Okay?"

Briggs nodded. "I got it."

"Arms on the table." Chris instructed. "Join hands."

Mick and Briggs positioned themselves for a round of arm wrestling.

Chris stood between them. "Ready to cheer, Tig?"

"Ready!"

Chris placed his hand over the joined hands of Mick and Briggs. "On three. I'll count, raise up my hand and you two go."

"We got it, do this," Mick instructed.

Chris genuinely smiled. "One … two … three!" He lifted his hand and let the big men battle.

JOURNAL ENTRY

I had my first day of school yesterday, it was pretty cool. I didn't think I'd be so anxious to raise my hand to answer a question. There were only six of us big kids. Jake wasn't there, but they keep telling me he's fine. He looks fine. They let me see him through a window.

Gonna go to school again today. Take Tigger, get Emmie, and wait for my turn. It'll help keep my mind off of things. Mick is leaving to go to Maryland to shut down a lab that has this really deadly virus. I'm nervous for him, but I know he can do it.

He won't be around for a couple days cause I know after he gets back he is gonna want to storm the rebel camp and get back his mom.

He better. I love Rose. She is the best. It makes me sad to think that she is hurt. But at least Lars is there and Mick will get them both.

Jonah Briggs is trying to come up with an attack plan on the camp. He said not to worry, they'll get Rose and Lars out safely. I believe him.

I'm gonna go and say goodbye to Mick. I want to give him my lucky two headed coin, but I don't want him taking it to where there are deadly germs. What if a germ gets on my coin? I'll wait and give it to him when he goes and gets Rose.

I got Mick and Jonah Briggs to wrestle. Well, sort of. They arm wrestled last night. It was really cool and took a long time. Tigger was cheering, I was cheering and they both broke a sweat. Man, were they going at it,

But I promised I would never say who won. That no one would know.

And I won't. Not even here.

17. LEG OF THE JOURNEY

October 18th
Damon, NY

Mick's arms held tight to both Chris and Tigger. He didn't want to let go, but at least this time before he left, he was more than positive that they were safe. He kissed them both and stood. "Okay, go to school. I'll be back before you go to sleep."

"Be careful out there, Mick," Chris said. "It's bad."

"I think me and Doc will be fine. Besides, I get to blow something up and you know how cool that is."

Chris smiled. "You're the best, Mick. I am so glad you're the one going to do this. You know why?"

"Why?"

"Because you're the only one I trust to do this right. Now, get going and don't waste time, you have to get your mom."

"I know that." Another kiss to Chris and Mick lifted Tigger.

"Hey!" Tigger squirmed. "I'm not a baby."

"You'll always be my baby." Mick gave a quick hug and kiss to Tigger.

"Aw, man, Mick," Chris complained. "Now why'd you have to go and get all mushy like? You better get going before you lose the macho badge after your arm wrestling match with Jonah Briggs."

Doc stepped into the conversation. "We're ready to go." He pointed to the jeep. "You and uh, Jonah had an arm wrestling match?"

"Yes." Mick nodded then pointed to Chris. "Remember your promise."

"I swore," Chris said. "Ain't telling no one."

Mick flashed a grin to Doc, told him he'd meet him at the jeep and then he walked to Briggs. "Hey."

Briggs extended his hand. "You have instructions from the virus guys on what to do?"

"Yep, and my phone is charged. Hopefully, the signal extends to there and I can call them.

"Good. And we'll keep in touch as well."

"Sounds good." Mick paused. "Briggs, I know this is an easy thing. And I'm sure everything will turn out fine. But on the outside chance something happens to me, can you make sure my boys get home to the rest of their family?"

"Absolutely. And Mick, awesome show of strength last night."

Mick grimaced and grumbled 'Humph', extended his hand to Briggs and headed to the jeep. He waved once more to the boys as he opened the door.

Doc stood outside of the jeep.

"What are you waiting for?" Mick asked.

"Who won?" Doc asked.

"You will never know."

"Seriously, come on. Who won?"

Mick simply tightened his lips in a snide smile, shook his head and got in the jeep.

* * *

Erie, PA

Lars performed what he called a 'raw surgical procedure at best' on Rose. He did what he could with what he had. He set the bone, cleaned out the infection, sealed the wound, hooked her up to antibiotics and hoped for the best.

She was resting now, much easier than she had been.

The young woman named Lola stopped by and Lars asked her to keep an eye on Rose while he stepped out. He'd learned that, until his arrival, Ace had been keeping her captive in the room with Rose.

It was a brisk day; he imagined a lot of the colder air was coming from the lake. The evening before, not surprising to Lars, Ace's men had brought three children to him to examine, stating they were found while on supply runs.

That was another reason Lars left Rose. He needed to find Ace.

He walked around for a good hour; no one seemed to care or notice him. Then again, most of those in the small four block militarized section were all Ace's men. A few women, not many.

He was just at the end of the blockage, where the main road left the tourist area and headed toward a residential area and downtown, when Ace called to him.

"Where are you going?"

"Actually looking for you." Lars saw Ace emerging from the Dairy Queen. "Oh, you were having ice cream."

Ace looked behind him. "Are you always this sarcastic?"

"Yes, comes with the territory. Tell me, dear tyrant, why is the Dairy Queen so heavily guarded? Are we protecting the last of the chocolate and vanilla?"

Ace bit his lip and moved in a storming manner to Lars. "I would prefer you to stay contained to one area, please."

"I'm not a prisoner, remember? And while I prefer to be in my quaint little house in Lodi, I cannot. So since can't, I would like those three children to be sent to Lodi."

"What children?"

"The ones you brought me to examine last night."

"They are orphans."

"Really? Because one of them told me they were at a campsite and it was raided. By your men, who killed almost all of the adults and took the children. Two of the camp's survivors are in Lodi, and one of the children here gave me their names. When I send for someone to get Rose, the children leave too."

"You're really demanding."

"How is sending children where they belong demanding?" Lars asked. "They don't belong to *you*."

"I am doing a great service for this country. Building, making it strong, getting people together. Organizing."

"So burning towns, killing innocent people, kidnapping children and raping women are a good service? These are reports I get from people."

"Steps are taken. Sometimes they're right, sometimes they aren't, but they're all for a good cause," Ace argued. "Sometimes it takes strength and chaos to bring peace."

"In whose world? I believe your motive is to strike terror into everyone. For what? So you can rule the country? How absurd is that? Are you holding the city of Erie hostage as well?"

"No, actually they're grateful, things were falling apart there."

"Then allow me to check. I'm sure some may need medical attention. Someone may need help."

"They have their own doctors."

"Then why do you need me?" Lars asked.

"You have a purpose here," Ace stated, and began to walk away.

"I'm not finished speaking to you. I need to call Lodi and ask for a trusted opinion on Rose."

"Whatever." Ace tried to walk by him. "I suggest you do your job."

"And what job would that be?"

Ace didn't reply. He looked once over his shoulder then

didn't look back again.

"Asshole," Lars murmured. And since no one really paid any attention to him, before he made that call to Lodi, Lars looked around a little more.

* * *

Las Vegas, NV

Slot Machine Charlie died. Despite the new respirator and Lexi's best efforts, he passed away from respiratory distress.

He was the only one so far that had died from SARS. Matt's mother was showing signs of improvement.

Charlie had died while Lexi was in the room. She tried her best to revive him, but it didn't work. She had just finished removing the medical items from him and covering him, when Matt walked in.

"They're back," he said through his facial mask.

Lexi exhaled. "I'll be right there." Hurriedly, she exited the room. She'd make plans for his removal after she spoke to Bill. She removed her gloves, gown and mask, then washed up and raced to the elevator and finally to the lobby.

Bill wasn't there. Her heart beat steady and strong, and she feared something had happened to him.

"I'm sorry to make you rush," Matt said. "When I said they were back, I meant they were pulling into town."

Hand to her chest, Lexi gasped then raced outside. The heat blasted her. As the wind whipped and sand blew in her face she saw the car pulling up.

When it slowed and Bill stepped out, Lexi raced to him and wrapped her arms around him. They embraced as if it had been days.

"Well?" Lexi asked.

"It was a hot zone. Like we knew," Bill replied.

"And you destroyed it?"

"Yeah," Bill said. "Burned the lab."

Lexi saw the look on his face. Was it concern? Exhaustion? "Bill, what is it? It's over. That part is over."

"No." Bill shook his head. "Lex, you should have seen the animals, the deer, the people. Those were the ones killed. Yeah, we may have burned out the virus in the lab. But all those animals that pass through, the deer that people shoot to eat. We will never get all the carriers."

Lexi's eyes widened. "It's an unending battle."

"For the time being. We stopped the bleed," Bill said, "but we far from healed the wound."

* * *

Lodi, OH

Tom was on phone duty while Henry and Kurt took a rest. The reports were starting to come in. Ethan returned, giving the good news that Kent still had power and it wasn't a hot zone. It had taken some effort to get into the secured lab which had bulletproof glass and a fingerprint security system. It was, like Ethan described, Fort Knox. They shut down power, went in through the wall, and were able to breach the system.

The generators kicked on, which provided a positive atmosphere. Once they managed to get into the lab, they were able to initiate the extinguishing system. Failsafe locked and loaded. They hurriedly initialized it, left the lab and waited outside.

It worked.

They stayed until they saw the explosion in the building. It was burning, but it was in the distance.

That was good news to Tom. So far, only two labs reported a breach and were a hot zone.

Lexi Martin's words stuck with him. Her fears that they hadn't contained the viruses, and that they had broken barriers already. That whatever escaped the lab was still out there, despite the fact that they burned the labs.

However, that couldn't stop them from hitting the other labs. In fact, Tom used Lexi's own words back at her, telling her that it was better to stop the bleeding then to bleed out, and that's what they had to continue to do. Step one, stop the labs. Set two would be to deal with and prepare for the aftermath.

Plus, they had to know where there was the most danger. There were five labs left and those were in Mick's hands. He was on his way.

Tom had the sense that the immediate threat would be over, because Mick was handling it. Tom knew Mick well, and he knew that, at any cost, Mick would successfully complete a mission.

* * *

Fort Detrick, MD

Mick knew right away that something had gone wrong, but not what they expected. As instructed, they suited up and were fortunate that Briggs had biohazard suits remaining from the flu epidemic.

The gate was up; the guard booth was empty.

Mick stopped the jeep and opened the door. "Radio on," he said as he got out.

"What's wrong?" Doc asked.

"Suit is tight. I'm okay."

"Just be careful."

"I'm good." Mick, leaving the jeep door opened, walked to the guard booth. There were no signs that anyone had been there. Leaves had blown in through the open guard booth door. There was one thing Mick did notice: despite how long the booth could have been open, the video monitors inside still worked. Images flashed and changed on all but one monitor.

"They still have power in there."

"That's good right? That means this isn't a hot zone."

"Hopefully." Mick tapped the dead monitor. "Building five isn't on. At least the monitor isn't." He stepped out of the booth.

"Is there a lab in there?" Doc asked.

"There's a lab in every building. Just a matter of which one."

"You know with our luck it's the weaponry one."

"Let's not think that way." Mick slid back into the jeep and drove through the already lifted gate arm.

They were armed with C-4 devices with timers and incendiary grenades for immediate problems. The clocks on their oxygen tanks were ticking and they had a lot of ground to cover.

* * *

Lodi, OH

Tom rushed into the Lodi Diner or 'war room' as Henry and Kurt called it. They were smiling. While things weren't all that optimistic in the west, they looked better in the east.

"Phone call," Tom announced.

"Tell us that is Mick with good news," Henry said.

Tom shook his head. "Nothing from Mick yet. This is Lars. You wanna take this?"

At Henry's nod, Tom set the phone down. "Lars? We have you on speaker. Are you okay?"

"Yes. Thank you. I'm well. They're treating me well," Lars replied.

Tom exchanged quirky looks with Henry.

"I've very pleased that Erie is so productive. Residents survived and are trying hard to move on from this tragedy."

Kurt mouthed the words, *"Does he sound odd?"*

Henry nodded. "Lars, what's up?"

"Well, I have tragic news. Rose Marie is not doing well. In fact, I am going to stay but I need you to get here in a few days to take her home so she can die with her family."

Tom's hand shot to his mouth. His heart sank. "Dear God."

Lars continued. "I'm going to give you a breakdown of Rose Marie. I have her stabilized here. Unfortunately, I'm not in a hospital. I am in an old breast care center that was used for a flu station."

"Can you get her to a hospital with better equipment?"

Lars chuckled airily. "I probably couldn't move her to the McDonald's across the street, let alone any further distance. But she has to come home to die. Until then, she has issues and maybe you can come up with a solution that can save her."

"We'll try, but you are Lars Rayburn. If you can't do it, I don't know what we could do here," Henry stated. "I'm sorry about Rose."

"Yes, tragic. I'm the mad scientist, remember? This is a bit out of my realm. Do you have a pen handy to write down what is wrong?"

"Yes, yes, we do, go on," Henry said.

"Okay, well Rose Marie definitely is complaining of discomfort in the smack center of the umbilical region. There are slight problems in the epigastria region, but as you well know, vital organs are above that, so that area has to be looked at cautiously. The left and right iliac along with the hypogastria regions are inconsequential. There may be a little blockage, but I think that's an easy fix. Her injury is located in the right lumbar region. There's a breach of skin there, an opening, but a slight tightening extends up to the right hypochondria. Biggest issue is, despite the open wound on the right, her left lumbar region is troublesome and thick and with what I palpitated as a small blockage in the upper left hypochondria. Got that?"

Henry blinked several times. "I wrote down everything you said. But Lars—"

"I have to go. I have to attend to Rose Marie. See what you come up with please. She doesn't have much time."

Before Henry could ask any further questions, Lars hung up.

"What the hell?" Henry dropped the pen.

Kurt reviewed the notes. "An injury and blockage? Maybe he is speaking about a clot."

"Or constipation." Henry shook his head. "I think they have him drugged."

Tom nodded. "I agree. He was very cold about an old friend dying and he kept calling her Rose Marie when he knows damn well her middle name is not … Son of a bitch! We're dumb." He swung out his hand. "It's code!"

"What?" Henry asked.

"Code. He said he would come up with a code and he did. Bet me. He gave us information."

"Kurt," Henry said, "he may be right. Grab a map of Erie and Tom, call Commander Briggs."

* * *

Fort Detrick, MD

They had to run. With only two hours on the tanks they underestimated the time it would take to get into each sealed lab room. The first lab in the first building was a test. In four buildings, the containment rooms were sealed. A small amount of C-4 was used to blow the secure door, and when they opened the biosafety cabinet, the cylinders were filled with the virus samples. Each cylinder contained six samples, each within a metal test tube structure and each of them contained a glass vial. All unbroken, all untouched.

They wrote down the inventory, secured a timed device to the cabinet, another in the room and moved on.

They had fifteen minutes when they rushed into the final building. Not a lot of time. At the security desk, Mick saw the reason for the black monitor. The entire panel had been destroyed.

"Something is up," he said. "Someone destroyed this on purpose."

"Why?"

"I don't know." As he had in the other buildings, he checked the location of the lab and ran with Doc that way. "What's our time?"

"Thirteen minutes."

Down the final corridor and a left into the lab, Mick stopped. He groaned.

"What the hell?" Doc blurted.

The door to the lab had already been blown, just like they had done elsewhere. It lay half off the side, amidst other debris.

"The cabinet." Doc said. "It's closed."

"That's a good thing. Let's check it. This has to be where the MHS is. We haven't found it yet."

"I got a bad feeling."

"Yeah, me too. Let's do this. Hurry." Mick charged forth toward the lab door climbing over the debris. The second he entered the containment room, he swore his heart stopped.

Rip.

Not only did he tear his suit, he felt a searing pain in his leg. He halted abruptly.

"What is it?" Doc asked.

"I ripped my suit."

"Oh my God, step out. Let's repair it."

"No time. No time."

"Mick, we have to repair and disinfect."

"No time everything is going to blow." Mick paused only briefly to look at his leg. He knew it was bleeding. He flew to the cabinet and opened it. The carriage lifted. "There aren't many in here. H5N1." Mick pulled the cylinder.

"Check. Accounted for." He moved to the next. "Zaire95" Pause. "Check." He grabbed the next. "MHS." He lifted the cylinder and opened it. "Fuck!"

"No."

"Gone. All the internal cylinders are gone."

"All six?"

Mick nodded. "What's our time?"

"Where'd they go?"

"I don't know. What's our time?"

"Six minutes. Mick …the antidote. It should be marked."

"Here." Mick lifted the cylinder out and opened it. "Gone. The antidote is gone."

"So everything else is accounted for but that. I guess we didn't need to be Einstein to realize someone blasted the door for something."

"Let's set that explosive." Mick pulled forth the explosives bag and crouched down.

"With that suit of yours ripped, at least we know the room wasn't …"

Mick put the C-4 on the tank. "What?" and grabbed the timer.

"Mick," Doc whispered.

"What?" Mick placed the timer.

"Look down."

Just as Mick attached the timer, ready to set it, he glanced down. There, by his foot, was a single metal internal tube. And beside it, a broken vial.

They were wrong. The room was hot.

* * *

The explosions sounded as they drove the jeep frantically out of Fort Detrick.

Doc repeated, "Two miles, two miles then pull the fuck over. I mean it."

Two miles at top speed didn't take long, and both men

moved quickly. The red bag was ready. They sprayed each other down with disinfectant, then ripped off the suits, quickly placing them in the bag. Again, they washed with the items they had brought, secured the bag, then immediately lit it aflame.

Doc wanted to tend to Mick's wound. He scrubbed the leg until Mick cringed and vocally expressed pain. The cut wasn't big, but that wasn't Doc's concern, and he told Mick that.

Mick's suit had ripped and not only was his skin exposed, he had an open wound.

They wiped down everything that they had touched in the jeep, steering wheel gear shift, everything, refueled the tank and drove off.

They had to call in. Another few miles away, they pulled over. Mick put on a brave front, acting tough, but Doc saw right through it. Doc was scared that he himself had been exposed, and his suit never even ripped. He could only imagine the turmoil Mick was feeling. He watched him, his jaw clenched, face red, but Mick's eyes stayed forward.

* * *

"Let me make the call," Mick said, and picked up the phone. He dialed and it didn't take long for Henry to answer.

"Mick, give us good news."

"I … I wish I could." Mick cleared his throat. "Power was still on, Henry. Cabinets were secure and sealed. We took out buildings one through five and accounted for everything but the MHS."

"Was it not stored there?"

"No, it was." Mick said gravely. "It's gone. The vials and the antidote were gone."

"Oh my God."

"Henry … I … I ripped my suit going in to the final lab.

Scratched my leg."

"But the cabinets were sealed, right? You disinfected, everything was clean. It wasn't hot."

"One of the MHS vials was on the floor. Whoever took it must have dropped and broke one when they were removing the inner cylinders."

"Did you seal the suit and disinfect right away."

"No. We set the explosives."

"May I speak to Dr. Kiddi?"

Mick handed Doc the phone.

"Yeah," Doc said sadly. "We're scared right now."

Mick shot him a glance.

"As well as you should be," said Henry. "Listen to what I am going to tell you about the MHS. Keep an estimated time of exposure. When you get back, pull a blood culture from both of you and examine them. Seal the room you work in and use precautions. Check the blood, this thing is visible right away. If it is there … if it is in your blood, Mick's blood, you both have 72 hours before you become ill. You have less than two days before you must leave wherever you are, because after forty-eight hours, you are highly contagious and are walking bombs. Do you understand the severity of this?"

"Yes, sir."

"Conditions of your testing must not be compromised. If the tests come up positive, incinerate the samples, right away."

"Yes, sir."

Mick cleared his throat again. "Tell him not to tell anyone."

"Mick asked that you not tell anyone," Doc said to Henry over the phone.

"You have my word. And please, get back to me."

"Yes, sir." Doc disconnected the call, and his hand trembled as he put the phone down. "We may not have it."

"You don't have it. I do." Mick said. "I know it. I feel it in my gut."

"Let's not give up, okay? Let's get back and check."

Mick nodded. "Call Briggs, tell him we're on our way back. Make sure he doesn't tell the boys we're returning. Just have him meet us at the clinic."

Doc agreed and picked up the phone. It was going to be a long ride home.

* * *

Lodi, OH

There was heavy silence in the room after Henry informed Kurt of what he was told on the phone call. Kurt had to know. He knew the virus almost as well as Lars. He protested it when he learned of it.

Even though Henry promised not to tell anyone, he had to inform Kurt because Kurt was right there.

"What will happen to them if they have it?" Henry asked. "I know they'll get internal—"

Kurt held up his hand and shook his head. "This makes me sick. It makes me physically ill to even think of it. Our flu will look like a picnic. The only saving grace is that this thing is fast. Two days. High fever, a burning rash, but the rash is like an iceberg, nothing compared to what will happen underneath the skin. Cold symptoms, stomach flu symptoms."

"Maybe they don't—"

"Do you remember how many scientists and techs died of this thing, just from touching a contaminated surface? Hopefully, they will be spared."

Henry lifted the phone.

"Who are you calling?"

"MHS is missing." He dialed. "I'm calling Lars." A few seconds passed and Henry requested with emotionless authority, "I need to speak to Lars Rayburn." Pause. "Do not give me that. He called for my help. I am calling back." His voice raised. "Let me speak to Dr. Rayburn. Now!" His eyes closed and he waited. After a few moments, he said, "Lars."

"Ah, good to hear from you," Lars said. "My roommate the guard was none too eager to put me on the phone. Did you come up with a diagnosis for Rose Marie?"

"Lars, we did. But that's not why I'm calling." Henry sighed. "It's gone, Lars. The MHS is gone. Someone took it."

* * *

Erie, PA

"Where is it!" Lars raged at Ace. After his phone call he had stormed past the guard and screamed Ace's name in the street until the leader arrived and pulled him aside.

"What are you screaming about?"

"Where is it?" Lars asked again. "You know what I am talking about."

"Actually, I don't."

"Let's try this again. You were with Homeland Security, you know if it, you know the location, you are the logical culprit. Where is the MHS?"

"I don't have that."

"The hell you don't and you show me where it is."

Ace laughed. "If I did have it, why would I show you where I'm keeping it?"

"Because you brought me here for it. I'm not here to be a doctor, I'm here for the MHS. Isn't that right? Now if you have it, you damn well better show me where you have it. Because if you are going to keep us all, all of us around the world's most deadly germ, I need to make sure it is secure! Your little 'dominate the world' plan will go out that window if that germ stands an inkling of escape. Now, I'll ask again. Where… is …it?"

* * *

"I should have known," Lars said, smacking his head. Something was up with the Diary Queen, it drew too much attention and had two guards on the building.

It was empty as Lars followed Ace across the small store and to the back. "How ironic. A place that symbolized something so sweet holds something so bitter and deadly."

Ace said nothing. He unlocked a door and left it open for Lars, and stepped into the room.

Lars followed. "You're keeping it in the basement of Dairy Queen?"

"I'm keeping it safe and secure and you'll see that." Ace led him across the empty basement and to a single silver door.

It was apparent it was a walk in cooler.

"This door is air tight," Ace said as he opened it.

"Do you just have the virus perched on a shelf next to old produce?"

"Don't be ridiculous."

"Me? You have a deadly virus down here and you call *me* ridiculous?" He stepped inside.

"Pull the door closed," Ace instructed. "We won't be locked in."

The freezer was emptied except for a single, small stand up freezer placed in the center of the room. Ace placed his hand on the lid. "They're in here."

Lars walked to the case and hesitated in his reach for the lid.

"Go on, check to see if they're safe. I assure you they are," Ace said. "They aren't just glass tubes. The vials are inside metal tubes as well."

"The antidote?"

"There as well. Look for yourself."

Lars lifted the lid. The stand up freezer had a shelf inside, and placed on it were five metal tubes and five vials. "There should be more."

"There should be," Ace replied. "That's why you're here. I need you to make more antidote."

Lars laughed. "How would I have the means to do that?"

"I'm working on that."

"We're not even sure the antidote works."

"It does," Ace said. "I know for a fact. I was pulling the vials and I dropped one of the metal cases. When I went to retrieve it, I notice the top had broken and the vial inside had smashed. I was exposed. I immediately took the antidote. As you can see, it worked."

"How unfortunate." Lars shut the lid to the freezer. "This is insane. You realize that, right? Destroy this now."

Ace shook his head. "I won't do that."

"Do you honestly plan on using that?"

"If I have to, yes." Ace nodded. 'How do we know what's out there, on the other side of our borders? Outside our country? We don't."

"I can almost assure you, it isn't people waiting to start a war or kill us. Not now and not for a long time. My God, an influenza pandemic has decimated our world. Billions are dead. Our country, *this* country, is struggling to hold on to what life remains, and you want to possibly use a weapon that can kill off what remains of this country or a good part of it."

"No, Lars. I don't want to use the weapon to kill off this country," Ace said. "I want to use the weapon to control it." He walked to the door and opened it. "Let's go."

"You're insane. Completely and utterly insane."

"Actually, I think I'm pretty smart." Ace motioned his hand for Lars to walk out. "I mean, it takes smart man to think of this as a means to get what he wants."

"No it doesn't. It takes a cold blooded killer to even conceive the idea." Lars walked past him.

* * *

Damon, NY

They made it back faster than they took to get there, but once they got to the hospital and settled into the quarantine area near the Ebola patients, time dragged.

It seemed as if it took hours, when actually it was only a little over one.

Mick sat in the hall, his elbows to his knees, face buried in his hands. All he could think about were his boys. He thought for the longest time about their lives and how it was possible he would never see them grow up. He was angry; it was never his intention to cause them any more pain. All he wanted to do was ensure they had a future, one without the threat of a deadly virus wiping them out again. At least one controlled by man.

Briggs showed up shortly after Doc had drawn Mick's blood. At first he bolted down the hall with childlike enthusiasm, sputtering off about how Lars gave them vital information on how to infiltrate the camp. He was proud of how easily he deciphered the message. And then Briggs finally noticed where they were and put two and two together.

They talked the entire time they waited on Doc.

"And you're sure?" Briggs asked.

"Positive. We need to infiltrate that camp, with minimal loss of life to civilians, take out his entourage and get that germ. Top priority. That's what needs to be done and I know my part."

"But—"

"No buts. If you were me, what would you do?"

"I don't know, Mick. I don't know if I'd give up hope."

"With this thing? Is there any hope?" Mick asked. "No. I don't want my boys to know if I'm sick, I don't want them to even think I'm sick."

"But you never know what can happen. You don't. Look,

we had people who should have died of the flu, they didn't. Miracles happen."

Mick chuckled. "Why does that sound so odd coming from you?"

"You don't know me," Briggs said. "Get to know me. You'll see. Rethink—"

"No." Mick grunted and stood. "God. This wasn't supposed to happen. None of this. Why didn't I just listen and stay home with the boys? Why did I decide to take this stupid road trip?"

"To save them. To save your town."

"What do you mean?"

"Maybe it was psychic. Maybe it was fate. God's intervention. Who knows? But had you not taken the road trip, you would have not known what was out here. How do you know Lodi isn't supposed to be the recipient of the missing virus? You could have been sitting ducks and anything could have happened to your town. Why? Because you believed that all was good in the world, you never would have seen the bad coming."

"You're reaching."

"I'm trying to be reasonable," Briggs said. "And we still don't know."

At that second the door opened and Doc stepped out looking tired and worn. His face was drawn.

As soon as Mick saw him, he knew. He exhaled and closed his eyes.

"I t-took a while," Doc stuttered, "because I had to incinerate the ..." He cleared his throat. "Mick ... Mick, I'm sorry."

An ache seeped from Mick and he dropped to the chair.

Briggs asked. "And you Doc?"

"I'm good. It's only strong in Mick's blood."

"Double check," Briggs instructed.

"I did."

"Then check again."

Mick stood. "No. We knew. We both did. It was Doc we were unsure of. Briggs, I was exposed. I was cut and I stood inches from the broken vial. I knew." He slowly turned and began to walk.

"Mick?" Briggs called. "Where are you going?"

"The way I see it, I have three days tops until I am sick. Two days until I'm contagious. I'm not gonna gamble. Mick dropped his voice to near whisper. "So I don't want to take a chance on infecting my sons. That means I have just a little bit of time left with them. Make the plans for tomorrow, Briggs. Tonight … tonight I just want to hold my kids. I'm gonna absorb every moment left that I can." Again he turned, only this time, Mick didn't look back. He kept walking, strong and tall even though, emotionally, he was torn up inside.

* * *

"Our scouts told us that the first blockade is set up on 90 just before Wattsburg Road," Briggs said, pointing to a map as he stood that night with twenty men in the room. "You gentlemen will be in charge of your own squad and we are storming this town, but we have to do so with caution. 90 is the first blockade. I believe that is what Dr. Rayburn is calling the left lumbar region. The right lumbar region, I am placing here at the 79 and 80 interchange. Sgt. Nelson will handle that, along with the right hypochondria areas." He saw Jon raise his hand. "Yes, Jon?"

"The iliac regions and hypogastria regions? Are we joining forces with Nelson?"

"Negative," Briggs said. "Sgt. Hems will take out five squads at first light and plan a southern trip coming up fifteen miles to meet those regions. Our entrance is here." He pointed west of Erie. "This is what I believe to be the tight left hypochondria. Three quarters of a mile is McDonald's, that's where Mrs. Owens and Dr. Rayburn are. That's where

I believe the bulk of the troops are. This main center of town, north, has to be the vital organs. I'll move with my men to the lower left lumbar region. Mick Owens and an elite squad will infiltrate the left hypochondria taking out the men there. Mick will enter the camp, radio us when he is in and unseen, and then we synchronize an attack, unless of course there is trouble."

Jon nodded. "Wait — if Mick is that vital, where is he?"

Briggs lowered his head. "He knows what he needs to do. And I believe he has a more important place to be right now." He exhaled and returned to the map, but Mick and the boys were never far from his mind.

* * *

Mick stood in the door of the room, watching the boys. They didn't even know he was there. Chris argued with Tigger over a game, so reminiscent of the arguments Chris used to have with Dustin.

"Are not," Chris said to Dustin.

"Are too."

"Are not."

"What the heck is wrong with you?" Dustin asked. "They aren't gonna do something like that."

"Are too. Gonna build a super highway right on top of Lodi, and we're gonna be able to look up and see it. Cars will be going by all hours of the day and night."

"Are not. Mick's the chief of police; he would never let them do that to our town. He would sign a petition, he would fight it. He wouldn't let them build a highway over Lodi." Dustin paused. "Or would you, Mick?"

"No." Mick grumbled. "And it's bullshit. Where did you hear this from?"

Both boys at that second pointed to Dylan.

"That's what I heard," their mom said. "All the talk down at Connie's beauty shop."

"Well, keep the talk at the shop and don't get these boys started. It'll get them started on their back and forth and it drives me nuts."

What Mick wouldn't give for one more moment of Chris and Dustin fighting, Dylan being the catalyst, and Dustin standing up for Mick then tearing him down. All that was gone and life was far from done changing for Chris.

* * *

"Mick's back!" Tigger exclaimed.

"Hey, Mick!" Chris rushed to him. "Did you get the germ? Are we good now?"

Mick sniffed.

"Oh, no, you didn't," Chris said.

"No, no we got it. We're good." Mick winked.

"We waited up for you to eat," Chris informed him. "I made sliced beef in a can. Not that your eggs weren't all that good, they were, you know, but I wanted sliced beef in a can."

Tigger argued. "Maybe Mick hates sliced beef in a can."

"Oh, Mick eats everything. He don't hate sliced beef in a can. Do you, Mick?"

Mick's heart thumped in his chest so hard he swore he heard it. "I eat everything."

"You okay, Mick?" Chris asked.

"I'm just tired from the trip and want to spend some time with you guys before tomorrow."

"That the big day?" Chris asked, enthused. "Are you gonna go get your mom?"

"I am." Mick nodded, then exhaled. "Let's eat, I'm hungry."

Chris jumped excitedly. "You're gonna eat my cooking now. Hope you don't get sick. Come on, it's in the cafeteria." He grabbed Tigger's hand and they ran by Mick.

Hope you don't get sick. Chris' words echoed in Mick's

thoughts. His entire being sank but he had to keep his spirits up, he didn't want anything to distract from every second he had left with the boys.

Mick planned on taking in every second, holding them, appreciating them and making just one more memory.

This night was the last night Mick would have with his sons and the last night, unknowingly, they would have with him.

He was going to make the best of it.

MICK'S LAST LETTER

Chris and Tigger:

It's a difficult task. Many soldiers and men and women who have sacrificed for our country have written a letter like this. This is by far the hardest letter I will ever write. It is my hope that you never have to read this. But if you do, if you get this letter, then I am no longer with you. It breaks my heart to even think about never seeing you two grow up, be men, fall in love, have children. My entire life has been spent loving you with every breath of life I take.

All I ever wanted to was to be there for you. I will always be there, watching, but not the way I want, you want or any of us need. It is the best I can do.

I am so very proud of you both. The greatest gift was the day each of you were born. My flesh and blood or not, you boys, all three of you, never will be less than my own sons.

My life has been complete. Please know that everything I have done, especially the past few months, has been for you boys. I did it without regrets.

It kills me to know that you will feel any more pain. It was not my intention, because God knows you boys have had enough pain for a lifetime.

You deserve a good life. A safe life, and one that is open to many opportunities. The world has changed since the days when I changed your diapers, took you to school, talked about space travel and wrestling. The days of dreaming of great things are not over, they are just different. Remember that.

Both of you boys are destined for greatness. You are remarkable young men and I know the path you choose will be good and honorable. You have it in your hearts to make this world what it needs to be, make it a better place.

This world is a new place and has changed. Please promise me it will not change you.

With all of my heart I love you. I love you more than I could write on this paper.

Be strong. Be brave. Live life for every single second. It's too short.

Again, I am proud and I love you.

Mick

18. FINAL BATTLE

October 19th
Damon, NY

Forty men left at dawn. Two hundred and ten lined the streets of Damon. Every vehicle was utilized. They were determined to defeat the rebels and exterminate the threat of the virus.

Even Doc was suited up to go, he had to. They didn't doubt that there would be injuries. They expected them. The midnight scouts estimated over a hundred rebel soldiers. The plan was simple. Outnumber them, outgun them, and outsmart them with minimal casualties. Take prisoners if need be. Life was too scarce to lose any more. There was only one life that wasn't sacred and that was the life of Shane 'Ace' Drummond. For him there was no mercy, but that mercy had to be given if Mick didn't locate the virus.

"Mick," Briggs walked by him. "We're ready."

Mick nodded. He stood with the boys.

"You're scared, aren't you Mick?" Chris asked. "It's okay. Maybe scared isn't a good word."

"Yeah, I'm scared," Mick told him honestly. "Scared can be a good thing. We're going into battle, there's always a risk. You know that right?"

"Yeah," Chris waved his hand dismissively, "but it's you. You're the mighty Mick Owens. I'm not worried. And just to show you how much I have faith in you …" He reached into his pocket and handed Mick the coin. "I didn't give it to you when you went for the virus. Didn't want a virus attached to it. But this is for you."

Mick's hand closed around the coin. "Oh, God. Chris."

"What?"

Mick shook his head. "This means a lot. And just in case ... you know …" Mick hugged Chris into him. "I love you."

"I love you too, Mick."

Mick looked down to Tigger. "I know you hate it, but can I lift you up, one more time for a good hug?"

Tigger raised his arms. "I'm sure it's not gonna be the last." He wrapped his arms tight around Mick's neck.

"I love you, Tig. Be good." Mick closed his eyes, one arm holding tight to Tigger, the other wrapped around Chris. He didn't want to let go. He didn't want to walk away. But his internal clock was ticking. "I …I gotta go boys." He tried hard to keep his emotions in check. "I'm sorry."

"Why you apologizing, Mick?" Chris asked. "Gosh, don't do that. We understand. We'll see ya soon."

Mick kissed his sons one last time.

Just as he turned, Chris called out. "Hey, Mick?"

Mick looked over his shoulder.

"Remember, you got this. You're our hero, you know."

Every muscle in Mick's face tensed up and his throat closed. That was it. The last he'd hear Chris' voice, the last he'd see his boys. He lifted his hand in acknowledgment and turned around.

His guts swirled with an echoing, screaming pounding to get out with every step he took. His eyes welled and glossed with tears and his face grew red and hot. Mick was in agony. He said his last goodbye.

He wanted to look back one more time but he didn't. He couldn't. He just kept walking.

* * *

Las Vegas, NV

"I can't thank you enough," Matt told Lexi after stepping from his mother's room. "She is doing great. Both of you, I thank you."

Bill looked to Lexi then to Matt. "We need to talk, Matt."

A look of worry immediately crossed his face. "You're leaving. That's what it is, isn't it? Is there anything I can do to get you to stay?"

Lexi said, "I have no plans to leave. We have too many that are ill. But Matt, is there anything we can do to get *you* to leave?"

He produced a half smile. "Why would I leave?"

"Not just you," Lexi said."Everyone. This whole damn place."

"What? That's insane."

Bill added. "And it's insane to stay here. Eventually we can all return, but for now, it's too dangerous."

"SARS is highly contagious," Lexi said. "It's carried by animals, insects, rodents, you name it."

"But you shut the lab down," Matt said.

"Animals, birds, they all got through," Lexi explained. "I know this is your home. And you know what? Come back. It could be crazy to leave here and you could very well wait it out. But in the last two days we have had nine more cases of SARS."

"What if we all have it?" Matt asked. "We'll carry it wherever we go."

"Start packing," Bill suggested. "Isolate the sick, care for the sick. Start moving. Most incubation periods are a week to ten days. We move further east, away from the threat. Wait. Then move again, until the time frame has passed and no one is sick."

"That really sounds kind of crazy," Matt said.

"Your choice," Lexi said. "As a health professional in this

field, I recommend we all go. Bill and I will stay the course with you. We'll travel with you."

"Go where?" Matt asked. "Do you know how much we have?"

Bill nodded. "It'll be a big move. Heck, send scouts out now, look for a town, a place, one that's vacant. Staying here is not the answer."

"Do you honestly think it isn't safe?" Matt asked. "With everything you believe, is it dangerous?"

"I wouldn't say go," Lexi told him. "Your pilgrimages will eventually stop. The location of that lab will carry everything west with the wind and the animals and so forth will bring it here. So much escaped that lab. The only way to stop this thing from going any further is for all of us to leave. Leave it behind."

"Sad as it sounds," Bill interjected, "the painful truth is, the west is a biological wasteland right now and we need to leave."

* * *

12 Miles West of Erie, PA

Dylan's eyes were bright and smiling as she held on to Dustin in the picture taken on the Fourth of July.

"I'm sorry, baby," Mick whispered as he stared at the picture. "I wanted to raise the boys, I wanted to be here for them. I'm sorry. But I'll see you soon. Both of you." Mick brought his lips to the phone, looked once more, then powered it down.

The convoy had pulled over.

It was the point where Mick and Briggs parted ways. Mick's squad was ready, and before he veered off with them, he approached Briggs.

Briggs inhaled and lowered his head. "Are you sure?" he asked Mick.

"Yeah. It has to be done. Got my weapon, got the incendiary grenades. I'm ready. This is where you and I say goodbye."

"Radio when you're in and have your mother and Lars. We'll start timing the coordinated attack once you search for Ace and the weapon. Weapon first."

"I got it," Mick said. "Listen, there's something I need you do to."

"What's that?"

Mick grabbed Briggs' hand and placed the phone in it, along with the coin. "Give those to Chris. I don't want them on me any longer. Can't take a chance I'll contaminate them. And this …" He reached to his back pocket and handed Briggs the letter. "You give this to them tomorrow or the day after, okay? Not today. Not … today."

Briggs swallowed. "I will. We all owe you a debt of gratitude for this."

"Don't give me credit yet." Mick said, his voice coarse with sorrow. "When it's done, then you can say thanks." He winked and extended his hand to Briggs. "You're a good man, Jonah Briggs. Get my boys back to Lodi and then if you can, keep an eye on them for me."

"It would be my honor, Mick Owens."

Sniffing hard through his nostrils, Mick gave one last look to Briggs, locking eye contact and conveying gratitude and respect. Then Mick joined his eight man squad. Their route to battle would be on foot, and Mick led the way.

* * *

<u>Lodi, OH</u>

"It's pretty cool here, Pap. I started school again. I'm not having school today," Chris rambled fast in a conversation with Tom. 'It's like a big praying day. I think I'll join them. Tigger made a friend. Speaking of which, we're bringing two kids home with us. I know you're like the community dad now. You'll like them."

"Wow, Chris, you sound excited. Now, when do I get to see you? When you guys coming home? Any idea?"

"Oh, sure, Pap, soon. They're having, like, a war not far from Lodi. You know that, right? Bunch of bad guys taking everyone hostage. Of course you know that they have Rose. Anyhow, as soon as that's done we'll be home. When Mick comes back we leave."

"When Mick what?" Tom asked.

"Comes back. He went and fought with them, you know."

"No, I didn't," Tom said and then changed the subject, silently seething over Mick's leaving and going off to fight. Tom finished talking and said his goodbye, then he had Joey keep an eye on Doe and headed down to the war room. Not for a meeting but to vent.

Henry was there and so was Kurt. As expected, they were monitoring everything. Tom didn't say hello, he stormed in complaining.

"Did you two know?"

"Know what?" Henry asked.

"That Mick went into battle with them."

Henry looked at Kurt then back to Tom. "No, we didn't."

"Son of a bitch bastard!" Tom barked. "I don't like to swear, but this just gets my goat. He leaves them and they are on the run, he leaves again, taking a chance to go to the labs in Maryland. But darn it, leave the fighting to the others. He doesn't need to go in there. What the hell are those boys gonna do if something happens to him?" He literally growled. "Oh, wait. I am gonna kick his big ass for leaving them boys alone again. He didn't need to take them from home. When he gets back, I'm killing him."

"Tom," Henry's voice cracked. "Mick won't be coming back to Lodi."

"What do you mean?"

"We didn't know he went," Kurt explained, "but it makes sense. This is all more than likely a suicide mission for Mick."

"What? Why is he going if it's a suicide mission?" Tom asked.

"Mick's dying, Tom," Henry answered. "There was a breach in Maryland, his suit ripped and he was exposed. No one knows. The boys don't know. Mick's infected with the superbug. I think he's probably doing this so the boys won't see him get sick."

"Oh my God." Tom dropped to a chair and his whole being sank. "Can't you fix this? Can't you help him?"

Kurt shook his head. "Not with this, no. I'm sorry."

Tom's hands shot immediately to his face. As angry as he was, that was how quickly he became sad. Tom was devastated. He didn't know what to say or if he even could speak.

It was Mick. *Mick.* It couldn't be. It wasn't fair. He had known Mick his entire life. To Tom, he was losing yet another child.

* * *

Erie, PA

According to the scout report, four men were posted at the northwest blockade. When Mick arrived there were six men and four trucks were horizontally parked, blocking the road. Ten yards from that blockade, Mick and his eight men took positions. They all, including Mick, had crossbows.

No guns. No gunfire. A silent hit.

"Again, repeating," Mick whispered, "on my call fire. Then we charge. We don't want to give them time to radio for help or pull their guns. Disarm them, detain them, kill them if they are a threat. Then you and you ..." he pointed to two men, "will go in with me. You two will head north toward the city. I'm heading to the southern tip where we think the hostages are located. I need two more of you to stay at this blockade, and the rest will meet up with Briggs. Got that?" He got their agreement. "Be accurate, gentlemen and be careful. Engage weapons."

They knelt in a line and all of them set their crossbows.

"Take your target." Mick called quietly. "On my call. One … two … fire."

There was a synchronized line of clicks followed by a single whistle sound as the arrows sailed through the air fast and furious.

Quietly, the nine arrows hit five of the men in deadly areas, the sixth took a shot to his leg and dropped forward.

"Charge!" Mick ordered and they all raced forward. Except Mick. He reloaded, aimed, and shot at the sixth man, taking him out.

He motioned to the two men to go in with him and as Mick crossed the barricade, he noticed one man reaching for his rifle. Mick kicked the weapon, bent down, covered the man's mouth, and ripped the arrow from his chest. The arrow pulled ligaments and blood flowed upward in a rush. Quickly, Mick shifted and stabbed the man in the throat.

At that point, he didn't have time to think 'humanity' and Mick charged through the barricade.

It was quiet. No one was around. The sneak attack had sounded no alarms and Mick waved his hand for the two men to go on.

"I'm in," Mick whispered into the radio as he ran. "All good. Six down. No one the wiser."

"We'll wait. Let us know when you get a position."

"Actually," Mick spotted the golden arches, "quarter mile. I think I see our fast food restaurant. Be back." Holding tight against the buildings, Mick followed the bright yellow 'M' as if it were the North Star. But staying out of sight was increasingly difficult as the buildings and businesses were further and further apart.

He came around a back street through a car wash and halted, his back against a wall, and peeked. Men carrying guns walked down the street. They weren't patrolling, they were walking. In fact, every man carried a weapon.

Mick pulled his radio to his mouth. "Don't respond, just listen. We have hostiles up and down the main street. They are armed but not in any ready position." Mick's eyes shifted to the blue sign above his head on the building. It read: 'Patient Parking only,'. "I think I found it. Hang tight."

He inched his way forward. Would the men even notice him? No one seemed to pay any attention to what was going on. As he hit the main sidewalk, he looked to his right and up.

It was the Breast Care Center.

Waiting until he had a clear shot, Mick darted from the side of the building and raced as fast as he could to the door. Revolver raised, he blasted through the door holding out his weapon.

The door closed on its own at the same time Mick saw Lars.

Lars spun around. "Mick!" He grinned.

"Michael?" Rose swung her legs from the cot.

"Mom!" Mick rushed to her. "Oh God."

Rose weakly got to her feet. Her legs wobbled but Mick grabbed on to her.

"Mick." She placed her hands to his face. "Thank you. I knew you'd be the one to get us." She kissed him over and over.

Mick smiled. "I've seen you look better though. Lars, how is she?"

"She's been better, but she'll heal." Lars stepped to him. "Mick, what is happening?"

"Hold on." Mick lifted his radio. "Briggs, found the hostages. Give me three minutes."

"Roger that," Briggs responded. "Let me know when you have it."

"Roger. Out." Mick clipped his radio. "Lars, listen to me. Take my mom out the back. Make a left, follow that street for a block then take a right. It'll bring you to the Left Hypochondria."

"I know exactly where that is."

"I know you do. You did great giving us intel. We own that now. Our men are there, Take my mother."

Rose asked, "What about you?"

Mick moistened his lips. "I don't have time to go with you. There something in this town I need to find. Find it, take it and destroy it."

Lars asked. "Are you talking about the MHS?"

Mick nodded.

"I know exactly where it is. It's at the Diary Queen a block and half down the road. In the basement, inside a stand up freezer. Be careful."

Mick's head tossed back with a grateful nod. "Thank you. Okay, get my mom out of here. We're running out of time and an attack is gonna happen any minute. It will no longer be safe for you."

"Then you'll meet us. Right?" Rose asked.

Mick took his mother's hands. "Mom, that's not gonna happen. You need to know how much I love you and how much you have been a great mother. Please watch the boys."

"Michael?"

"Mick?" Lars asked. "What's going on?"

"Lars, go," Mick said firmly. He struggled to pull his hands from Rose.

"No. No," Rose shook her head. "You are my son. What are you doing?"

"Yes, Mick, what *are* you doing?" Lars asked.

"Lars, go,"

"No!" Lars yelled. "Not until you tell me what is up."

"I have the virus!" Mick snapped. "My suit ripped. The room was hot. I have it. Confirmed. In less than 8 hours I'll probably be highly contagious. I can't let the boys know, I can't let them see me die like that. I won't be able to touch them, hold them. So …this is my last stand." He looked at Rose. "I'm sorry."

"No," she wept. "You're my son. My son. I'm going to stay with you. I don't care about the virus. I don't."

"I do," Mick said passionately. "I care about you and I care about those boys. They need you."

"What are you going to do, Mick?" Lars asked in irritation. "Take care of the heroics and when that is done, go off to the woods and die like a sick dog?"

"If I have to, yes. Or …" Mick touched the grenades strapped to his belt, "go out in a blaze of glory."

"You can't do that," Lars argued.

"What choice do I have!" Mick blasted.

"You can't be serious?" Lars said. "You stand before me and ask that. Let me help."

"You are the great Lars Rayburn, but not even you can beat this."

"How do you know!" Lars yelled. "How? Give me a chance at this, Mick. This is what I do. Get the antidote. It's with the virus."

"It needs to be taken within two hours you know that."

"But it's something for me to work with," Lars said. "It's a base to start with. The virus is heat resistant and I'll stick you in a sauna if I have to slow it and buy us time, but for God's sake don't do this. Don't give up. Let me try. For those boys, your mother. For all of us," he pleaded, "Please, Mick, let me try."

Before Mick could reply, gunfire rang out in the distance. "Fuck. We're too late. Battle started. Go. Go! Get her out."

Lars took hold of Rose. "What are you going to do?"

Mick closed his mouth tightly, leaned to his mother, kissed her and stepped back. "First thing's first. I get the MHS." He pointed outward and shouted. "Go!" and she flew through the door and out to the street.

He emerged unnoticed onto the street. Men and women

with weapons rushed toward the other end of the street. Mick could only guess they were headed to the front lines. He blended in so much no one noticed he was the opposing force.

"Wrong way!" someone yelled at Mick. "The fighting is that way."

"Gonna check the other barricade!" Mick replied as he ran.

The Dairy Queen. He saw it. Picking up the pace, Mick charged to the former ice cream store and inside. The door clanked as he slammed though it and it echoed in the hollow empty store. The basement door wouldn't be in the main dining area, so Mick hurried to the back hall. It wasn't there, then he turned to the kitchen.

He spotted the door and saw it was open. He ran down the stairs and the single metal freezer door was directly in the scope of his vision. That too was open.

He pulled his revolver and quietly made his way to the door. Back against the unit, he peeked in. A man was in the standalone cooler. After a long blink and knowing that it had to be Ace, Mick rolled shoulder first with a step into the freezer and shut the door. "Hold it."

The gray haired man peered over his shoulder with the snidest of looks. "Son, I don't think you have a clue what I'm holding."

"Oh, I know what you're holding," Mick said, eyeing the pouch.

Ace shut the lid to the cooler. "Step aside."

"I don't think you realize I'm holding the gun. Hand me the pouch." Mick held a steady aim.

Ace held out the pouch, but with a grin, retracted it and showed a vial. "Step aside, big man." He inched around Mick toward the main freezer door.

"Or what?" Mick laughed. "You're gonna pop that cap? I have news for you. You broke a vial at Fort Detrick. I got the virus, so expose me, go on, I'm already a dead man. But you aren't getting away with that. On my life I promise you, you will not leave this room with the virus."

Ace made his way to the door. "Go on, shoot me. This vial drops and you won't get it in time before it breaks. That means, you open this door for more than three seconds, you stand a chance of exposing everyone around this building. The second they step in they're dead. Just like you."

"You drop that vial, you expose your men and yourself."

"I got the antidote, I'm not an asshole. And listen to it up there." Ace raised his head to the gunfire. "I'm pretty sure that's not my men doing all the shooting. They'll be more men out there." He put the strap of the pouch over his shoulder.

"You honestly think I'm letting you walk out the door?"

"Actually, I think you are. I'm holding the weapon. My men, your men. You don't want them exposed. Do you?" He reached behind him for the door. "Three seconds. I'm using them now." His exposed hand opened and the vial dropped, smashing to the floor.

There was zero hesitation and the split second that the vial broke, Mick fired a single shot, directly to his head and Ace flew back against the door, dropping before it and right by the virus.

Quickly, Mick stepped to Ace, grabbed the pouch, used his foot and rolled Ace's body over the vial. He opened the pouch and looked inside. Four metal tubes and five bottles which Mick could only figure were the antidote doses.

Even though he had what he came for, the walk in freezer was quickly becoming a viral bomb.

Mick looked at the door, then looked at the incendiary grenades on his belt.

* * *

Lars and Rose had made it almost to the destination, though they had to move slowly. Rose could barely walk.

Lola had run to them, but Lars urged her to keep going, to leave. They'd get there.

He crossed the street with Rose, and before he could register a man pointing a gun at them, a bullet sailed into the man and he dropped. Lars looked for the shooter, and a soldier flew around the corner. He aimed, lowered his weapon and used it to point in a direction. "Almost free, keep going. Watch your backs," he told them.

After just one more step into the street, an explosion rang out. It wasn't loud, it didn't rock the ground, but it stood out amongst the firing.

Lars knew. He turned to look and another explosion occurred. This one sent flames shooting upward and not far from them.

The direction of the fire told him all he needed to know. Rose nearly collapsed and with a heart wrenching sob, her knees buckled and it took everything Lars had to hold her up. She rolled into his embrace and Lars lowered his head with saddened eyes and whispered, "Mick."

19. COMING HOME

THREE DAYS LATER
October 22nd

"They're back!" Jake screamed into the schoolhouse church."They're coming up the main roadway!"

Chris dropped his pencil and even Mary stood.

"Hold up everyone." She walked slowly and focused from around the desk. Chris heard her squeak out a moaning scream and he saw Doc walking in alone.

"Fai," she rushed by Chris and the kids to Doc. "Oh, God. I thought when you didn't call that—"

"No, we're good. We're good," he said. "We were successful. It took two days. We have to go back, " his head lowered. "We had losses. We did."

"I'm sorry," Mary said.

Chris wasn't waiting for permission. After hearing Doc, he flew from the church, out the door and down the steps.

The convoy of cars had pulled on to the street and he saw the first vehicle. Faster than he believed he had ever run in his life, he raced to the cars.

He saw Jonah Briggs step from the first vehicle and walk around the front. He spotted Chris and they made eye contact.

Where was Mick? Chris looked about, he didn't see him. He had to be in the back. He hurried to Briggs.

"Jonah!" Chris ran up to him.

"Chris," Jonah said softly. "Where is your brother?"

"Oh, he's in the playroom. I didn't even think about getting him."

"Let's … let's go find your brother."

Chris felt Briggs' hand on his back and he froze. "Where's Mick, Jonah?"

"Chris …"

Chris looked around. "He's here, right? Mick's somewhere. Is he lagging behind? What?"

"Chris." Briggs cleared his throat. "Listen to me. Let's find Tigger." He reached for Chris.

"No." Chris pushed his hand away. His body trembled and with desperation he looked around. Somewhere, in all the men, Mick had to be there. "Where is Mick? Where's my father?"

Briggs stared at him.

"No." Chris shook his head, his words shook, and his insides cramped up in pain. "No. Not Mick, please, not Mick." Eyes filling with tears, Chris eked out the words. "Please, not Mick. Please." Sobbing, he stepped into Briggs. "Not Mick."

Briggs wrapped his arms around Chris. "We need to talk, Chris."

Chris lifted his head. He could barely breathe. "Where is he, Jonah? Where's Mick?"

Briggs pulled him back into the embrace.

20. LOST CAUSE

October 24th
Cleveland, OH

"Oh, stop it. It's not that bad." Lars spoke with irritation, wiping the sweat from his brow. "You think this is a picnic for me?" he walked over to the bed. "Every time I step in this room, I'm reminded of the tropics. Oh, by the way, no trace at all of MHS in Erie. So that was a positive." He reached down to touch the arm.

Mick cringed in pain. "Every time you touch me, I swear to God, you do it on purpose 'cause you know it hurts."

Lars smiled.

Mick was only covered by a sheet. His body was red and a rash covered his chest and arms. He groaned again. "I thought I should be dead by now."

"You should have been. Apparently you are not," Lars said. "Temperature is still high. Fluid in the lungs, but the rash hasn't begun to bubble or pus, so that's a good sign. It's definitely slowed down. Who would have known that half-brained theory of mine about baking you would have worked? Certainly not me."

"This is the worst I have ever felt in my life."

"And you are by far the worst patient I have ever had."

"Why didn't you let me die?"

"Same reason you didn't blow yourself up. You didn't

want to die, and I didn't want you to die. Although, baking myself every time I come in here makes me moody."

"You're not the one that's sick."

Lars sighed. "No, I am not. The antidote worked on me. And I am developing antibodies, Mick, so hang tight." He tapped Mick's arm.

Mick screamed.

"God, you're such a baby." Lars stepped back. "I have to be away from home, I wish this could be more tolerable for both of us. Now I have to get back to the lab." He walked to the door. "Do you need anything?"

"No." Mick shook his head.

"Make sure you respond back to the message from Chris," Lars told him. "I know your fingers are swollen and hurt, but he knew it was me writing it the last time because I used punctuation."

"I'll call him instead."

Lars reached for the door. "Just try not to do that Mick moaning and groaning thing, the boy is worried enough."

Mick grunted. "Lars?"

"Yeah?"

"Be honest. How are we doing with all this? Was it worth it?"

"Absolutely, Mick. I'll be one hundred percent honest with you. You still are not out of the woods and we may yet lose you, but damned if we both aren't fighters. Plus, we're getting close. We are getting so close."

Lars took another look at Mick, who had suffered through an illness that should have killed him days earlier. It was a tough road, and Lars wasn't the most confident, but he was determined.

Whether his efforts would work remained to be seen and only time would tell.

21. MOVING FORWARD

Fifteen Years Later
Erie, PA

Jonah Briggs paused in his walking the stairs. His knees hurt. When they went bad, he didn't know. He was able to get some fishing in earlier, the weather was nice, but it was back to work. Things weren't too bad. Biggest problem was with the wheat crops and some of the manufacturing.

He returned to his office a few minutes earlier, carrying a box.

"Tigger, damn it," Briggs said as he opened his office door. "Get out from behind my desk."

"Really?" Tigger slid from the chair. "No, 'hey how are you'? How was Virginia? Glad to see you back?"

"You called every day. Everything okay?"

Tigger was in uniform. A tailor made uniform to fit his size. He was proportionate but still small. He had never really grown much through the years. "Yeah, good. Just like Farmer Joe said."

"Farmer who?" Briggs set the box on his desk and sat down with an exhale.

"Farmer Joe, the guy who runs the big tobacco farm."

"That's Joseph Farms."

"Same difference. Why are you grunting? You getting old?"

"Yeah, Tig. I am. I want to retire, but Wentworth won't take over."

"I can."

Briggs laughed. "Uh no. Napoleon had his reign, we don't need a repeat of history."

"Oh man, is that dig toward my size?"

"No, it's a dig toward your tyrant attitude, asshole."

Tigger laughed. "Anyhow, field is clean. They were right. Those goofy half-dressed Indian acting things were raiding the fields. Man, you'd think it was corn or weed. Which by the way—"

"No." Briggs snapped off a reply. "Don't ask again."

"Can I have a drink?" Tigger pointed to the bottle on the desk.

"Go to the bar. It's open."

"You are tough on me." Tigger shook his head.

"Someone has to be. Everyone else is scared of you. Three reports last month of you pushing your weight around."

"You reprimanded me. I took the punishment." Tigger tossed up his hands. "Anyhow, I'll go to the bar. I wanted to see Chris before he left. Can I see it before you give it to him?"

"No." Briggs replied. "And he should be here any—" He smiled at the knock. "That's him."

Chris stepped through the door. He was tall and thin, his hair wavy and short. He wore a tee shirt and jeans, not a uniform like Tigger. "Hey, Jonah Briggs."

"Chris." Briggs said in greeting with a smile.

"Tig." Chris nodded a greeting. "Thought you were in Virginia?"

"Was. Done. Back. Heading west in a few days. I'll stop home."

"Pap will be glad. He's been having some problems lately, and isn't moving around. Still goes to the store every day though."

"Is he renting the movie I made?" Tigger asked.

"Yeah. It's always rented."

"Sweet." Tigger looked at Briggs. "And you said no one would wanna see a documentary of us training."

"What else is there? Not many people make movies and they ones that do get made are bad," Briggs replied then glanced at Chris. "What's wrong with Tom?"

"Diabetes is out of control again. Lars wants to put me on working on a new form of insulin, but he knows I suck in the lab. I'm better with patients."

"He wouldn't ask if he didn't think you'd see something."

Chris shrugged. "I guess. Anyhow, what's up?"

"When we moved here years ago, I had boxes I never opened. The other day I was wanting to clean things out and look what I found. You left this in Damon." Briggs reached into the box and pulled out a notebook.

"Oh my God." Chris took it. "Oh my God. My journal."

"Thought you may want to look through it. Mick's last letter is in there too."

"Wow. Thank you."

Another knock came at the open door and Mick called, "Hey, ready to head out?"

"Yeah," Chris replied. "What took you so long coming up?"

"Fucking steps are killing my knees."

Briggs nodded in agreement. "I hear you."

"You guys are old," Tigger said.

"What's up, Tig?" Mick motioned his head. "Haven't seen you in a few weeks. Still reigning terror?"

"Absolutely. Someone has to."

Mick shook his head. "Figures."

"Hey, Mick?" Chris with a smile, holding up the notebook. "Look what Jonah found."

"Oh, wow, that's awesome. I'd love to read it if you wanna share."

"Sure."

Briggs added, "Me, too."

"Me as well," Tigger said.

Chris grimaced at his brother and looked down at the book. "This is so cool. I was so young…" He flipped through the pages. "Oh, wow. The arm wrestling match." He looked at Mick, then Briggs. "Wait, I didn't write down who won."

Briggs asked. "You don't remember?"

Chris shook his head. "Not really. I mean, I think I do. But I changed it in my mind so many times. Tig, do you?"

"I was six. Not really." Tigger said.

"Who won?" Chris asked.

"You really don't remember?" Briggs peered at Mick, then Chris. "Mick did." He winked.

Chris looked at. "You won?"

"I thought Briggs did. Not sure."

Chris grumbled. "It'll come back to me." He tucked the notebook under his arm. "Ready." He walked around the desk to give Briggs a hug, then hugged his brother. "Get your ass home, Tig. Seriously."

"I'll be there." Tigger raised his hand.

Mick exchanged handshakes with Briggs, and he walked out with Chris, shutting the door behind them.

"Alright, I'm out of here," Tigger said. "Hitting the bar."

"Tigger," Briggs called him. "You don't miss a trick. How do you not remember who won that arm wrestling match?"

"Oh, I remember," Tigger opened the door. "Just that, two big men, two big egos. I didn't want to dredge up the pain of that night." He flashed a smile. "See ya."

Briggs laughed. Tigger drove him nuts, but for over a decade, Tigger had kept him going. He sat back in the chair, hands folded behind his head and swiveled to the window. He peered out and watched as Chris and Mick got in a car, and Tigger darted out of the building.

Things were finally on track. Some semblance of life had returned. There were problems here and there, but Briggs couldn't complain. To him, life was good.

JOURNAL ENTRY

I can't believe it has been fifteen years and five months since I have laid eyes on this journal. Reading it brought back not only memories, but feelings I had back then. The pain, the fear, everything. But I left it open, unresolved and I thought I'd fill in the blanks. Not really for me, but maybe in the years ahead, should I have children and they want to read it. 'Cause I'm pretty sure, just like the arm wrestling match, things will be pretty distorted in my memory.

After the battle and Jonah Briggs returned without Mick, I thought he was dead. Even though I was certain there was no way, no how Mick would die in battle. Not him. Jonah pulled us aside, because he didn't want others to know. He told us that Mick had that super virus and Lars was going to try to beat it.

Lars didn't know if he could or would, but he'd try. After all, it was Lars Rayburn. After about fifteen days, he declared Mick out of the woods and took him from quarantine right before we had our first Thanksgiving. Mick was pretty scarred up from the sores, all over his neck and arms, but those battle scars were worth him living. I don't know what I would have done without him. I was very proud. It was a long month. We stayed a couple weeks longer in Damon, then Pap came and got us. He said we had to get home.

Unfortunately, Rose didn't live to see the first Thanksgiving. She had a ton of complications from her accident. She got to see Mick one more time. That was good.

Despite how much I was attached to Emmie, I couldn't handle a toddler, not at fourteen. Doc and Mary asked if they could raise her and it broke my heart to tell them yes. But I did. I got to see Emmie often because they moved to Erie, which is pretty close.

Jake moved in with them as well. He's doing well. All grown and married. Has two kids last we talked.

Pap took care of Baby Doe. We called him John and he turned out pretty good. A teenager now. Ethan is prepping him to be a teacher. Pap is still kicking, man, we have good genes.

Erie took a while to clean, but it was thought to be the best location for headquarters. First summer after, Jonah Briggs moved there and was running things. Been bitching about it since. Both he and Mick bitched a lot. Despite what he always said, Mick ran Lodi, but joined forces with Jonah. They had to work together.

Before the first winter, a huge pilgrimage with close to a thousand people showed up. They were led by some guy named Matt and a former CDC doctor that Henry knew. They waited until it was safe and then they went back to conquer the west. Lexi stayed behind a couple years because her and Bill had a daughter and they didn't want to leave while she was a baby.

They're out there now. We keep in touch.

Power was able to stay up but only in pockets of the country. Close vicinity communities. A lot of small ones are in the dark and have learned to live like that. Prefer to live like that.

The internet never came back. I thought it would. One day. Tigger will probably bring it back.

Tigger. Wouldn't believe it, but man, when he turned thirteen he became a handful. Nothing that Mick did. He just got bad. Running into abandoned towns. Bringing back souvenirs. I think he was twelve the first time he got drunk. Mick kicked his ass couple times, but really how much would Mick kick Tigger's ass? He was still little. So the summer before his fourteenth birthday, Jonah Briggs offered to take Tigger in and 'work' him as he put it.

It backfired and Tigger loved it. He was the youngest soldier in Briggs' army. Started serving small stuff at fifteen and went up against the "Dins," as Tigger named them, at sixteen. He's good at taking them out. He calls them that because they are survivors who try to act like the old school Indians. They never see Tigger coming. He's the best man for the job. Tigger is fearless and I fear Tigger one day taking over for Jonah Briggs. I think Jonah has the good sense not to allow that. God help us all if he does.

Me, well, I made the grave mistake of praising Lars Rayburn for saving Mick. I told him he was my new hero and I wanted to save people like that. At the time I did, all in his glory for saving the man who was a father to me. But I was like thirteen, come on. Lars knew that had to change. Unfortunately, Lars immediately took me under his wing. I went to the Lars Rayburn School of Hard Knocks. We started with basics, stuff you learn in school, and recess was anatomy and medical stuff. Kurt and Henry started dividing their living time around all the communities. When they were in Lodi, Lars made me learn from them. I can remember Kurt telling him, "Lars come on let the kid go play." And Lars would say I can play when I'm older.

Really?

I still have yet to go out and play like I did. But I am grateful for Lars because I am reluctantly the next generation of doctors. People call me the next Lars Rayburn. I don't see it. Growing up, everyone wanted to be like Lars, not because he was this brilliant guy, but because he shook the president's hand. In our small town, that was a big thing.

Perhaps I'll be a legend as well for something other than medicine. That would be cool. Actually, I just may be. Six years ago, I achieved a big dream of mine and it wasn't being a doctor.

Like with Lars, maybe one day parents will say to their kids, "You wanna grow up to be like Chris Roberts, don't you?"

And instead of saying, 'he shook the president's hand, you know'. They'll say, 'He's the one who brought back professional wrestling.'

PERMUTED PRESS

14

BY PETER CLINES

Padlocked doors. Strange light fixtures. Mutant cockroaches. There are some odd things about Nate's new apartment. Every room in this old brownstone has a mystery. Mysteries that stretch back over a hundred years. Some of them are in plain sight. Some are behind locked doors. And all together these mysteries could mean the end of Nate and his friends. Or the end of everything...

PERMUTEDPRESS.COM

DAY BY DAY ARMAGEDDON

GREY FOX

BY J.L. BOURNE

Time is a very fluid thing, no one really has a grasp on it other than maybe how to measure it. As the maestro of the Day by Day Armageddon Universe, I have the latitude of being in control of that time. You have again stumbled upon a ticket with service through the apocalyptic wastes, but this time the train is a little bit older, a little more beat up, and maybe a little wiser.

PERMUTED PRESS

PERMUTED PRESS

THE INFECTION

BY CRAIG DiLOUIE

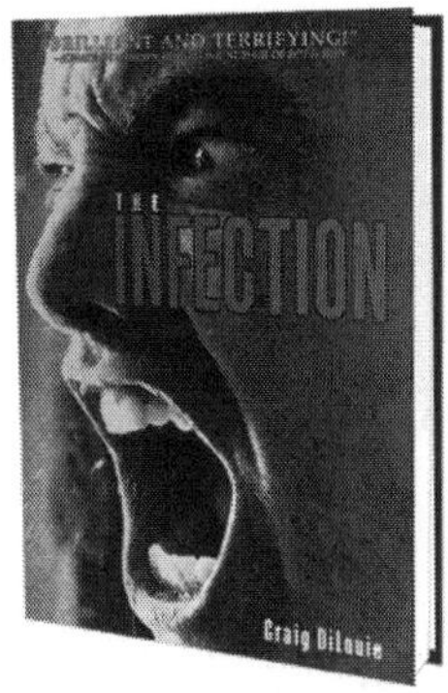

The world is rocked as one in five people collapse screaming before falling into a coma. Three days later, the Infected awake with a single purpose: spread the Infection. A small group—a cop, teacher, student, reverend—team up with a military crew to survive. But at a refugee camp what's left of the government will ask them to accept a dangerous mission back into the very heart of Infection.

PERMUTEDPRESS.COM

THE KILLING FLOOR

BY CRAIG DiLOUIE

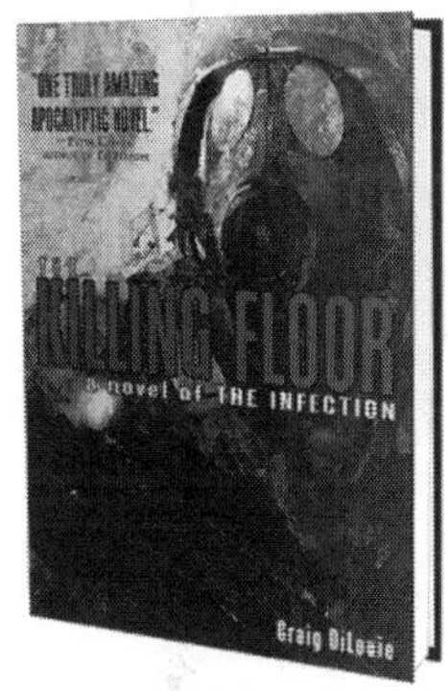

The mystery virus struck down millions. Three days later, its victims awoke with a single violent purpose: spread the Infection. Ray Young, survivor of a fight to save a refugee camp from hordes of Infected, awakes from a coma to learn he has also survived Infection. Ray is not immune. Instead, he has been transformed into a superweapon that could end the world … or save it.

PERMUTEDPRESS.COM

THE INFECTION BOX SET

BY CRAIG DiLOUIE

Two full #1 bestselling apocalyptic thrillers for one low price! Includes the full novels THE INFECTION and THE KILLING FLOOR. A mysterious virus suddenly strikes down millions. Three days later, its victims awake with a single purpose: spread the Infection. As the world lurches toward the apocalypse, some of the Infected continue to change, transforming into horrific monsters.

PERMUTED PRESS

PERMUTED PRESS

DOMAIN OF THE DEAD
BY IAIN MCKINNON

The world is dead, devoured by a plague of reanimated corpses. Barricaded inside a warehouse with dwindling food, a group of survivors faces two possible deaths: creeping starvation, or the undead outside. In their darkest hour hope appears in the form of a helicopter approaching the city... but is it the salvation the survivors have been waiting for?

PERMUTEDPRESS.COM

REMAINS OF THE DEAD
BY IAIN MCKINNON

The world is dead. Cahz and his squad of veteran soldiers are tasked with flying into abandoned cities and retrieving zombies for scientific study. Then the unbelievable happens. After years of encountering nothing but the undead, the team discovers a handful of survivors in a fortified warehouse with dwindling supplies.

PERMUTEDPRESS.COM

DEMISE OF THE LIVING
BY IAIN MCKINNON

The world is infected. The dead are reanimating and attacking the living. In a city being overrun with zombies a disparate group of strangers seek sanctuary in an office block. But for how long can the barricades hold back the undead? How long will the food last? How long before those who were bitten succumb turn? And how long before they realise the dead outside are the least of their fears?

PERMUTED PRESS

PERMUTED PRESS

ROADS LESS TRAVELED: THE PLAN
BY C. DULANEY

Ask yourself this: If the dead rise tomorrow, are you ready? Do you have a plan? Kasey, a strong-willed loner, has something she calls The Zombie Plan. But every plan has its weaknesses, and a freight train of tragedy is bearing down on Kasey and her friends. In the darkness that follows, Kasey's Plan slowly unravels: friends lost, family taken, their stronghold reduced to ashes.

PERMUTEDPRESS.COM

MURPHY'S LAW (ROADS LESS TRAVELED BOOK 2)
BY C. DULANEY

Kasey and the gang were held together by a set of rules, their Zombie Plan. It kept them alive through the beginning of the End. But when the chaos faded, they became careless, and Murphy's Law decided to pay a long-overdue visit. Now the group is broken and scattered with no refuge in sight. Those remaining must make their way across West Virginia in search of those who were stolen from them.

PERMUTEDPRESS.COM

SHADES OF GRAY (ROADS LESS TRAVELED BOOK 3)
BY C. DULANEY

Kasey and the gang have come full circle through the crumbling world. Working for the National Guard, they realize old friends and fellow survivors are disappearing. When the missing start to reappear as walking corpses, the group sets out on another journey to discover the truth. Their answers wait in the West Virginia Command Center.

PERMUTED PRESS

PERMUTED PRESS

DEAD LIVING
BY GLENN BULLION

It didn't take long for the world to die. And it didn't take long, either, for the dead to rise. Aaron was born on the day the world ended. Kept in seclusion, his family teaches him the basics. How to read and write. How to survive. Then Aaron makes a shocking discovery. The undead, who desire nothing but flesh, ignore him. It's as if he's invisible to them.

PERMUTEDPRESS.COM

AUTOBIOGRAPHY of a WEREWOLF HUNTER
BY BRIAN P. EASTON

After his mother is butchered by a werewolf, Sylvester James is taken in by a Cheyenne mystic. The boy trains to be a werewolf hunter, learning to block out pain, stalk, fight, and kill. As Sylvester sacrifices himself to the hunt, his hatred has become a monster all its own. As he follows his vendetta into the outlands of the occult, he learns it takes more than silver bullets to kill a werewolf.

PERMUTED PRESS

PERMUTED PRESS

INFECTION:
ALASKAN UNDEAD APOCALYPSE
BY SEAN SCHUBERT

Anchorage, Alaska: gateway to serene wilderness of The Last Frontier. No stranger to struggle, the city on the edge of the world is about to become even more isolated. When a plague strikes, Anchorage becomes a deadly trap for its citizens. The only two land routes out of the city are cut, forcing people to fight or die as the infection spreads.

PERMUTEDPRESS.COM

CONTAINMENT
(ALASKAN UNDEAD APOCALYPSE BOOK 2)
BY SEAN SCHUBERT

Running. Hiding. Surviving. Anchorage, once Alaska's largest city, has fallen. Now a threatening maze of death, the city is firmly in the cold grip of a growing zombie horde. Neil Jordan and Dr. Caldwell lead a small band of desperate survivors through the maelstrom. The group has one last hope: that this nightmare has been contained, and there still exists a sane world free of infection.

PERMUTED PRESS

PERMUTED PRESS

MAD SWINE: THE BEGINNING
BY STEVEN PAJAK

People refer to the infected as "zombies," but that's not what they really are. Zombie implies the infected have died and reanimated. The thing is, they didn't die. They're just not human anymore. As the infection spreads and crazed hordes--dubbed "Mad Swine"--take over the cities, the residents of Randall Oaks find themselves locked in a desperate struggle to survive in the new world.

PERMUTEDPRESS.COM

MAD SWINE: DEAD WINTER
BY STEVEN PAJAK

Three months after the beginning of the Mad Swine outbreak, the residents of Randall Oaks have reached their breaking point. After surviving the initial outbreak and a war waged with their neighboring community, Providence, their supplies are severely close to depletion. With hostile neighbors at their flanks and hordes of infected outside their walls, they have become prisoners within their own community.

PERMUTED PRESS

PERMUTED PRESS

DEAD MEAT

BY PATRICK & CHRIS WILLIAMS

The city of River's Edge has been quarantined due to a rodent borne rabies outbreak. But it quickly becomes clear to the citizens that the infection is something much, much worse than rabies... The townsfolk are attacked and fed upon by packs of the living dead. Gavin and Benny attempt to survive the chaos in River's Edge while making their way north in search of sanctuary.

PERMUTEDPRESS.COM

ROTTER WORLD

BY SCOTT M. BAKER

Eight months ago vampires released the Revenant Virus on humanity. Both species were nearly wiped out. The creator of the virus claims there is a vaccine that will make humans and vampires immune to the virus, but it's located in a secure underground facility five hundred miles away. To retrieve the vaccine, a raiding party of humans and vampires must travel down the devastated East Coast.

PERMUTED PRESS

12304475R00178

Made in the USA
San Bernardino, CA
13 June 2014